ALBATROSS

David Stroud

TSL Publications

First published in Great Britain in 2017
By TSL Publications, Rickmansworth

Copyright © 2017 David Stroud

ISBN / 978-1-911070-84-9

Cover photo: David Stroud
Albatross: pixabay.com/en/albatross-running-new-zealand-bird-2417603/

For my son
Javier

Acknowledgements

A huge thank you to the three mentors who guided me through the writing of this debut novel: Siobhan Curham, Hill Slavid and Barbara Towell.

Also heartfelt thanks to:

Gabriela Harding, writer and friend, for your passion for the story which kept me going whenever my enthusiasm waned.

Mike Deller, writer and actor, for reading *Albatross* aloud, bringing the story to life.

John Hudspith, literary editor, for your hawk-eyed corrections, encouragement and suggestions.

Paquita, my wife, for your support and opinions during this long process.

Anne Samson, publisher, for piloting me through my first publishing experience, making it seem almost easy.

You, the reader, who makes it all worthwhile.

Chapter 1

"So much for strolling in the Cotswolds." Fiona was gazing at the rain streaming down the stone-framed window of the hotel. "You wouldn't believe it could rain so much in August."

"You would if you came from the pisspot of Wales," I said.

"How can you talk about your home town like that?"

"Like what? A term of endearment for us Swansea Jacks, that is."

The edges of her mouth turned down. "Well, I think it's disgusting."

Her yellow summer dress had pulled tight on her the year before, but now it hung elegantly from her soft shoulders. The Jane Fonda exercise video and Weight Watchers were working. I felt chubby compared with her and wished I'd put on a shirt with vertical rather than horizontal stripes. Too many of these, I thought, putting my pint back on the table. Her shoulder-length hair, swirling upwards at her neck, was light brown, while mine was steel grey. She looked more than her four years younger than me.

She clicked her tongue. "We're so unlucky."

I moved the cut-glass vase with the red rose a few inches to one side and covered her hand with mine.

"Oh, I don't know. We might be lucky later on."

"What do you mean?"

"Well, you know. Wedding anniversary, romantic break in the country-side …"

Her hand shot away as if it were attached to an elastic band. "That's all you think about."

After that, silence. She sipped her Moet Premier Cru and I my Taunton Ale.

"You are ready to order?"

We both looked up at the waitress with the foreign accent.

Fiona's face lit up as she asked, "*Êtes-vous française?*"

"*Oui, madame,*" the waitress replied, handing us leather-bound menus. "*Parlais-vous française?*"

"Oh, *oui,*" Fiona giggled. "*Un petit peu.*"

A French waitress. Perfect. Fiona had been studying French for some years. My first thought had been to take Fiona to France this weekend but I had to be at the university the next day and it didn't seem worth crossing the Channel just for one night.

While Fiona was studying the menu, I snapped mine shut. "I'll have the steak."

"*Moi aussi,*" said Fiona. "*Avec frites.* And you, Owen?"

"No thanks, I'll just have chips with mine."

She glowered at me.

"And the *bifteck*, how would you like it, sir?"

"Medium for me," I grinned.

"*Et pour moi, saignant, si'l vous plaît,*" said Fiona, adding in English, ostensibly for my benefit, "I can't stand seeing blood in it."

The waitress looked confused. "So, *madame*, you mean *bien cuit?*"

It seemed like there was absolute silence in the restaurant until Fiona replied, "Oh, yes." It was one of the few times I'd seen Fiona blush. "Of course that's what I meant."

I resisted following the waitress with my eyes as she walked away. "You see," I said to Fiona, "I even threw in a French waitress for you."

She smiled. That was a good sign. "How did you know she'd be here?"

I shrugged. "Just a matter of asking the right questions in the right places."

"Shows what you can do when you try."

The surprise trip, the flowers and the oversized anniversary card waiting for her in the hotel room, the champagne in the ice bucket beside the table, and now this. The cards were stacking up in my favour. The glow inside me was like the orange-yellow flame of the candle on the table between us.

But then she leaned towards me and hissed, "If you'd told me, I could have brought my phrase book."

The glow faltered and almost went out.

"But then," I said, intertwining my fingers, "it wouldn't have been a surprise."

"True," she conceded, and I sighed with relief.

The smell of sizzling garlic made me look up. As the waitress leaned over to place the plate in front of me, I observed every detail about her. It was a habit that had grown from years of celibacy with Fiona. The black and white uniform. Dark hair tied up in a bun, a few strands escaping, a fringe over her blue eyes, pupils dilated with the subdued light of the dining room.

Fiona cleared her throat. "Excuse me."

Her eyes and tone of voice told me that she'd been trying to get my attention.

"Oh, I was just wondering ..." I said, "how do you say another pint of beer, please – in French."

Her scowl transformed into a smile as she turned to the waitress. "*Puis-je avoir une autre bière, s'il vous plaît.*"

My eyes felt unnaturally wide as I kept them unblinkingly on Fiona while the waitress walked away. But later, when Fiona was explaining some point of French grammar to me, I noticed the waitress behind her. As she reached for a bottle high in a tall wine-rack, her skirt rode up her thighs. Fiona twisted to see what I was looking at.

Turning back to me she smirked, "You don't leave one standing, do you?"

I suddenly became very interested in my steak. But the truth is, it had lost its appeal.

As we passed Reception on the way back to our room, Fiona paused. "I'd better phone home to make sure Bradley's okay."

"Of course he's okay with your mum and dad."

She twisted her mouth to one side, but before she could say anything I added, "It's only for one night."

I took her arm and was surprised that she let me lead her up the stairs.

"Fancy something from the mini-bar?" I said after locking the door behind us. I opened the little grey door beneath the TV.

"I think you've had enough already, Owen."

"Well, it is a special occasion." I knelt on the floor in front of the mini-bar.

"Some water would be good." She always liked to have a glass of water beside her bed during the night.

"Sparkling water … sparkling water …" I read as I moved the bottles and cans around.

"No, still water."

"I know, but – oh, here you are." I held the bottle at arm's length, squinting at the label. "Still water."

Fiona looked up at the ceiling, then back down at me, crossing her arms. "When will you admit that you need glasses?"

When I went into the bathroom to clean my teeth, she was standing in front of the mirror in the hotel's white bathrobe removing her makeup. The bright light from the vanity unit shone in my eyes as I watched her from behind. Then I wrapped my arms around her, snuggling into her back. "Daddy sheep loves ewe."

"If only you knew," she shrieked, wriggling free, "how childish that sounds."

"You thought it was funny when we got married."

"That was a long time ago."

"Only ten magnificent years."

She glared at me as if to say, *That's not funny.*

"Anyway, it feels like a lot more than that," she said, and that definitely was not funny.

When she came out of the bathroom, I was pushing the twin beds together. "What are you doing?" she demanded.

With a hairbrush in her hand and a white bandana circling her forehead she looked like an adolescent tennis player.

I tried to sound casual. "You'd think they would have given us a double bed on our anniversary, wouldn't you?"

Her eyes narrowed. "Don't get any ideas. These walls are paper-thin."

"You must be joking." I thumped the wall beside the heavy, velvet curtains with the side of my fist, making a dull thud. "These walls must be ten inches thick."

"The outer walls may be," she said, rapping the wall beside one of the beds with her knuckles, making a hollow sound. "But not where these rooms are partitioned off."

Resigned to spending the night alone, I lay on my back with my hands under my head. But not really resigned; I couldn't believe that all my efforts had been in vain. When a change in Fiona's breathing signalled that she was asleep, an audacious thought occurred to me. I got up and, carefully pulling her sheet back, slipped in beside her. She woke up as soon as I put an arm around her.

"Owen, I told you …!"

"It's been so long, Fiona. I just thought that …"

"No, no! It's wet enough outside without you wetting my sheets with your – your –" she struggled to find an acceptable word, "nonsense. Besides that, you smell like a brewery."

She turned her back on me, pulling the sheet tight around her.

I was eating a full English breakfast when Fiona came into the conservatory next morning.

"How can you eat all that?" she asked, sliding into the chair opposite me. "After what you got through last night."

"Shall I order you a stick of bread and a glass of water?"

She glared at me through half-closed eyes. "I'll just have a black coffee."

I leaned forward. "I'm sorry." My tone was soft now. "I really thought this would work."

"What?"

"That – that things could be like they were before …"

"Didn't stop you fancying that French tart, though, did it?"

As I poured her coffee, I murmured, "Who could blame me under the circumstances?"

"You don't need circumstances."

I shrugged. "You didn't even remember it was our anniversary."

"It's hardly surprising after what I've been through."

"I went through it, too." I wanted to take her hand, but felt I wouldn't be able to stand another rejection. "But I still remembered."

"You certainly remembered." She gave a quick, sarcastic laugh. "And we all know why, don't we?"

As I watched her holding the cup under her nose, breathing in the aroma, I said, "I never dreamt it would end like this."

"It hasn't ended." She sipped her coffee. "Yet."

There was hardly a cloud in the sky as I lifted our suitcase into the boot of the car. The ground was completely dry, so we could have gone walking in the hills. But I just wanted to get back to London, and I was sure Fiona felt the same.

Neither of us spoke as I drove through the countryside to the M5. As Fiona liked to keep the car windows closed to protect the pallor of her skin from the sun, the only sound was the quiet hum of the Audi's engine. Hundreds of seagulls followed a tractor that was ploughing a field, like the wake of a ship.

A ship.

I remembered leaning over the stern of the *Albatross* and gazing at the white water being churned up by the propeller, the cold handrail between my fingers. With my tongue, I felt the new, raised wound on my lower lip.

"You okay?" Fiona's voice, louder than usual, cut across the image.

I turned to look at her. "Huh?"

"Oh, my God, Owen – keep your eyes on the road!"

I looked straight ahead.

"You want to stop?" she queried. "Have a coffee?"

"Why, do you?"

"I just want to get back to Harrow in one piece."

I nodded. "I know. Tiredness kills. No, I'm okay."

Back in our own bed that night, I was still reading when Fiona clicked off her French language cassette and took out her earphones. She listened intently to make sure there was no sound from Brad's room. Then she switched her bedside lamp off and was soon asleep, leaving me staring at the now meaningless text in my hands.

I couldn't believe it when she hooked her foot around one of my legs and pulled me towards her. Was she dreaming? I clicked my light off and turned to her, so close I could feel her breath on my face. My hand followed the contour of her thigh. Then I began to carefully lift her nightdress.

"Oh, no ..." she moaned, still asleep.

Her breathing became shallower and, although I couldn't see her, I knew her eyes were now wide open.

"What are you doing?" she demanded.

I pressed my mouth against hers. "Fiona, darling!"

"Leave me alone!" she shouted, pushing me away.

I rolled onto my back, staring up into the darkness.

"You know I don't feel anything anymore." Her voice sounded like it came from the bottom of a well. "You're so insensitive."

After a long pause, I said, "Do you think she would have wanted this?"

"What sort of a question is that? Shame on you. She was just a child."

I closed my eyes tightly. Holding back the tears got harder as she began to sob at my side. I wanted to reach out to her, but I knew I couldn't touch her in any way. Then she got up and felt her way around the bed to the door. It opened and then slammed shut. It must have woken Brad. It must have woken the neighbours on both sides. I lay there waiting for her to come back.

She didn't.

Chapter 2

While I stood by the dining room table carving the leg of lamb, I looked down at Brad, hunched up over a sketchpad with his coloured pencils. The fingers of his left hand disappeared into his hair as he supported his head, concentrating. Auburn hair, like mine before it started changing colour.

A bowl of mint sauce under my nose. The smell took me back to my childhood in Wales where we had a roast dinner every Sunday, not occasionally, like now, when Fiona's international cuisine took precedence. My mother would send me or one of my sisters out into the garden to pick a bunch of mint for her to make the sauce. She wouldn't have dreamt of buying it.

The phone rang as Fiona was bringing in a steaming dish of carrots. "I'll get it," I said, putting the carving knife and fork down on the greasy plate.

After a minute I came back and reported, "That was your mum, checking if we're going there for lunch next Sunday. I told her I probably won't be able to with that lot to get through." I nodded towards the pile of folders on the coffee table and sofa.

She put a jug of diet orange squash on the table. "Squash or water?" she asked me.

"I think I'll just have a beer."

"And go to sleep after lunch?"

"Very likely."

"*Sacre bleu!* That means we'll have that lot" – now it was she who nodded towards the folders – "cluttering up the sitting room for another week."

I resumed carving the meat while she glared at me with one hand on her hip, until I finally broke and said, "Okay, I'll take it up to my room straight after lunch."

"I'm surprised they still invite you, anyway," she said, laying out plates and cutlery, "after the way you behaved last Christmas."

That was not long after my mother died of liver cancer and I was not in a festive mood, despite her parents trying to jolly me along. "For Christ's sake," her father had said in the end, opening another bottle of mulled wine. "That was months ago! It's time you snapped out of it. Think of your wife and son instead of yourself for a change."

As irrational as it was, I had already been feeling that it wasn't fair that I had lost both my parents while Fiona still had hers.

"I'll try to make it on Sunday," I mumbled.

"It's okay if you can't. I'm sure they'll get over it."

I asked, "Who else is coming?"

"Just us and Mum and Dad."

"No, I mean now – today."

She looked at me. "Just us – you, Bradley and me. Why?"

"You've laid four places."

Her eyes widened as they scanned the table. Then, with fire in them, they darted back to me. "You bastard!"

That was only the second time I had heard her swear. The first time was just after Susan died, and that was at me, too.

Brad's head jerked up as she slammed the dessert spoons on the table and dashed out of the room.

"What's wrong with Mum?"

"She made a mistake with her sums, that's all."

"She got upset about *that?*"

"Yes. Look, you get on with this," – I lifted a couple of slices of lamb onto his plate – "and I'll go and see how she is. Okay?"

"What is it?" he said, wrinkling his nose.

"It's lamb. You've had it before."

His mouth turned down. "I'm not eating a little lamb from Wales."

"It isn't from Wales," I said, spooning some vegetables onto his plate. "It's – it's from the freezer."

I knocked on Fiona's bedroom door and waited. I could hear her crying.

"What do you want?" she responded at last.

"I just wanted to make sure you're okay. Can I come in?"

"Of course I'm okay." After a silence, she added, "Come in, then – if you're still there."

Not for the first time, it struck me as strange that I had to ask permission to enter her room, whereas she just walked into mine without knocking.

"Don't sit here," she said as I lowered myself onto the bed next to her. "Use the chair."

I straightened up from my semi-sitting position, then brought over her wicker chair. She frowned as I sat squarely in front of her.

I took a deep breath before saying, "Fiona, it worries me when you do things like that."

"Like what?"

"Behaving like Susan is still with us."

Her knees were pressed together. She reminded me of a gazelle with her fragile features and wide eyes. Dabbing those eyes with a tissue, she said, "I don't know why, but sometimes I forget ..."

Her hand tensed up when I put mine on top of it. She stared down at my badly cut fingernails until I folded my arms to hide them.

In the silence that followed, I looked around the room. It had been a long time since I'd been in here. My eyes rested on a photo of Fiona and her friend

Maureen receiving their Reiki Master's certificates at the end of a residential weekend. They were standing with their hands clasped over their genitals like footballers in a wall. They were flanked by two men who had their hands behind their backs. The elderly Reiki teacher was next to Maureen, while his young assistant was next to Fiona.

"I thought things might change when you took up Reiki," I ventured.

"They did, enormously."

"I mean, between us. Back to as they were before Susan ... Reiki was like a new lease of life to you."

"I don't know what I'd have done without it, that's for sure."

"You were so enthusiastic, laying hands on anyone who had the slightest problem, physical or mental. Channelling universal energy into everyone. It was good to see you so involved again. You stopped crying in bed every night."

"You knew about that?"

"I heard you if I got up in the night. When the crying stopped, I thought it was a sure sign that you were going back to your old self. I expected you to say you were moving back in with me any day. Instead, you had this put in." I nodded towards the fitted wardrobe.

"You couldn't expect me to use a portable rail forever."

"That's just it – I didn't expect it to be forever. Fiona, come back." I was pleading, and I hated it.

"No."

"Why not?"

"I've got all my things here ..."

"Just say the word and they'll be back in the other bedroom."

"Everything is just as I want it here now ... Besides, you snore."

"I've always snored." I could hear my Welsh accent getting worse. *Worse?* Well, that was how Fiona's father would have described it.

"Not like you do now, with that," she glanced at my belly.

"That's just another thing you don't like about me, isn't it?"

"You've just let yourself go ..."

"That's comfort eating for you."

I stared at her mouth. She wasn't wearing lipstick as I had thought at first – it was just the natural redness of her lips. The tip of her nose was like a sign pointing down to her mouth saying *Kiss here*. It was only when she moved back a little that I realised I was gradually leaning towards her.

"You can't stand me touching you, can you?" I was trying not to get angry. "Even if I brush against you in the kitchen, you tense up. And as for kissing ..."

"Oh, leave me alone! You're talking like a teenager."

"I need to know!"

She sighed. "Owen, you do know."

"Why don't you want me to kiss you?" I insisted.

She stared down at the carpet. "It's your disfigurement."

I felt a sudden pain, as if someone had punched me in the stomach. "What about it?"

She carried on studying the carpet until I put my hands on her shoulders and made her look at me. I had almost forgotten how wonderfully soft she felt. "What about it?"

"It feels … uncomfortable."

"It never bothered you before."

"Things were different before."

"Before Susan died?"

"Take your hands off me!" She was beginning to raise her voice.

"Why?"

"Because I don't like it. It feels like you're interrogating me."

She struggled to get free. It would have been so easy to carry on holding her, to pull her closer, to press her against me. Frighteningly easy.

"Perhaps I am," I said.

"I thought you just came to make sure I was all right!"

"I did." I removed my hands from her and put them on my lap. "But now I need to sort this out once and for all."

"You need, you need!" She was shouting now, her eyes drilling into mine. "All you care about is what *you* need!"

"I care about *us*. And what about this?" My hand was shaking as I brought it up to my mouth. "Why do you find it repulsive? Why now?"

"I don't know." Her voice was suddenly quiet. "I suppose I didn't notice it so much before, but now … Another thing – you've never told me how you got it."

"You never asked." I regretted saying that instantly.

"It's a matter of trust. If you trusted me … some time or other you'd have told me."

"Do you really want to know?"

"No. It doesn't matter now."

"But it did before?"

"Maybe I was curious before. But not now." She squeezed her eyes and mouth shut, as if trying to block out some intolerable pain.

I rested my hand on her arm. "Fiona, perhaps we should have another child."

She jerked her arm away and her eyes narrowed as they focused on me. "What?" The harshness was back in her voice.

"It might help you get over Susan."

"You think we can replace her? Is that it?"

"I know there'll never be another Susan. I just thought it might be time to, you know, move on."

"*Move on?*" Her tone was mocking.

"Yes. Move on." I shrugged. "Have another baby."

She imitated my shrug. "*Have another baby.* Just like that?"

"We wanted to have two children. That was the plan, remember?"

"Well, the plan went wrong, didn't it?"

I felt like shouting: *It wasn't my fault!* Instead I said quietly, "I just thought it might help you."

"Or you?"

"*And* me."

She gasped. "We don't even sleep together, for goodness' sake!"

"Through your choice," I reminded her. "That could change at any time."

"Oh, no. I think not!"

"We should think about it."

"You can think about it as much as you like, but don't count on me."

I nearly put my hand on her arm again, but caught myself just in time. "Don't you want me anymore?"

Her eyes shone with incredulity. "Are you stupid, or what?"

I looked away.

"Make no mistake about it," she said, getting to her feet. "I'm only staying for the sake of the children."

I expected her to correct herself, but when she didn't I said, "The *children*, Fiona?"

"That's right. Otherwise I'd be long gone."

She opened the door and stood there waiting for me to leave. I put my hands in my pockets and crossed the room to her as casually as I could. I was going to remind her that the house belonged to both of us and that she came into "my" room whenever she pleased. But her eyes were so cold, so lifeless.

The door slammed shut behind me.

And I never went into that room again.

Chapter 3

A year passed. Then one night I woke up trembling, with sweat running down the back of my neck. I wasn't sure how much was from the dream and how much from the heat of that summer night. I had dreamt I was taking a shortcut home across the railway tracks in Swansea when someone changed the points, catching my foot between the rails. I tried to shout for help, but no sound came. I heard the whistle of the approaching train and felt the vibration of the metal that gripped my foot like a vice. I'd had this nightmare a couple of times before.

As soon as I went out onto the landing I knew from the smell of Chanel No. 5 that Fiona's door was ajar. I saw her sitting up in bed, bedside light on and decorative Reiki notebook on her lap. Her fingers were tracing a Japanese symbol in the air. This was not the first time I had seen her doing it. She had called it *The Bridge*. A bridge between the sender and receiver of healing energy, she'd explained. She'd likened it to a telephone line, and once I asked her if the energy went to someone else if she was a digit out. She wasn't amused.

When I'd asked her about these signs she said, "They're secret. Anyway, they cost me two thousand pounds when I became a master, so I'm not going to show them to just anyone."

That said it all. I had become just anyone. Perhaps it didn't occur to her that the two grand had come out of our joint bank account, and although there was some income from Reiki, it was very little.

I stood there in my boxer shorts. She had one leg outside the sheet, bent at the knee. Seeing her in bed like that, barely covered, reminded me of how she looked when we were on holiday in Marseille the year after we got married. Only then she was wearing a skimpy nightdress and holding a glass of white wine. She had a little smile on her face as she waited for me to come out of the bathroom. Things were different then.

If she knew I was looking at her, she didn't let on.

Through force of habit, I peed silently onto the side of the bowl at first. Then, in an act of rebellion, straight into the middle. A good, full stream – worthy of a wild stallion on the Brecon Beacons. It was the colour of the beer I'd been drinking. It even developed a frothy head.

I paused outside Fiona's bedroom again on the way back to mine. Now her eyes were closed and she had both hands in front of her as if she were trying to hold back the tide. Distant healing. This was the part of Reiki I found most difficult to swallow. She opened one eye and glared at me until I shrugged and carried on back to my bedroom.

That afternoon there was a timetabling error, meaning that my class was supposed to be in two places at the same time. I was happy for them to be in the other place – at a control and restraint workshop – while I went home early.

A delicious smell hit me as I opened the front door. One of Fiona's exotic recipes. French, Spanish, Italian ...? Not Indian. I would have recognised that. As I put my briefcase on the coffee table, the oven bell rang. I waited for Fiona to come running from somewhere. She didn't, so I called up the stairs for her. No answer, so I went to her treatment room. The door was closed.

With a twist of the handle, I entered Reikilandia. The smell of lavender, a colourful, glossy poster of the chakras on the wall, a glass cabinet containing cast iron dragons and wizards. The sun glinted off two blue glazed pots from Italy and water chortled from a miniature fountain onto white pebbles from a Spanish beach.

A man lay face down on the treatment couch, stripped to the waist. Fiona

was standing with both hands on his back, wearing her white uniform.
They both looked at me in surprise.

"Sorry," I mumbled. "The 'Do Not Disturb' sign wasn't up."

Of course, I thought. She hadn't bothered as I wasn't expected home at that time.

"Well, what is it?" she snapped.

"The oven bell – it rang."

She had obviously forgotten about it. "Is it cooked?"

"I don't know."

"Can you check it for me? I can't leave my client now. I've got his chakras open."

The man glared at me as if to say, "Can't you see that, you arsehole?"

I hesitated, feeling foolish.

"Just switch the oven off and leave it," she said, waving me away.

Then she turned back to her client and joked, "It's impossible to find decent help these days."

He sniggered and turned his head the other way as I closed the door behind me.

I sat on the cream-coloured sofa staring at my briefcase on the coffee table. I heard the budgie rubbing its beak against the bars of its cage. I heard its swing move up and down once. The briefcase was full of assignments to be marked, but all I could think about was that man – that Adonis – in the other room with Fiona's hands on his bare body. Perhaps I should make an appointment for Reiki with her, I thought.

Chapter 4

My eyes scanned the boardroom. Hospital staff surrounded the long table, which was covered with a white tablecloth. On top was food, drink and the entrails of party poppers. Then I saw her – Irene, the ward sister from Birmingham. She was with Sonal, the Indian staff nurse, standing under a long banner with multicoloured letters that read: "Merry Christmas and a Happy New Year". I picked up a can of beer and pulled the ring opener back as I edged my way towards them.

"Fancy seeing you two here!" I exclaimed.

Sonal eyed me in mock cynicism. "We seem to be seeing a lot of you lately, Mr Roberts."

"Well, as link tutor I am responsible for your ongoing education."

"Irene must be the most educated sister in the NHS, then."

Irene smiled. That was the first time I'd ever seen her without her uniform and with her brown hair down, cascading over her shoulders.

"Can I get you guys a drink?" Young women liked to be called that, I found. I remembered when only guys were called guys.

"I'm all right," said Sonal, raising her glass of orange juice.

"How about you, Irene?" Her glass was empty. "Shall I fill you up?"

She shot me a glance, apparently not sure if it was a *double entendre* or an innocent question. I wasn't sure myself.

"Okay." She handed me the glass. "Martini, please."

"*Rosso* or *bianco*?"

She looked confused for a moment and then said, "The red one."

Sonal nudged Irene. "Posh, ain't he?"

Irene wasn't there when I got back with her drink.

"Gone to the loo," Sonal said. "You've got a soft spot for her, haven't you?"

"For who?"

"For her – Jasper Carrott with tits." She giggled. "That's what the doctors call her."

I can see why, I thought as I scooped up a handful of dry-roasted peanuts.

"Don't tell me your interest in her is purely professional," she went on.

"No, I wouldn't say that." I popped a few peanuts into my mouth. "I suppose we are friends, too."

Sonal grinned. "Was it Oscar Wilde who said men and women can't be friends?"

"I don't think that's true. Especially at our age."

"*Our* age? Speak for yourself, dear!"

"Okay, my age. Besides, we're both married with kids."

She was giving me that cynical look again.

Irene came back and picked up her refilled glass. "Did I miss anything?"

"No," said Sonal. "We were just talking about you."

"Nothing new there, then." Irene knocked back half the contents of her glass.

"I was just saying, Irene," I said, "it's nice to have friends of the opposite sex who don't want to just get you into bed."

"You mean you don't want to get me into bed?"

I laughed and shrugged.

"No, come on," she insisted, her Birmingham accent getting stronger. "Why don't you want to get me into bed?"

I laughed again, for longer this time, trying to show that it was a joke.

"I won't let go of this," she persisted, and it was then I noticed she was a bit tipsy. "Why don't you want to get me into bed?"

She was raising her voice and people were beginning to look at us. Sonal opened her eyes wider as she backed away, merging with the crowd behind her.

"I think we need to talk," I whispered.

"No, I want to know. Come on, out with it." Her eyelids looked heavier than usual.

"Let's go and have a coffee."

Irene was not aware of me gazing at her in the staff cafeteria as I waited for the coffee. She was sitting on a sofa, her eyes turned down thoughtfully. Under the cold, glaring lights a few nurses sat at Formica-topped tables eating hospital food. A white-coated junior doctor was making notes from the British National Formulary as he ate. The only sound was the occasional clatter of plates or cutlery and the hiss of the coffee machine. It was a miserable scene, but I was glowing inside.

Irene looked up and smiled as I put the cups on the coffee table in front of her. She was still wearing an orange paper hat and had some tinsel clinging to her shoulder.

"Sorry about that, back there," she said.

I laughed. "It's okay. I knew you were joking."

She cradled her cup in her hands. "Sometimes we say things as a joke and they are true."

"Many a true word, and all that."

"Yes, that's it."

Picking up my coffee from the low table, I looked at her feet. She was wearing peep-through shoes and had the same crimson nail polish on her toes as on her fingers. "I love that colour," I said.

She smiled. "I only do it to stop me biting them."

"Don't tell me you do that?"

"No, not now. It wouldn't be the thing to see a ward sister biting her nails."

"I imagine it wouldn't go down well in the ward round," I agreed. "Especially your toenails."

She gave me a mock punch on the arm, then after a pause, said, "I'll miss you over Christmas."

"I'll miss you too."

"No, I'm not just saying that." She sipped her coffee to get away from my gaze, and the cream left a faint moustache. "Lately, I can't stop thinking about you, Owen."

I handed her a paper serviette. Instead of using it to wipe away the cream, she dabbed her eyes with it.

"The nights are the worst," she added.

"Hasn't your husband noticed anything?"

"He doesn't even notice I'm there half the time."

This was suddenly getting too deep for me.

I put my hand on her arm. "If we weren't both married, it might have been different between us."

Her eyes glazed over as she stared at me. She nodded slowly as the meaning of what I'd said sank in.

"Well, I'd better be getting home," she said, reaching for her handbag and coat on the chair beside her.

Her short steps beat a rapid rhythm as we walked along the main hospital corridor. Holding the collar of her long coat around her neck with her leather-gloved hand, it seemed she was avoiding eye contact with me. As we went down to the ground floor, she nearly tripped on the stairs. I took her arm to steady her.

"Drank too much, said too much," she giggled.

"How much?"

"Talk?"

"No, drink."

"Two Martinis." I must have looked surprised, because she added, "Never could hold it, though. That's the thing."

"Come on, I'll give you a lift."

"There's no need – really."

"I don't want you travelling on the underground like this."

When we got to Neasden, I said, "You'll have to direct me to your house from here."

I glanced at her when she didn't answer. "Well, which way?"

"Why don't we stop somewhere quiet first?"

The suggestion took me by surprise. A bit old-fashioned, perhaps, but I wished I'd said it instead of her. "Yes, okay."

She directed me to a lane behind some gardens, which was lined with garages. It was dark by then. I stopped about halfway down.

I turned the engine and lights off. "How did you know about this place, then?" I teased her.

"Me and Barry used to come here before we were married."

As I held her close for the first time, I realised that this is what I'd been missing all these years, and I felt a pang of regret.

"I haven't been with a woman like this for so long."

"Neither have I. With a man, I mean."

"Except for your husband …?"

"No, not like this. Sex, yes – when the mood takes him. But not like this."

As we kissed, I imagined Wencheng, my unofficial conscience, looking at me questioningly. I deliberately shut him out of my mind. I wanted this so much. I fumbled to unhook the back of her bra under her jumper.

"Shouldn't we wait?" she whispered, while still kissing and caressing me.

"For what?"

"I don't know. Till we find somewhere to go?"

You're right, you're right, I thought. In the dim light, I saw her as I'd never seen her before – face taut, eyes wide. She sort of cooed as I lifted her breast to my mouth.

I half expected her to stop me when I tried to remove her panties and tights, but she lifted herself up slightly to facilitate me.

"I won't be able to look at you next time you come to the ward," she mumbled.

Then I was kneeling in front of her in the cramped space. Her left leg resting on top of the glove compartment and the right on the steering wheel. Besides the sound of our breathing, it was eerily silent.

"Barry!" she cried out.

"Where?" I struggled to pull my trousers up.

"No, I mean someone just walked past."

I rubbed the misted windscreen until I could see through a patch. A man was standing in front of a garage, taking a bunch of keys out of his coat pocket.

"It's okay," I whispered. "He didn't see us."

Irene looked sceptical.

"Well, if he did, he doesn't care," I went on.

As I leaned towards Irene to kiss her again, there was a screeching as the garage door rolled upwards. I grimaced and pressed my hands over my ears. But I still heard the clang as the door hit the top of the metal frame. To me it was the deafening sound of that freak wave wrenching open a hatch on the *Albatross* all those years ago.

Later, as we drove on, I said, "Can't believe you called out your husband's name while we were … you know."

"At least it wasn't somebody else's."

I laughed, then went on, "I feel a bit guilty, though."

She arched her eyebrows.

"After all, you had been drinking."

"So had you," she protested.

"But that's different. I feel I've taken advantage of you, in a way."

"Chauvinist pig!"

I turned and looked at her in surprise.

She went on in a softer tone, "It takes two, you know."

After a few minutes' silence, she asked, "Owen, what spooked you back there?"

I felt the muscles around my mouth tighten. "Memories. That's all. Just memories."

There was another silence. She must have realised that it was something I didn't want to talk about.

"You'd better drop me off here," she said at last.

I stopped the car and looked down the row of terraced houses. "Are you sure? It's quite dark."

The way she looked at me I thought she was going to call me sexist again. Perhaps she was. But instead she said, "It's okay. Really. I don't want you to drive up to my door. Good night, Owen."

"Good night, Irene." I thought of the folksong with that title, but felt it would be too corny to refer to it.

Chapter 5

We arranged to spend Christmas Day at The Cedars, Fiona's parents' house in Stanmore. They felt it would be nice to be at home for Christmas for a change rather than away on one of their exotic holidays. We had asked them to come to our place, but her father said he would find it claustrophobic. That was his favourite word when talking about our house. Claustrophobic.

Coloured lights illuminated the house when we pulled up outside at eight o'clock in the morning. Brad pointed excitedly at the reindeer and sleigh on the roof and the brilliantly white snowmen on the front lawn.

"How on earth does he manage to do all this?" I marvelled, as we got out of the car.

"It's the gardener," said Fiona. "He does most of it since Dad fell off the porch roof, tangled up in fairy lights. Lucky it wasn't the main roof ... Don't know what you're laughing at. It's all for Bradley, you know."

I turned to look at our son on the back seat. He was staring at the scene with his mouth open.

Martha hugged her daughter and grandson and mwah-mwahed my cheeks. Grinning down at Brad, she said, "I think Father Christmas has been. Shall we see if he's filled all those parcels under the tree?"

She took him by the hand and led him into the sitting room which was the size of the whole of our downstairs. The Christmas tree almost touched the ceiling, a mass of sparkling coloured lights.

"Ho, ho, ho," came from behind us. I turned, expecting to see James, Fiona's father, dressed as Santa Claus. Instead he was wearing a white shirt and grey flannel trousers. No doubt he would appear as Santa Claus with surprise additional gifts after lunch. Martha and Brad sat on the carpet in front of the wrapped presents.

James stepped forward and reached for a wrapped present that could not have been anything but a book. "This is for you, Brad," he said. "I'm afraid we've had to cut down this year, as I'm retired now." It was a variation of the joke he said every year. Brad feigned an expression of disappointment mixed with gratitude, knowing that his main present would emerge later.

"It must be a struggle on a surgeon's pension," I put in.

Fiona shot me a warning glance. James pretended he hadn't heard me.

There was a gold necklace for Fiona and a silk tie for me. It was always either a tie or a bottle of something for me. Last year it was a bottle of brandy, so I should have expected a tie this year. At least I drank the alcohol – I hardly ever wore the ties.

James prepared to carve the enormous turkey while we all sat around the table. With his white shirt and thick-rimmed glasses, I imagined that he was operating on one of his patients. He paused as he noticed me looking at him. After a few aperitifs, I had probably stared longer than I realised. "Nice shirt," he commented. "Although pink isn't a colour you'd normally associate with a man."

"Just think," said Martha while we were eating, "this time last year we were in Kerala."

I cleared my throat. "I read a report about Kerala."

"Really, Owen?" said Martha.

"Yes. Kerala is a unique place in many ways. Sociologists call it the 'Kerala phenomenon'."

"Why so?"

"For a start, it's the only truly communist place on earth. People there have very little, but what they do have they share with each other."

"More turkey?" James asked her.

"Not at the moment."

"Although there are different religious groups, there's never been any conflict between them," I went on. "And although it's very poor – it's even the poorest state in India – begging isn't usual there."

James chuckled. "Well, what about that guy with no legs who kept popping up at that restaurant in Kovalam? Eh, Martha? I reckon he hadn't read that report."

I picked up my full glass of red wine to throw over him. Instead, I put it to my lips and didn't stop drinking until it was all gone. It was as if I were trying to swallow my feelings.

James excused himself after lunch. He reappeared in the guise of Father Christmas, wheeling in a tinsel-covered bicycle for Brad. "Sorry," he laughed, "I forgot to leave this earlier."

Brad couldn't wait to try out his bicycle. While his mother and grandmother helped him keep his balance, James lit one of his Havana cigars.

By the evening I needed to escape for a while. I kept wondering what Irene was doing at that moment. Was she asking herself the same question about me? Probably. I was fed up with hearing about James and Martha's holidays and watching the videos. And the wine was making me sleepy. As it began to get dark, I remembered Irene's words: "Nights are the worst."

Returning from the upstairs toilet, I stopped in the hall to put on my overcoat. Standing in the sitting room doorway, I said, "Just going out for a walk."

Fiona looked at me as if I were crazy. "In this weather?"

"Yes. It's invigorating."

"Take Sultan with you," said James. "His lead is hanging by the front door."

Brad jumped off the sofa and rushed to his new bicycle. "I'm going, too!"
"No you're not," said Fiona.
"Why?" asked Brad.
"It's too cold," his mother replied.
"He'll be all right if he wraps up warm," I said.
"Haven't you seen the ice on the road?" She went on, "The icicles hanging from the roofs?"
"I want to see them!" Brad wailed.
"Now look what you've done," Fiona chided me.
"He'll be all right. The fresh air will do him good."
Fiona folded her arms, staring at me.
James winked at me. "You'd better do as she says."
"You mollycoddle him too much," I said to Fiona, turning to go.
As I attached the lead to Sultan's collar in the hall, I could hear Brad still protesting.
James came into the hall. "You can let him have a run on the green," he told me.
"Okay, will do."
He looked dubious when he saw my black woolly hat with 'Cymru, Wales' on the front. "Don't know what people around here will make of that, though."
Outside, the cold air was indeed invigorating. Sultan was pulling at the leash. Instead of slipping it when we got to the common, I ran with him, letting him lead me. The grass crunched under my feet and I laughed, thinking about Irene.

Chapter 6

Bright sunlight shone over the top of the ill-fitting curtains, allowing me to see the mass-produced photo of the Taj Mahal on the red and gold embossed wallpaper. The rumbling of a train reminded me that we were only five minutes' walk from Wembley Park underground.
Irene tapped me on the shoulder. "It's okay. You can get off now."
I rolled off her and reached for the coffee flask and cups on the bedside table. "So," I said.
"So, what?"
"So you still haven't told me. If you've ever been with anyone else since you've been married."
"Why do you want to know?"

I ran my finger down her nose. "I want to know everything about you. You've been married much longer than me – even though you're younger –"

"A *lot* younger."

"So I just thought *you* might be able to teach *me* something for a change."

"Well, if you must know ..." she teased, examining the back of her hand. Then she laughed and shook her head. "No, I haven't."

"Never?"

"Never. Bet you have, though."

I hesitated, then nodded.

"Who was she?"

"An administrator at the university."

She attempted a whistle of admiration. "An administrator!"

I laughed. "That's not as grand as it sounds. She was a glorified secretary. Anyway, it was hardly more than a one-night stand."

"How many nights, exactly?"

I screwed my eyes up at the ceiling. "Oh, let's see. Three, I think. It was a long time ago."

"But after your daughter ...?"

I looked down at the worn bed cover.

"Are you angry?" she said.

"No, no. Of course not. It's just that I don't know why you have to keep bringing that up." Hearing the harshness in my voice myself, I went on more softly, "Yes, it was a couple of years after."

"So what happened? Why was it so brief?"

"Didn't really seem to mean anything. I decided it wasn't worth the guilt I felt."

"Do you feel guilty about me?"

I held her hand, stroking the back of it with my thumb. "No – strangely, I don't."

"What was her name?"

I tucked my chin in. "Rather not say."

"Do I know her?" She sat up straighter, supporting herself with an elbow on the brass-plated headboard.

"It's extremely unlikely."

"So?" She smiled as I stayed quiet. "You're not the type to kiss and tell?"

I laughed. "It was a bit more than kissing!"

"But you don't tell." She snuggled up to me. "That's good. Makes me feel safe."

"You don't tell either?"

"Me? Of course not. Women don't."

"So if there had been others, you wouldn't say. Right?"

She grinned, her eyes half closing.

"Anyway, you know I'd never do anything to hurt you," I said, stroking her hair.

"I know. Not intentionally, anyway."

After a long silence, she said, "What are you thinking?"

"Nothing."

"Why do men always say that?"

"Why do women always ask that?"

"I feel you hold things back about yourself, as if you don't really trust me. For instance, you've never told me how you got this," she ran her finger along my lower lip. I guided her finger into my mouth and bit it gently. She giggled.

"You were quiet, too," I said. "What were *you* thinking?"

"That's typical of you – trying to divert the attention away from yourself!" Then she sighed, suddenly becoming serious. "I was thinking about that young patient who was readmitted today. A bone marrow aspiration has come back with some abnormal promyelocytes floating around."

"What does that mean?"

"It means he's going to die."

"It must be so difficult working on an oncology ward."

"You get used to it. But every so often you get a case that knocks you back. I suppose I'm trying to make sense of it – why this should happen to someone like him."

"Do you think there is some reason?"

"There has to be, otherwise what's the point of –" she waved her hand around the room, "of all this?"

"All this?"

"Life. What's it for? Haven't you ever asked yourself that?"

"Sure I have. I suppose everyone does at some time or other. I've probably thought about it more than your average Joe Blogg –"

"Joe *Blogg*?"

I laughed. "That's Wencheng-speak. I went through a phase of reading about various religions and philosophies."

She folded her arms. "Well, what did you come up with?"

I chose my words carefully. "Every religion expects you to believe in something that is, frankly, ridiculous. Especially when it comes to salvation. Take the resurrection. At a given signal, all dead believers will return – not only in spirit, but in body as well. Right?"

"Oh, my God, I've been sleeping with an atheist!"

"I'm not exactly an atheist. Deep down I feel there might be a supreme intelligence behind everything. It's religion that I don't believe in."

We heard a man speaking an Asian language as he passed our door, the sound trailing off.

Irene sniffed. "I smell curry."

I turned my head to the door and took a deep breath. "Looks like he's put us next to the kitchen this time."

"Are you hungry?" she asked.

"I am now. I'll go and get our take-away."

I swung my legs out of the bed. Through the corner of my eye, I could see her watching me as I got dressed. She rubbed the end of her nose with the knuckles of her right hand.

I gazed at her with my head to one side. "I've been wondering what you remind me of. Now I know – a rabbit!"

She laughed and rubbed the tip of her nose again, this time crinkling up her face.

"Just make sure you bring some of those lamb samosas," she said as I left.

We ate lunch and drank white wine on the bed like castaways at sea. Then we made love again. This time on the little chair with worn fabric that squeaked as Irene, squatting over me, moved up and down. Fiona popped into my mind and I wondered what she was doing now. Irene had her eyes closed, so I glanced at my wrist watch. She'd be picking up Brad from school. I pushed the thought of them out of my mind.

Irene moved faster until I gasped and she cried out, throwing her head back. Then she leaned forward and down, pressing her mouth against mine. Drawing her mouth away, she traced a finger along my lower lip, staring down at me questioningly.

"Does it bother you?" I asked.

"Of course not. I'm just curious."

"Well, if you must know, I cut myself shaving."

For a moment she remained silent, not sure if I was serious. Then she said, "Oh, sod off!"

She stood up, easing herself off me. I refilled our wine glasses before we lay on the bed again.

"This is nice," she said, licking her lips. "What is it?"

"Just their house white."

She sipped some more wine, then sighed. "I don't think I can cope with this much longer, you know."

"With what?" A pointless question. I knew what she meant.

"Meeting in dingy hotels like this. It's so sordid."

"You used to find it okay."

"That was at the beginning."

"I know it's not a fortnight in Ibiza, but it's got to be better than the back seat of the Cortina." I grinned.

She frowned. "I don't like the way the owner looks at me – as if he's wondering how much I charge."

"Well, at least he never asks any questions."

"That's because you always pay him up front. But I can tell by the way he looks at us that he knows we're not married."

"Does he?"

"Of course. You don't think he buys that about us going to catch a plane at Heathrow – with just an empty holdall between us? He really gives me the creeps. He's like an Asian Uriah Heep. "Welcome to our 'umble abode," she said in an East London accent. "I take it you don't need 'elp with your luggage, hnnn?"

"Hey, that's good. Can you do a Brummie accent as well?"

"But seriously, Owen." She propped herself up on one elbow. "I know you don't like talking about it, but it's time we looked at where this relationship is going."

"You mean about leaving our partners?" I was playing for time. I felt I couldn't tell her that what frightened me was the thought of losing someone else, even though things with Fiona were lousy.

"Well – yes. If we're going to carry on with this."

"It's difficult, having a child."

She raised an eyebrow. "Tell me about it! I have two."

"But they're older." I tried to get more comfortable on the bed. "Brad is only ten."

"Believe me, it won't get any easier."

"Okay, I'll think about it."

"No you won't. You've said that before. As soon as we leave here that's the last you'll think about it. You know why? Because it's easier not to think about it."

I tried to smile. "Looks like I've taught you too well."

"How are things with her now, anyway?"

"Same as always."

"She still doesn't want to ... you-know?"

"No – nothing."

"I can't understand a woman like that," she said, staring blankly at the gaudy wallpaper on the opposite wall. "She seems so – I don't know ... selfish?"

"I don't think she can help it, after what happened to ... to ..." After complaining about Irene bringing up Susan, I didn't want to do the same thing.

"In that case, she should've left you." Irene grinned and wrapped her arms around me. "Then we could've been together before now."

I rested my hand on her bare hip for a minute. Then I said, "Okay, I know you're right. Let's do it."

I leaned over to kiss her, but she quickly drew back just out of reach, leaving me kissing the air.

"When?" she asked.

"When?"

"If we don't decide now, we'll have to go through all this again next time we have a love-in."

I laughed. "A *love-in?*"

She couldn't help smiling. "That's what you used to call it in the sixties, wasn't it?"

"I never thought about it like that. But yes, it was."

We were silent again for a while, then I said, "Next Saturday."

Her clear hazel eyes searched my face.

"I'll leave next Saturday," I said.

She wrinkled her brow. "Are you sure?"

I nodded, perhaps too forcefully.

"When will you tell her?"

I hesitated. "After I've left. I'll pack while she's at the college, giving her Reiki class. I can leave my case in the boot of the car. I'll go when she gets back. I'll pick you up at – what? Four o'clock? If you're not on duty."

"I'll make sure I'm not." She cuddled up to me. "Are you sure you can do it, Owen?"

I nodded. "Absolutely. Now that I've decided. It's the right thing to do. It's the only thing to do."

The sky was low in the sky when we were leaving, casting long shadows. I quietly put the keys on the reception desk.

"I was just thinking," Irene said, looking back at the hotel.

"Glad to see my visits to your ward paid off."

She smiled. "These love-ins will be a thing of the past soon – when we have our own place."

That sounded good. I put my arm around her waist as we walked to my car.

As she got out at the corner of her street, I said, "Goodnight, Irene. I'll see you –"

"In your dreams," she finished for me, laughing. After glancing around to make sure no one was in sight, she poked her head back into the car to blow me a kiss from the palm of her hand.

Chapter 7

Although the refectory was packed, I managed to find one of those small tables near the window free. I unloaded my lunch from the tray. Opening a writing block, I drew a line down the middle of one page. On the top of the left column I wrote "Advantages of leaving home" and on the right "Disadvantages". Between mouthfuls, I jotted items in the columns. The Disadvantages were heavily outweighing the Advantages. Fiona had a lot of good qualities. Sophisticated, educated, rich parents (yes, I had to be honest); then there was Brad; and then there was our house, security, stability ... I sat back and looked out of the window.

Returning to the list, I wrote SEX in the right-hand column.

"Can I join you, Owen?" It was Charity, peering at me from under her woollen peaked hat.

I sighed. "Of course."

"Are you sure? I can look for somewhere else if you ..."

"No, no, please –" I indicated the chair opposite me.

"You shouldn't be doing that, you know," she said as she put her tray on the table.

My hand automatically covered what I'd just written. "What?"

"Writing while you eat. You'll never lose weight that way. You are still on a diet, aren't you?"

"Sort of."

"Well, you must eat consciously, chewing each mouthful at least thirty-two times." She glanced at the writing block, apparently not noticing my hand obscuring part of it. "What's so interesting, anyway?"

"Oh, I'm just working on my autobiography."

"What, you're writing a book?" Her Zimbabwean accent always came out when she was surprised.

"Yes, it's based on my experiences as a general student nurse."

She looked impressed. "What's it called?

"The working title is *Just a Little Prick*."

"You're incorrigible," she laughed. "But they don't say that anymore. Now they say, 'Just a little scratch'."

"I wonder why."

"Yes," she said, looking at me from the corner of her eye. "So do I."

While I was putting my writing block away, she went on, "How did the meeting with the visiting professors from Milan University go? Did I miss anything?"

"Not really. Except me upsetting Dean Martin."

"Dean Martin?"

"Aka dean Martin Crawford."

She laughed. "Oh, not again! What did you do this time? You didn't call him Dean Martin in front of everyone, did you?"

"No. What happened was one of the professors presented a case study of foot fetishism. His patient had been arrested for touching women's feet on the Milan underground. Afterwards, Martin asked each of us to comment. You should have heard the psycho-dynamics that were flying around! When it came to me, I said I would advise the patient to take up chiropody."

Charity's belly moved up and down as she laughed. "How did they take that?"

"The Italian professor stroked his beard – which was just like Freud's, by the way – and said, '*Molto interessante* ...' Audrey did her sucked lemon routine."

"She's a right jobsworth, that one. And she's supposed to be preparing students for a caring profession!"

"Martin looked as if he was going to kill me. The only one who laughed was Les."

"That doesn't say much. He'd laugh at anything."

She winked and impersonated Les, "*You know what I mean?*" followed by a rendering of his jolly laugh.

Suddenly serious, she went on, "Martin feels you're not very politically correct."

I pulled a face. "And *you* are?"

"No, I don't say that. But you have to be careful who you joke with."

"I can't imagine what you mean."

"You're always winding him up the wrong way." I was never sure whether she was deliberately mixing her metaphors. "I think Martin can be dangerous."

I shrugged. "He can't do anything to me. As much as he'd like to."

"I wouldn't be so sure. He is the dean, after all. Given half a chance, he'd have your balls on a plate."

After eating in silence for a minute, Charity looked over my shoulder and said, "Talk of the devil. Don't look. He's by the counter. Oh, no! He's seen us. From the expression on his face, he might kill you yet. Oh my God, he's coming over!"

Charity kept her head down, apparently struggling with her chicken breast.

The dean paused at our table, holding his tray in front of him. "Your inane comment to our visitor was out of order," he said, riveting me with his eyes. "A professor from one of the oldest and most prestigious universities of Europe deserves our respect. I can't see any reason for you to feel superior. You've only just finished your Masters. Not a great accomplishment at your age."

I looked at his plate and said, "Meat balls, Martin?"

Charity put a hand to her mouth and started coughing to disguise her laugh. The dean observed her for a moment, then scowled at me. "I don't know why I waste my breath," he hissed.

"He's not a happy bunny," I observed, watching him walk away.

Charity looked at her watch. "Oh, my God, I've got to go. I've got to be at St Mary's by two o'clock to see Nudge."

"Nudge?"

"The charge nurse."

I gave a short laugh. "Is that what he's called?"

"That's his nickname. His name's Nigel. He keeps nudging you when he talks. And he's so condescending to us in education. He keeps referring to *the real world*. Like, *that might be so in theory, but in the real world ...* That gets on my tits."

Putting down her knife and fork, she said, "And it's such a drag – having to go there, I mean. It's in the opposite direction from where I live. I have to drive all the way back here to get home. I don't know why you don't change clinical areas with me, Owen. St Mary's is much closer to where you live …"

I shook my head.

"But why?"

Her puzzlement was understandable. What she was saying was true. But I couldn't tell her the reason I didn't want to change with her was because of Irene. Seeing her on those weekly visits was too precious for me.

"I'm sorry," I said.

She stared at me for a moment, then picked up her handbag. "I'm sure you must have a good reason."

As she rushed away, I looked at the list in front of me. A wave of anxiety came over me as I reminded myself that in three days' time I would be leaving Fiona and Brad to go to live with Irene.

Chapter 8

On Saturday I lay in bed until I heard Fiona closing the front door behind her. Then I heaved myself out of bed. I couldn't face her that morning. Not with what I was going to do.

Through my bedroom window's net curtains, I watched her opening her red Micra. Her skirt momentarily tightened around her thighs as she stepped inside. I couldn't help thinking how elegant she looked for her age. She put her slim black briefcase containing incense sticks and Reiki paraphernalia onto the passenger seat, checked herself in the rearview mirror, then drove off.

I went down to the kitchen, made some coffee, put a couple of slices of bread in the toaster and plonked a tub of crunchy peanut butter on the worktop in readiness. Not an ideal breakfast for someone trying to lose weight, but I just wanted something quick and easy.

Getting the milk for the coffee, I saw the note on the fridge door under the magnet from Paris. This had become Fiona's preferred way of communicating with me. The notes usually told me to do something or complained about something I had or hadn't done. This one read: 'Sweep up the cherry tree petals today – before someone slips and breaks their neck'.

My first thought was to write underneath it, "Not today, dear. Today I am leaving you for another woman". Instead, I screwed it up and threw it in the bin.

Feeling even heavier than usual, I carried my breakfast upstairs and put it on my chest of drawers. Thankfully, I had already brought a suitcase down from the attic. That was good forward planning, I thought. It was very unlikely that Fiona would see it under the bed. I pulled it out and opened it on top of the bed. As I began to pack, pausing to eat or drink from time to time, I imagined how I was going to break the news to Fiona about Irene. That would be when I came back for the rest of my things. Yes, in a week – maybe two – I'd come back, sit her down and explain everything to her. Straight from my Adult ego state, as Wencheng would have put it.

I picked up the silver-framed photo of Fiona, Brad and myself on Mumbles Beach, wondering if I should take it. It was a perfect photo of a perfect family. Fiona was proudly pregnant with Susan. I'd said, "There'll be four of us in next summer's picture." Fiona had put her hand on her belly and replied, "There are four of us already." After Susan died, the photo disappeared from the mantelpiece. I came across it later at the bottom of a linen drawer and brought it up here.

I put it in the case, wrapped in a hand towel.

Then I opened the wardrobe, and my first thought was that most of these clothes didn't fit me anymore. I ran my eye along the rail to see what was worth taking until, in the full-length mirror in the door, I saw a short, plump middle-aged man staring back at me. He was like a stranger. I was surprised to see beads of sweat on his forehead.

At least I'll be travelling light, I thought, as I selected a few things from the wardrobe. The rest could go to the charity shop.

While packing, I glanced out at the cherry tree. Just two weeks ago it was ablaze with deep pink flowers. Now you could see the grey sky through its branches. I moved closer to the window and peered down at the petals that had fallen on the concreted front garden. A gust of wind sent another flurry floating down. It reminded me of the *Albatross* as she cleaved her way through the dark Norwegian Sea, the snow turning pink by the port navigation light.

"Where are we going, Dad? On holiday?"

I spun around to see Brad standing behind me in his pyjamas, rubbing his eyes.

"Nowhere, Brad. I mean, you're not going anywhere. I'm going on my own."

"Where?"

"I'm not sure yet."

He blinked a couple of times. "When will you be back?"

This was the big one. I finished folding a shirt and laid it in the case before answering. "I won't be back – I mean, not like now."

I sat on the bed to be more at his level and put my hands on his shoulders, looking him in the eye. "I don't know if you've noticed, Brad ... things between your mum and me aren't as they should be ..."

"No, I haven't." His eyes half closed as he struggled to understand. "You don't quarrel or anything."

My mouth was getting dry, so I took a sip of tea. It had gone cold.

"But that's not everything," I said. "People need to be compatible."

He stared back at me. How could I expect a ten-year old to understand a word like that? I tried again, "I still love you and Mum … but sometimes grown-ups need to separate. You'll understand one day." I tried to smile, but it was false. And he knew it.

"I don't want to understand! I just want you to stay."

The room had gone darker. Was it just my imagination? But then I heard the rain beating against the window. The sides of Brad's mouth were beginning to turn down. I had been all right up until then.

"Hey, we'll still see each other." Now I was trying to cheer him up. A cheap trick, I thought.

"Please, Dad – don't go."

I stared back at him. Then I got up, clicked the suitcase closed and walked to the door with it. Brad rushed past me and slammed the door shut. He stood in front of it, barring my way. Tears welled up behind his eyelashes. Then he started crying. It was at that moment I knew I couldn't go. Not then. Not ever. Maybe Fiona would leave one day, but I wouldn't.

"It's okay," I said, putting the suitcase down and taking him in my arms. "I won't go."

"Is that true?"

"Yes, it's true. You go back to bed. I'll bring you some breakfast. What do you fancy?"

"I don't know. Boiled egg?"

"With soldiers?"

He nodded. After giving me a searching look, he turned and made his way back to his bedroom.

I mis-dialled Irene's number twice. Wencheng would have said that meant I didn't really want to make that call. The next time I dialled, her answering machine came on. It was her husband's voice. *"We can't take your call at the moment –"* I dropped the receiver onto the cradle.

Backing away, I glared at the phone as if it were a living thing. Then I went into the kitchen and made Brad's breakfast. I took it to him on the wooden tray with folding legs, which he liked so much. Sitting up in bed, he smiled when I walked in. Then I came back down and hit the redial button on the phone. This time I was ready for the machine.

"This is a message for Irene." I tried to sound casual, but I could feel the tension in my throat and my eyes were getting blurry. "Hi, Irene. I'm ringing from Riverside University. I'm afraid today's event has been cancelled. I mean – the whole affair has been cancelled. I'm sorry … Take care."

Putting the phone down, I covered my face with my hands and took a deep, shaky breath.

As I unpacked I wondered if I was doing the right thing. I shook my head, muttering, "I don't know, I don't know." I would hurt Irene by not going, and I'd hurt Brad – and probably Fiona – if I did. I froze when I heard the budgie ruffling its feathers violently, remembering how Fiona had always maintained that it could sense nervous tension. I also thought of how the budgie had always been *it* to me, but *he* to Fiona and Brad. "We don't even know if it's male or female, for goodness' sake," I'd said to her once.

I went down to the sitting room to clean out *its* cage. It was one of the few times I did it without Fiona telling me to. It began making a rapid noise with its tongue. I was convinced it was saying, *Fuck you, fuck you, fuck you!* My hands were shaking as I replaced the paper at the bottom of the cage and topped up the water and seed.

The phone rang. I tried to steady my breathing before lifting the receiver.

"Come to the park near your house," said Irene. I could tell she was trying to control the hysteria in her voice.

"Irene, I can't –"

"Come to the park!"

"I'm looking after Brad –"

"At least you owe me this."

I glanced upstairs. I didn't want to leave Brad alone in the house. But he was happy with his breakfast in bed. He should be all right for ten or fifteen minutes.

"Okay," I said.

"Don't be long – it's pouring down."

"Where are you?"

"Near the duck pond."

I glanced upstairs again, then whispered into the phone, "I'll be right there."

Rain was bouncing off the parked cars and gushing along the gutters as I hurried along the street. The cherry and copper birch trees shook frantically in the wind. A forked flash lit up the dark grey sky above me, followed almost immediately by a crash of thunder. I struggled to keep my black golf umbrella in the direction the wind was coming from to stop it blowing inside out. It reminded me of a scene from *The Omen*. The only thing missing was a church and a lightning rod to be struck by lightning and come down to impale me.

I found Irene by the long boarded up toilets, sheltering as best she could from the rain. Her drenched hair hung down over the collar of her raincoat, as if she'd just got out of the shower. She was wearing her leather boots. Her flimsy pink and white umbrella hung uselessly from her hand, blown inside out and destroyed.

We just stood looking at each other at first, then I said, "I'm sorry."

"Owen." Her umbrella fluttered to the ground as she reached out for my hand. "I can't go on without you."

I took a deep breath, trying to control my emotion. "And I can't go on with you, Irene."

"I don't understand. What happened?"

"I just can't do it. It's too difficult."

"Nobody said it would be easy."

"I know, but –"

"Perhaps you need more time."

"No, Irene. It has to end."

"But we can still see each other. As friends, at least."

I shook my head. "No. We must make a clean break. I'll stop coming to your ward. That'll make it easier."

"You can't do that!" It sounded as if she were losing control.

"Yes, I can. I can swap clinical areas with Charity."

"No, I mean you can't do it – for my sake." Tears mixed with rain as they ran down her cheeks. "Didn't it mean anything to you, Owen?"

"What? Those sordid hotel meetings?"

"*Sordid?*"

"That's what you called them."

"All that matters is to be with you. It doesn't really matter where. Don't you feel the same?"

"No, Irene. We should just be grateful we were never caught out."

"*Caught out?*" They seemed to be foreign words to her. "I thought we loved each other."

"Maybe it meant more to you than me." It wasn't true. I just thought if I was harsh with her it might have made it easier for her in the long run.

She stared at me with her mouth slightly open, water trickling down her face. I tried to read what was going on inside her – shock, bewilderment, defeat?

"It's nine," she murmured.

"Nine …?"

She nodded. "The pain I'm feeling now. It's nine."

Then I remembered. As we sat on the bed in the Wembley hotel, eating chicken curry and drinking white wine, I was explaining how she could use a subjective pain scale on her ward.

"At least it's not ten," I said, because I didn't know what else to say.

She wiped water away from the tip of her nose with the back of her hand. "That's only because I can't really believe it yet."

I needed to get back home, but I hated leaving her like this. I pressed the handle of my umbrella into her hand. She just stood there holding it, unblinking, like an alabaster mannequin in a shop window.

As I ran back to the house in the rain, soaked through and feeling water running underneath my upturned collar, a terrifying thought occurred to me. Something might have happened to Brad in my absence, like with Susan. Maybe that was to be my punishment. Retribution for my infidelity. That would have been infinitely worse than being killed by a falling lightning rod.

With the front door open and with a pool of water forming at my feet, I yelled up the stairs, "Brad, Brad!"

"I'm here," he said, coming out of the sitting room. His eyes were wide with fear as he looked at my drenched clothes and muddy shoes.

I swept him into my arms and lifted him up. "Thank God you're all right!"

"Stop," he protested, prising himself away from me. "You're making me all wet."

Chapter 9

My arm was still in a sling after the accident at the gym the week before. Luckily it was my left arm, so I could still function reasonably well, although I couldn't drive. Fiona was waiting for me when I came downstairs that morning. As soon as I saw her standing there, leaning back against the dishwasher with her arms crossed, I knew something was wrong.

"I saw Aisha go into Bradley's bedroom this morning," she started.

"So?" I said, filling up the kettle. "Coffee?"

She ignored my offer. "She came out of the bathroom in her dressing gown. Went into his room, closing the door after her."

"So?"

Fiona sighed in desperation. "It means they're sleeping together. And if you say *so* again, I swear I'll smash you over the head with this saucepan."

"But it's been months since they stopped pretending to sleep apart when she stays here." I immediately thought that maybe I shouldn't have said that.

"You knew?"

"Yes, of course." The only thing to do now was brazen it out. "He doesn't even bother to throw a blanket on the sofa anymore."

"And you didn't tell me?"

"I assumed you knew. It was pretty obvious."

"I didn't know," she said through clenched teeth, and I thought she was going to reach for that saucepan after all. "I didn't think Indian girls were like that."

"Like what? That they had sexual feelings? Everyone has." I added pointedly, "Well, almost everyone."

Her eyes radiated hatred. "It's your fault he's turned out like this."

"Mine?"

"Yes, yours! Because of your attitude. The way you look at young women in the street, the way you flirt with anything in a skirt."

I pretended to be concentrating on making my coffee.

She went on, "You know you've become a laughing stock at the gym?"

I looked up before I could stop myself.

She nodded, "Oh, yes, Rita told me what happened."

"I told you what happened," I said. "I fell off the running machine."

"But she told me why you fell off." Her thin smile was sadistic. "She saw you ogling that young woman, the one who dresses like a slut. She told me how you turned to look at her as she passed behind you, losing your balance. Oh yes, she saw you. And she wasn't the only one. Pathetic!"

My face was becoming hot with embarrassment as I stared down, stirring my coffee. Eight years had slipped past since Irene and I broke up. At first I'd missed her terribly, but I gradually resigned myself to life as it was with Fiona. Just recently, though, my interest in other women had reawakened. For some reason I became attracted to the way they smelt – not their perfume, but their natural smell.

"Will you stop stirring your coffee like that!" Fiona brought me back to the present. "It's beginning to sound like a fire alarm."

"Getting back to Brad," I said, putting the spoon down, "I think it's a matter of accepting things as they are. After all, they are eighteen."

"Exactly. They are still children."

"It's normal at their age. I mean things have changed since our days, when –"

"Don't tell me about our days! I only care about their days! What would her parents say if they knew?"

"Well, they sleep together at her house." I bit my lip, realising I'd said the wrong thing.

"How do you know?"

"I don't know. That's just the impression I get."

"You're immoral!"

"No – it's not that, Fiona."

"Yes, it is that, Owen. They've never given *me* that impression."

"They are probably careful not to, knowing your feelings about these things."

I suddenly remembered my dread that one day Fiona would confront me about packing to leave her when Brad was a child. Sooner or later, I'd thought, he was bound to tell her. But he never did. And he never mentioned it to me again. It was as if it never happened. I never knew whether he had decided it was the wise thing to do or his mind had blanked it out.

Fiona tutted. "I can't believe her parents allow her to behave like that."

I shrugged. "I suppose they accept things as they are."

"They can accept whatever they like. They are not going to carry on like that under my roof!"

"So what are you going to do?"

"Me? You're his father. What are *you* going to do?"

I felt her eyes piercing the back of my head as I put a slice of bread in the toaster. "Oh, all right," I said, yielding to her silent pressure. "I'll talk to him."

"Talking isn't enough. You have to tell him he's not allowed to sleep with her anymore."

I thought of Irene again. Sex was good with her. I knew I would miss it. I missed it so badly that it was me who caved in after a couple of months, not her. It was me who phoned her home and was told she no longer lived there. It was me who asked Charity about her, and was told that she had left the hospital. Perhaps it was for the best in the long run. It wouldn't have been right to risk hurting her again.

Fiona was staring at me as if trying to fathom out what was going on in my mind.

I turned my eyes to her as if coming out of a dream. "How can I tell him that? Do you really think he'd take any notice, anyway?"

"At least you can tell him not to do it in here. I don't care what they do outside. Well, yes, I do care, but ..."

"So? Wouldn't it be better to let them do what they want to do? Rather than doing it behind our backs?"

She was beginning to look unsure, so I continued, "If we succeed in stopping them from doing it here, they'll only do it somewhere else – and that might be less safe."

"Safe? That's another thing that worries me. I wonder if they take precautions ... If he uses something."

"You mean rubbers?"

"Don't be crude! But yes, that is what I mean. You know that unprotected sex nowadays is very dangerous. And besides that, I don't want him involved in a shotgun wedding."

"I didn't think they do them anymore."

"Okay," she said after a brief silence. "I'll allow it on one condition."

I raised an eyebrow.

"That you tell him the facts of life," she said.

The urge to laugh was almost uncontrollable. I nearly spilt my coffee.

"A responsible father would have done it years ago," she snapped.

"Okay, okay. I'll talk to him."

I tried to do it that afternoon. And that evening. And the next morning. But every time I went into his room I ended up saying things like, "Are you going to watch the football this afternoon?" or "How are you getting on with your assignment?"

In the end he said, "Do you want something, Dad?"

"Well, yes, Brad. I do. I think it's time we had a little chat."

I closed his bedroom door behind me.

"About what?"

"I won't beat about the bush, it's about – about ..."

"Oh, my God, don't tell me it's about – about ..." he imitated me in mock horror.

"Well, yes, it is."

"It's a bit late for that, isn't it?"

"It's never too late to learn, Brad."

"Okay. What do you want to know?"

I forced a laugh, then cleared my throat. "I was just wondering ... You know, it just occurred to me ... can you get free prophylactics at your university?"

"You mean condoms?"

I nodded and swallowed hard. "It's just that our students can."

"Yes, we can. But I usually just pop into the Family Planning Clinic down the road."

"Oh. Right. Great." I reached behind me for the door handle. "Well, if there's ever anything you want to ask me – anything at all ..."

"Sure, Dad." He grinned. "It's a great comfort to know that."

Chapter 10

I kept thinking about the conversation with Brad over the next few days. My son had sex without commitment, while I had commitment without sex. It wasn't fair – but even as I thought that, I realised it was irrational.

There were at least a dozen people waiting for the lift on the ground floor, most of them female. The observation of Philip, a senior lecturer in Mental Health like myself, but much younger, taller and with a ring in his ear, came back to me: "Out of any ten women you see – anywhere – one of them is always on heat and yours for the taking. The tragedy is you don't know which one."

Then I noticed that Karolina Czech was amongst them. That wasn't really her last name, of course. I'd seen her real name on the register when I did a series of workshops for the Maternity Branch and found it unpronounceable. She was from the Czech Republic, so she became Karolina Czech in my mind, to distinguish her from Carolina Murphy, head of the Assessments Office. She smiled when she saw me, then edged her way to me and kissed me on the cheek.

In a low voice, I said, "Can I have a word with you?"

Her smile faltered. Then she frowned. "Oh, dear. Am I in trouble?"

I was a bit disappointed that she saw me as an authority figure. "Not at all. It's only if you have time ..."

"I have, I have," she rushed. I could see that she was anxious to know what it was about.

"The refectory?" I suggested.

She nodded.

I had sworn that I'd never again hurt anyone as I did Irene. But as we walked to the refectory I reminded myself that there was nothing vulnerable about this attractive young woman who emanated confidence and talent. The world was her oyster, I thought. I imagined her swinging in a giant oyster shell, her legs hanging over the side, a glass of champagne in her hand.

Even though it was the lull between coffee and lunchtime, I chose a table where we would probably not be overheard. The large window caught the warmth of the morning sun. I devoured her with my eyes as she unbuttoned her long, black coat, revealing a white blouse above her jeans. She hung her bag on the back of her chair, then turned back to me questioningly.

How should I begin?

"I was just wondering …" I said, "how you are getting on?"

"Fine." She was looking at me in a strange way.

"Your course – it's going okay, then?"

"Yes."

"And your essays? With English not being your first language …"

"Why? Has someone said something?"

"No, no. I was just wondering." I put my hands on my knees, arms rigid. "You said in one of the role plays that Czech grammar is very different from … thanks for volunteering, by the way. You're quite an actress."

"You're welcome."

Our relationship had always been so easy and enjoyable, but now she was cautious. I just hoped, as she stared at me, that she wouldn't see the hunger and emptiness inside me.

"You want a coffee?" I asked.

"No, thank you. We just had our coffee break."

"Oh, right. So did I." I tried a smile, but it turned out to be more of a grimace. "So I was just wondering. If you need any help … with your essays?"

She laughed nervously. "Are you going to write my essays for me?"

I laughed too, in the same way. "Not write them for you, no. But I could check them, suggest improvements … correct your English. I understand that your personal tutor doesn't do that."

Karolina laughed again, but more relaxed this time. "Audrey? No way!"

She was becoming more like her normal self, which gave me the confidence to say, "Look, I'll give you my mobile number – just in case."

I wrote it in my pocket notebook and tore the page out for her. She read it before thrusting it into her coat pocket. "Thank you."

"Ring me any time." I was hoping she would give me her number, but she just got to her feet and buttoned up her coat. "Audrey mentioned you've got an essay due in a couple of weeks," I continued, pretending not to be disappointed.

She pulled a face. "Yes."

"So I'll expect to hear from you soon." I hoped I didn't sound as desperate as I felt.

While she hesitated with a puzzled expression on her face, I stood up and took a step towards her. She stiffened slightly, offering me her hand to shake.

Chapter 11

I was on my own in the lift when Karolina Czech stepped in on the second floor, clutching a corrugated cardboard cup of coffee. At first we stared at each other in surprise, then she said, "Going up?"

I nodded. "Which floor?"

"Eight." She watched as I pressed the button. "A new job, you have?" she said, imitating my accent. "Lift attendant you are now, is it?"

I laughed and continued the joke, "Not come to that yet, it hasn't."

Noticing that I was looking slightly upwards as I spoke to her, I said, "You've sprung up since I saw you last."

"It's just my heels," she said, lifting and twisting one leg to reveal the thick, high heel that had been hidden by her jeans.

Aware that we might not be on our own for long, I said as casually as I could, "Lost my mobile number, did you?"

She blinked. "No. I think I've still got it here somewhere." She glanced at her bulging shoulder bag.

"It's just that when you didn't ring me ..."

She shrugged and sipped her coffee.

"Your essay must be due in soon?"

The lift tinged to signal it would be stopping on the next floor.

"Today, by three-thirty. I'm just going to pick up a submission form. Then I've got to check a few spellings, tidy up the references ..."

When the lift doors opened, a young student hurried in and hit one of the buttons. Forehead knitted into a frown, he flipped through a transparent folder with a yellow Assessment Submission sheet at the front.

I glanced at my watch and said to Karolina, "You're cutting it a bit fine," but the newcomer must have thought I was talking to him because he looked up with panic in his eyes.

Karolina smiled, "Lastminute.com is my middle name."

"So that's how you pronounce it?"

She looked confused for a moment, then laughed.

As the other student dived out of the lift on the sixth floor, he unknowingly jolted Karolina's arm, causing her to spill some coffee. I was going to say something to him, but I was mesmerised by the sight of Karolina's tongue catching the drips running down her cup.

The lift tinged again.

"Eighth floor," I announced. "Assessments Office and other Student Nightmares."

She giggled as she wiped her cup with a tissue.

"Good luck with your essay," I said.

"Thank you, Owen." She hesitated, then added, "You're a great teacher."

Before getting out, she leaned forward and gave me a peck on the cheek, leaving me with a warm feeling inside.

My mobile rang as I was getting out of the lift two floors higher up.

"Hello? Is that Uncle Owen?" At first I thought it was one of the students messing about, but she went on, "This is Siân."

"Siân? ... But aren't you in New Zealand?"

"Yes."

"You know this is my mobile?"

"Yes, I know. I called you at home, but there was no answer ..."

I felt the muscles at the back of my neck tensing up.

"Mam and Dad are here with me for a month."

"I know." My mind was racing. What was so urgent? Had something happened to Gwen or Roger there? "How are they enjoying it?" I said, trying to sound causal.

"Oh, they love it here on the farm. Especially Dad – he gets up early every morning to help feed the animals." For some reason I hadn't expected her to have a New Zealand accent.

"I'm ringing about Mam," she said. "Uncle Owen, I'm afraid we're not going to have her for much longer."

"Why? When is she coming back?"

"That's not what I meant." There was a long pause. "You know she hasn't been well for a while?"

"Yes." A cold feeling settled in my stomach.

"We took her to see our doctor in Auckland and he referred her to a specialist. She's got terminal cancer, Uncle Owen."

My hand tightened on the mobile.

"Are you still there?" she asked.

"Did he say how long ...?"

"A year. Eighteen months tops." She sniffled back a tear.

"And Roger, how is he taking it?"

"He's in complete denial. Says he'll sort it out when they get home."

"I don't know what to say."

"What can anyone say? ... What about you, Uncle Owen, how are things with you guys?"

"We're fine. No problems."

"I'd better go." It sounded as if she was starting to cry, and she wouldn't have wanted me to hear that. She had Gwen's strong personality. "Give my love to Auntie Fiona and Brad."

Ewelina, the Polish girl who had been with us for teaching experience for a couple of months, looked up as I passed her desk. She got up and followed me to mine and asked quietly, "Are you okay?"

"Yes, I'm okay," I said, sitting down.

"You don't look it. You look like you've seen a ghost."

I put my hands to my face and took a long breath in and out.

"Shall I take your blood pressure?" A recently qualified general nurse, this was one thing she knew how to do well.

"No, it's okay." I tried to smile.

She hesitated. "I don't know. It was a bit high last time." Then she added decisively, "I will do it."

Her blonde ponytail swung from side to side as she hurried away. I knew she was going to the Practical Floor to get a sphygmomanometer and a stethoscope. I got up and walked over to the window. I looked down at the roofs of other buildings. Some, in their day, must have been considered very high, but were now dwarfed by our fourteen storey building.

"Come to sit down," Ewelina called to me, drawing a chair up to mine for herself.

I did as she said, pulling up my shirt sleeve and extending my arm. She secured the cuff to my upper arm and put the ends of the stethoscope into her ears. As she pumped up the cuff, I gazed at her glassy blue eyes. She knew nothing about my home situation, I mused, although I knew a lot about hers, especially the acrimonious divorce she was going through.

Imagine if she knew how the death of Susan had destroyed my marriage, like a ship with a gash below the waterline. Or about the affair with Irene that had ended in heartbreak. That was one of the worse things, not being able to talk to anyone about it. Not even to Wencheng. And now there was this news about my sister.

Ewelina removed the stethoscope from her ears and let it hang from her neck. Taking the cuff off my arm, she said, "It's much higher than last time. You should get some medication."

"I'll try to see my GP next week," I murmured.

She swivelled her chair towards my desk and wrote on a piece of paper. "Show him this," she said. "And I think it should be today, not next week."

I folded the paper without reading it, mesmerised by the assertive side of Ewelina that I was seeing for the first time.

"Another thing," she added. "I thought you were going to lose weight."

Chapter 12

Shola, the Nigerian student, was on my mind when I woke up. Remembering what had happened in the empty classroom the day before, I felt a pang of anxiety grip my stomach.

As I buttoned up my shirt, I glanced out at the cherry tree on the pavement. It was ablaze with luscious flowers which, I knew, would start withering within the next week. A young Asian woman stopped under the tree, looking up at it. When she reached and snapped off a sprig, I put my hand on the window handle to open it and complain. But then, smiling to herself, she secured the flowers in her hair. The deep pink flowers against her black hair was stunning. Wherever she is going, I thought, she'll share the beauty of the tree, and I smiled inwardly.

Fiona was sitting at the kitchen table spreading diet marmalade on her crispbread when I walked in. "I wouldn't have been surprised to see crop circles on the lawn when I looked out of my bedroom window this morning," she said.

"Good morning to you, too."

My bedroom. She said it without thinking these days, as if it was normal for married people to sleep in separate rooms. I put a couple of slices of bread into the toaster.

"Where's Brad?" I asked.

"*Bradley*," she corrected me. "Where do you think he is at this time?"

"Not still in bed?" I dropped open my mouth feigning surprise.

"If you don't cut the grass this weekend," she said, going back to the crop circles theme, "I'm going to ask one of the Polish boys in number twenty-three to do it."

"Well, why not? You haven't bothered them for a while."

"It's no bother to them. They are always ready to earn some extra cash." She added provocatively, "They are such nice boys ... especially Jacek. The 'y' sound at the beginning is actually written 'j', you know."

"Oh, which one is he?"

"The one with the cropped blond hair and amazing blue eyes. The one who got rid of the old fridge freezer for us."

I stopped stirring my coffee for a moment as if pondering, and then said, "I thought they all had blond hair and blue eyes."

"No, not at all." If she saw any anger behind my remark, she didn't show it. "Take Lukasz —with a k and a z – his hair is quite dark and he has brown eyes."

Strange that she could still provoke jealousy in me even though there had been nothing physical between us for years. There had been nothing physical between me and *anyone* since Irene.

I extracted the Flymo from the shed at the bottom of the garden while she got ready to go to give her weekly Reiki class at the adult college. The shed was in a mess again. In desperate need of a tidy up and a chuck out. No doubt that would be the next thing Brad would want done after the attic had been sorted out. He was looking for things to do while on holiday from university.

The mower whirred hysterically as its rotating blade struggled with the long grass. I pulled it back and forth at the uneven flower borders, going blind under the petunia, busy lizzies and London pride. I always feared that some animal might be hiding there and imagined it crying out as it was minced alive.

Now that I was mowing in straight lines, my mind was free to wander. I wondered how Gwen was now, and when she and Roger would be returning from New Zealand. I thought about how I hadn't bothered to speak to my GP about my high blood pressure. And then I went over the events with Shola the day before. She had stayed in the classroom when all the other students went for lunch so I could help her with the fourth attempt of one of her essays.

"Let's sit here," I'd said, sliding behind one of the desks.

I took the essay out of my briefcase and placed it on the desk in front of me. She sat next to me so that we could look at it together, her beautifully plaited hair with occasional maroon and gold braids falling down to the desk.

"Will it pass?" she asked.

"In its present form, I would say no," I replied.

"But I thought it was nice now."

"Well, there are still a few things you need to work on. Things I've already discussed with you in the past."

"You're so patient with me, Owen. Not like some lecturers."

Ignoring her admiring gaze, I went on, "Firstly, you need to develop an academic argument —"

"I hate arguing," she interrupted. "Ask anyone. I just walk away."

"I don't think you quite understand the principle ..." I stopped as she treated me to one of her dazzling smiles. "Oh, I see. You're teasing me."

"You're so serious, Owen!"

"Maybe *you* need to be more serious, Shola, if you want to get through this course."

"I know. I wouldn't have got this far without you."

"Helping you with your assignments is one thing, but I won't be with you when you re-sit your final exam. For the fourth time. It must be soon ...?"

"Next month."

"Okay. Another thing is your use of language."

"But English is not my first language. That's why I always ask my husband to correct. His English is very good."

"That's not what I mean. You must learn to use academic language."

"Ho, academic language, academic language! I never understood what is that."

"Well, look," I said, flipping through the essay. Her perfume, which was unfamiliar to me, smelt stronger as she leaned towards me to see what I was reading. "Ah, here, for instance. 'I was gob-smacked to hear that he had taken an overdose'."

"Well, I was!"

"Maybe you were, but it would be better to say something like, 'The writer was surprised ...' or 'dismayed'."

Fiona slid back the dining room doors and stepped out onto the patio, bringing me back to the present. She was still wearing her dressing gown, but had put on her makeup. She flapped her hand for me to turn the lawnmower off. Then she said, "Don't forget to rake the surplus grass when you've finished."

"Yes, of course."

"Well, you didn't last time, and it went a horrible brown colour." She gave me a cautionary look before turning to go back indoors.

I remembered how tears had welled in Shola's dark, almost black eyes. She turned away from me and rummaged in her handbag for a tissue.

"All this academic rubbish," she said, dabbing her eyes. "All I want is to be a nurse."

"And I'm sure you'll make a good nurse. I know it seems unfair sometimes, all these academic demands ..."

She gazed at me imploringly and leaned forward. Then I felt her hand on my thigh. My eyes shot to the open door to see if anyone was around. I could have said something, or moved away. But I didn't. It had been so long since anybody touched me like that.

"I want to go home as a nurse," she went on, gently squeezing my leg. "I would do anything for that."

My reverie was interrupted again by the reappearance of Fiona on the patio, handbag dangling by her side, car keys in hand. "Okay, I'm going."

I stopped raking up the cut grass and gazed at her. She looked so pretty, standing in the sun with her straw hat and Ray-Ban sunglasses. But she seemed so far away, looking down as if from a stage. Not for the first time, I thought of how distancing herself from me was like a means of protecting herself.

"Okay," I said, turning back to the raking and thoughts about Shola.

Chapter 13

I was lounging on the sofa watching *The Wright Stuff* and finishing the barbecued spare ribs and rice from the night before when the phone rang. I grabbed the tea towel from the tray and wiped my hands as I went to answer it.

"May I speak to Mrs Owen, please?"

An African accent, it sounded familiar. I tilted my head to one side, trying to figure out who she was while I replied, "No. She's at the college, teaching Reiki. Are you one of her students?"

There was a hesitation, then, "Yes, please. When will she be at home?"

"Well, she usually gets back around two-thirty. You not at the class, then?"

"No. Thank you." She hung up.

About ten minutes later my lunch was disturbed again, this time by the doorbell. I groaned as I picked up the tea towel and went to open the door. I was wearing shorts splattered with paint, a souvenir T-shirt from Las Vegas, and flip-flops. I hadn't washed or shaved, either, so I must have looked a mess.

I didn't recognise Shola at first. She was wearing a smart skirt and jacket, black high heels, a silver chain around her neck and silver stud earrings. Her plaited hair, which usually hung loose, was tied back into a thick ponytail.

"Well, aren't you going to ask me in?"

I wasn't sure if I was. What was she doing here? I wiped my mouth with the tea towel and moved to one side. "Yes, of course. Come in."

As I led her into the sitting room, I asked, "How did you get my address?"

"It was easy. Electoral register."

I sat on the sofa and indicated the armchair to her, but she sat next to me on the sofa. I glanced at the tray on the coffee table in front of us, at the almost finished spare ribs and the glass decorated with brown fingerprints.

"This is quite a surprise," I said.

She looked around the room, then back at me, smiling, her perfect teeth brilliantly white.

"Nice house," she commented. "How long have you lived here?"

"Probably longer than you've been alive. Twenty-five years."

"Oh, I was alive. Eleven years old in Nigeria. Living with five brothers and sisters, my parents and one set of grandparents in a house no bigger than this room." She glanced around with a faraway expression.

I supported my chin on the back of my hand, waiting for her to answer the unasked question that hung above us.

"I needed to see you urgently," she said.

My eyebrows rose a fraction.

"I'm so worried about the final exam."

"I can understand that. But it's too late to worry about it now."

"Is it? You haven't marked the papers yet, have you?"

"No, that's future entertainment. In a couple of weeks."

"You'll mark mine, as I'm in your tutorial group?"

"Yes, but it won't have your name on it, only your student number. For anonymity. To prevent marker bias, and all that."

"You'll recognise mine. I've left a big space between each answer."

"Why would you do that?"

She hesitated, then looked me straight in the eye. "So that I can write in the answers when you tell them to me."

"What?" At first I couldn't take in what she had said. "Shola, I couldn't possibly –"

I stopped as she put her arms around my neck.

"It was you who phoned, wasn't it? To make sure Fiona was out."

"Is that her name? Yes, it was me. You mentioned in class that she goes somewhere every Saturday. I didn't know what time, though." She ran her fingers through my hair. "You'll really enjoy it with me, Owen. It's quite tight."

"*Tight?*" I echoed the word in surprise, not believing what I'd heard.

"Oh, yes. You might not have thought so, after having three children." She added quickly, "But not too tight – you won't have any problem."

I tried to laugh but ended up clearing my throat. "I can't believe it ..."

Her eyes opened wider. "You don't believe me?"

"No, it's – I mean, I can't believe this conversation ..."

"It's time, isn't it? Time to stop pussyfooting. I know you like me. I've seen you looking. Even when I don't see you looking, my friend Princess tells me, 'Oh my God, girl, whenever you turn around that teacher he is looking at your butt'."

I tried to laugh again. "Hey, come on! What an imagination!"

But I acknowledged to myself that her figure was like a magnet to a man's eyes. It was then I noticed that my erection was becoming visible. She noticed too and turned her eyes back up to me in mock astonishment. As if it were a cue, she then undid the top two buttons of her blouse, pushed the left side of her bra down and lifted out her breast.

"Do you suck?" she asked.

No, I don't, I thought, *but not through choice.* I recognised this as a point of no return. Up until now I had just played a passive role. But I felt a yearning in my gut, and a voice in my head was saying *why not, after so many years, why the hell not?*

She was looking at me expectantly, her lips curved into a question mark.

She sighed with satisfaction as I reached down with my mouth. At first I only licked her nipple and that circle around it, but soon I was like a dog drinking water from a tap. She chuckled.

A faint *tinggg* somewhere in the house made us both start.

"What was that?" she asked, eyes popping.

I turned my head to one side to listen and her nipple rubbed against my ear.

"Your son's not in?" she whispered. "I forgot about him!"

"No, he's at his girlfriend's." Then I smiled with relief. "That was the retaining ring on one of the kitchen lights. They're always dropping out … How did you know about my son, anyway?"

"Electoral register."

I felt a bit uneasy about her checking up on me like that, but just said, "Shows you can do research when you want to."

Shola treated me to one of her dazzling grins and, with one deft movement, exposed the other breast. I admired and caressed it for a full minute before giving it the same treatment as the first one.

Her hands on the back of my head, gently pulling me towards her, she said, "You can take me from behind if you like."

My mouth became still and I said to her right breast, "My wife will be home soon." I don't know why I said that – Fiona wasn't due home for at least another hour. Perhaps this was too sudden for me, and it was going too quickly. Fantasy was one thing, reality another.

"Oh." She sounded disappointed as she wriggled her breasts back into her bra. For a moment I thought they were not going to fit back in.

As we walked to the front door, I felt my head would burst with ambivalence. It had been an exquisite experience, but now another voice in my head, that sounded suspiciously like Wencheng, was telling me it was wrong.

"Do me a favour," she said as I opened the door. "Get those kitchen lights fixed before I come next Saturday."

She put her arms around my neck and kissed me on the cheek. As she walked along the garden path she turned to wave and caught me looking at her bum. She laughed and blew me a kiss from the palm of her hand.

Chapter 14

The following Saturday I decided that when Shola phoned I would tell her she could not come to the house and that there was no way I would collaborate in her proposed academic fraud. And that would be the end of it.

But she didn't bother to phone. I saw her through the net curtains of the sitting room window before she rang the bell. She glanced at her wristwatch, then rang again, keeping her finger on the bell longer this time.

Coming to the conclusion that she was not going to go away, I went to open the door. I wasn't sure if I really wanted her to go away. I opened the door and stood looking at her. She narrowed her eyes questioningly and mouthed, *Has she gone?*

I nodded. "But I want to make something very clear to you, Shola –"

"Are we going to talk out here, on the doorstep?"

"I just want to make sure you understand ..."

"I've come a long way, Owen. At least a cup of coffee?"

"No."

She leaned against the doorframe in a pose that accentuated her legs. "Why not?"

"Because," I said, feeling my resolve weaken, "one thing might lead to another."

"Oh, go on. What are we, a couple of teenagers?"

Fearing that perhaps I was being unreasonable, I moved to one side and motioned for her to come in. I followed her into the sitting room, where she dropped her handbag onto the sofa.

"Okay," I said. "I'll make the coffee."

She flashed me a smile. "I usually have mine afterwards."

"There's not going to be an afterwards, Shola. I mean that."

When I brought the coffee she patted the sofa beside her. But I sat on the armchair opposite. She crossed her ebony legs.

"So your feet are getting cold?" she asked.

"What? Oh, you mean am I getting cold feet?"

"I don't know. Are you?"

"I just don't think it's right," I said, then corrected myself: "I *know* it's not right."

"Who decides what's right and what's wrong? You remember that lecture you gave us on morals, with dilemmas and all that?"

"Moral development?"

"Yes, that's it. You said sometimes it's right to do the wrong thing, like stealing a drug, for example, for your partner if they are dying."

I nodded, then sat back, folding my arms. "So?"

"Well, take me. I'm really good on the ward, with practical things – ask anyone. So if you make sure I pass this stupid exam you'll be doing a good thing because the patients will have me to look after them."

I smiled. "You really believe that?"

"I believe because you told us. I know you wouldn't tell us nothing that wasn't true."

I shook my head slowly. "It's not that simple ..."

"I know it's not. That's why you told us the dilemmas an' all."

For a minute we sat in silence, sipping our coffee. Then she came and knelt in front of me, taking one of my hands in hers. Tears welled behind her long eyelashes. "I just want my family to be proud of me, that's all."

Her face collapsed into my lap. She made movements as if she were sobbing. When her hands moved to her face I thought it was to wipe tears away, but I became aware that she was unzipping my fly.

"Shola, what are you doing?"

She didn't answer. It was a pointless question.

"Look at that!" she said, having exposed me. "So he is interested after all."

She curled her fingers around it and began moving her hand up and down. *I can still stop it,* I told myself, *even now* ... but I just sat back with my arms at my side. She straightened up and pulled her jumper off, revealing a white bra. Leaning back slightly, the bra came off next and her breasts sprung forward.

As she hitched up her short skirt I saw her almost transparent panties, embroidered with lace. Then she put one knee on each side of me and lifted herself on to me. As she moved up and down simulating intercourse, I put my hands on her back.

We both froze as the doorbell rang.

"Don't answer it," Shola breathed. "They'll go away."

"No, I'd better check. It might be important."

"And *this* isn't?"

She reluctantly stood up so that I could go and look out of the window. A white van was parked outside. Then I saw two men in brown overalls standing on the doorstep. The middle-aged one, holding a clipboard, was tall with an enormous belly. The other, a teenager, was rakish with a pin through his eyebrow.

"Damn! I forgot about the delivery," I said. "Wait here."

The two men carried a large cardboard box in.

"Where do you want it, gov?" asked the older man.

"Here will be fine," I said.

"What, in the hall? Are you sure? Your missus said to put it in the living room."

"Oh, I er ..." My mind was racing.

The strain began to show on their faces as they waited for me to decide.

"It's just that I'm doing a tutorial at the moment ..." I tried to think what reason I could give to Fiona for leaving it in the hall.

The teenager's knees were beginning to buckle.

"Make your mind up, gov," panted the other one. "This is bloomin' heavy."

"Just bring it in here." I hurried into the living room before them.

"Sorry," I said to Shola, who was now fully dressed. "This won't take a minute."

The two men watched her smooth her skirt down, then looked at one another.

"Over there, against the wall," I said. "I think that's where she wanted it."

When they set it down against the wall, the older man turned to me. "Okay if we assemble it now?"

"Assemble it?"

"Yeah, your missus paid for it to be assembled. But if it's not convenient ..."

"Could you call back later?"

He flipped through the papers on his clipboard, then said, "Yep, next Thursday."

I imagined what Fiona's reaction would be to waiting that long. "Well, how long would it take to do it now?"

"Normally about twenty minutes. But this chap's new and he's not the sharpest tool in the box, so might be longer."

I moistened my lips and glanced at Shola.

"No problem, professor," she drawled, picking up her handbag and slinging it over her shoulder. "I'll see you same time next week."

I walked to the door with her. She squeezed my hand and smiled at me over her shoulder as she stepped outside.

"Right," said the guy in charge when the cabinet had been assembled. "Just sign here, gov – I mean, professor."

As they walked to the gate, I heard him chuckle and say to his workmate, "Tutorial? Is that what they call it now?"

I only half closed the door so that I could still hear them.

"I wouldn't mind giving that blonde girl in the office a *tutorial*," said the teenager.

"Watch it, mate! That's my daughter."

"Is she?"

"No. Just kidding." His laughter trailed off.

Chapter 15

Sitting at my desk, I might have looked as if I was working, but I was deep in thought about Gwen. How was she now? When would they be returning from New Zealand? I needed to go to see her as soon as I could. But at the same time I dreaded seeing her with a terminal illness. I started when I heard a voice behind me say, "Here's my lesson plan –"

It was Ewelina.

"Sorry," she went on. "I didn't mean to scare you."

"It's okay," I said. "I was just ... Lesson plan?"

"Yes, for this afternoon. You're observing my teaching session."

"Oh, yes."

"You forgot?"

"No, no. It's in my diary."

"Have you got time to look at it now?"

"Sure."

She handed me a couple of sheets of paper and pulled up a chair to sit next to me, crossing one leg over the other.

As I read, I asked, "How's your Cert Ed going?"

"Oh, it's going. I think. But it's difficult with two children and going through a messy divorce."

I nodded sympathetically. I already knew about her home situation. As I studied the papers she'd given me, the silence of the open-plan office was broken by a sound like air escaping from a balloon. Ewelina and I automatically looked in the direction it came from.

"Oops, sorry," said Les, another senior lecturer, looking up sheepishly.

Ewelina's blue eyes turned to me and she whispered, "In Poland that is very rude."

"He's our office slob," I whispered back. "Every office has one. They're often very creative people. But Les is just a slob."

"A student told me he even does it in front of them. I mean, is that normal?"

"Well, it's not compulsory."

She glanced over to the podgy figure of Les again, looking puzzled. "Apparently he always says that – 'oops, sorry'."

A BT jingle struck up from the other side of the office.

"That's my mobile!" she said, jumping up.

In her haste to get back to her desk to answer it, she bumped into Philip, who was making his way to the photocopier with a wad of papers.

"Hey, careful!" he said as several fell to the floor.

She said, "Sorry!" over her shoulder as she continued the dash to her desk.

As Philip bent down to pick up the papers, he muttered, "Damn!" His eyes following Ewelina behind his tinted glasses. If it had been anyone else, he would have said more than that, I was sure.

Grabbing her mobile from her desk, she gasped, "Hello." Then she straightened up and spoke quite formally. "Oh, hello. Can you hold the line a moment, please?"

As she walked out of the office, mobile in hand, she signalled to me with her index finger and thumb and mouthed, "two minutes".

Having made a few corrections and comments on Ewelina's work, I got up to go the loo. Outside the office, in the lift area, I saw her leaning against a wall. She didn't sound so formal now, holding the mobile close to her mouth, smiling and speaking softly. She nodded to me and waggled the same two fingers in my direction.

She was sitting at my desk again when I came back. I noticed her blonde hair shining in the sunlight, and she looked happy and relaxed.

"Manage to sort everything out?" I said, sitting beside her.

She looked at me quizzically.

"On the phone. Sounded important."

"Oh, that." She smiled, then looked down and blushed.

"Okay. Your lesson plan is quite good, but I think you're trying to cram too much into two hours."

"Do you think so?"

"It's a common mistake with new teachers, being afraid of not having enough to say."

"Yes, that's me."

"But with students turning up late, taking time to settle down, a coffee break …"

My words petered out as, through the corner of my eye, I saw Lisa, the dean's voluptuous PA, putting on her shoes. She always worked bare-footed at her station in front of Martin's room. Balancing herself on her desk, she put on one high heel after the other. This meant she was either going in to see him or leaving the office. Clutching a file under one arm and swinging the other, she marched between our desks to the exit, "leading with her tits", as Philip put it. The office seemed to resonate with her steps, the split in her long skirt flashing one leg, then the other.

Philip put down his pen and leaned back in his chair, hands clasped behind his head, to watch. Les seemed to reach out to steady his coffee mug as if the vibration might make the contents spill over. Audrey observed her sideways, eyes narrowed in disapproval.

I imagined the support pillar next to Audrey's desk being a stripper's pole and Lisa pausing to dance and writhe around it, looking straight at Audrey, who kept her head down to her work, turning puce with rage. The rest of us encircled Lisa, slow clapping …

I chuckled at the fantasy and Ewelina looked up from her lesson plan. "What?"

She looked down again, no doubt trying to see what I found funny about what she had written. Then she followed my eyes to the undulating figure leaving the office.

"Careful with your blood pressure," she said.

I cleared my throat and reached for the lesson plan. She moved it just out of my reach.

"What did your GP say?"

When I hesitated, she added, "You didn't see him, did you?"

"Not yet."

She shook her head slowly.

Chapter 16

Everything was going slow that morning. It felt like I'd been marking those final exam papers for hours, but as I dropped the second one onto the coffee table, I said to myself, two down, twenty-seven to go. I picked up another one from the top of the pile and stretched out on the sofa again. It seemed like Fiona was taking ages getting ready to go to her Reiki class.

It reminded me of how I used to try to catch the budgie to put it back into its cage. I would carefully bring my hand to within a few inches of the cornered bird, then try to grab it. At this point the wings and my hand would appear to move in slow motion. No matter how much I tried, I couldn't get my hand to move faster as it took off without being touched. That was before someone told me the trick was to darken the room so that it wouldn't fly.

Fiona's hair was short – cute, I thought. And her makeup was perfect. Why did she always have to be so immaculate? Was there another man? He was in for a shock when he found out she was frigid. Unless she was only like that with me, of course.

She put on her Ray-Ban sunglasses. I had never forgotten the make since Brad mentioned how much he paid for his. Her Prada handbag hung at her side. I remembered that name too as I was taken aback when I happened to see the price tag after her shopping expedition to Bond Street.

"Are you sure it's okay for you to mark papers slumming around like that?" she asked.

"What's wrong with it?"

"Well, you don't look professional. You should be sitting at your desk."

"I don't think it matters to the students what position I'm in when I mark their work."

"I wouldn't like to think of you making a decision that could affect the rest of my life so casually."

"It's not casual. I take marking very seriously, you know that."

She shrugged. "It doesn't seem professional, that's all." She sniffed the air. "Are you going out?"

"Me? No, why?"

"You've had a bath – and washed your hair."

"It may have escaped your attention, but I do wash occasionally."

"Not when you're working at home, you don't."

"And there was me thinking you don't take any notice of me." I resisted the temptation to add, "*What's it to you, anyway?*"

She gave me an angry glance.

Careful, I told myself. She might find some excuse to come back early from the college, even though she never had before. Even if she didn't care what I did, it might have been convenient for her to be able to blame me for all those loveless years. If I hadn't been nervous before, I certainly was now.

She put on her elegant straw hat and examined herself in the large mirror above the fireplace. "Try not to leave your paraphernalia all over the sitting room."

"I won't."

"Well, that's your usual *modus operandi.*"

She turned her head from side to side to check each profile.

"Okay," she said at last, "I'm out of here. *Au revoir.*"

"Have fun," I said without looking up, apparently engrossed in the current exam paper. But as soon as I heard the front door close I was up and standing by the window watching her walk down the path and along the street to her Micra. I wanted to be sure she had finally left. Fiona and Shola are so different, I mused. Not only in skin colour. Shola was bigger and louder in every way.

Would she come? Perhaps in the long run it would be better if she didn't, even though I was tingling with excitement. She'd been the soul of discretion at Riverside during the past week. More formal with me than usual, if anything. Even called me "Mr Owen" a couple of times.

I started when the phone rang.

This time Shola made no effort to dissimulate. "Has she gone?"

I was disconcerted by her directness, but in the end I said, "Yes."

"Are you sure?"

"Of course I'm sure."

"So why are you whispering?"

"I'm not whispering." Now I was aware that I *was* whispering.

"Okay, I'll be there in a minute."

Opening the front door, I saw that she was dressed very differently from the previous Saturday. A short denim skirt and high-heeled sandals made her legs look even longer. She was wearing silver hoop earrings.

She swayed past me. I glanced up and down the street to check that none of my neighbours were around before closing the door behind us. She didn't wait to be invited to sit down this time. Instead, she patted the sofa by her side, inviting me to join her. I hesitated.

"Playing hard to get?" she teased.

Feeling a bit foolish, I sat beside her.

"This is nice," she said, leaning over me to touch the colourful cloth draped over the back of the sofa. "Where is it from?"

"Mexico. We went there a few years ago."

She glanced around the room. "You've got many foreign-looking things."

"Souvenirs. We travel a lot. Fiona loves it. Fancies herself as a bit of a linguist."

"What languages does she speak?"

"English."

She looked puzzled.

"Although she's been studying French and Spanish for many years," I added.

"How about Africa? Have you been there?"

"We visited Fiona's cousin in South Africa many years ago."

She smiled. "I can't wait for my family to see me in my nurse's uniform. They'll be so proud of me."

As she spoke, she followed the contours of my face with her fingertips. They lingered on my lower lip.

"How did this happen?" she asked.

"Cut myself shaving."

Suddenly serious, her hand sprang away. "That's not funny."

"I know."

"So why did you say it?"

"I don't know. Habit, I suppose."

To my surprise, she looked thoughtful and sad. It was an unguarded moment.

But a moment later she laughed. "Oh, what's that?" She touched the protrusion in my jeans. "Your mobile phone?"

Then she was on her feet, hitching up her skirt. I'm not sure whether that was a crease in the material or the outline of her vagina that I could see. Whatever it was, my heart was pounding, and I wasn't sure if it was excitement or fear.

As she put her hands around my neck and lowered herself onto my lap, I said, "Wait, I've got to get something."

"No need." She reached for her handbag. "I've got them here."

While I put the condom on, she stood up again and started undoing her clothes. Her skirt dropped to the floor. Then her knickers, which she deftly kicked to one side. I wondered if this small movement was common to women all over the world. She paused, giving my eyes time to wander over her body. I noticed her stretch marks. Then she sat beside me, with her legs open. As I positioned myself on my knees in front of her, I was amazed by the contrast of our skin colour. Her curly pubic hair was jet black and as soft as silk.

She lifted her feet onto the coffee table behind me and pulled me towards her. As I leaned forwards to kiss her, a sudden pain caused me to catch my breath and put my hand to the left of my abdomen.

"Are you okay?" she asked, examining my face.

"Yes, it's nothing."

"Are you sure? I don't want you dying on me or anything."

"Just a muscle I pulled working in the attic."

Relaxing back, she moaned as she moved her legs further apart, and I heard the coffee cup being knocked over on the table. Glancing behind, I was horrified to see the brown fluid expanding on an exam paper.

"Oh, no!" I turned around and dangled the booklet between my fingers for the coffee to drip off.

"Just say you received it like that," Shola said, trying to pull me back.

"No, that wouldn't be fair to the student. Shit! I mean, I suppose it could have happened in the Assessments Department ..."

"Fine." She tugged at me again.

"But that wouldn't be fair to them."

I tried to separate the pages to assess the extent of the damage.

"Will you leave that damn thing alone," she snapped.

"You're not being very sympathetic, Shola." Even though I knew that sounded ridiculous, I continued, "It sounds like you don't care."

"Is it my booklet?"

"No."

"Then no, I don't care. Are you coming back here or not?"

"Maybe it won't be so bad when it dries out ..."

Sighing with resignation, she began to get up.

"No, wait," I said, putting the paper down and turning back to her.

She relaxed back as I took my position between her legs again. She gazed at me patiently as I looked down at the now loose-fitting condom.

"I'm sorry," I said.

"No problem." She leaned forward and kissed me on the forehead.

Gently pushing me back to give her room, she stood up. She pretended not to be aware of me staring as she put her clothes back on. Without looking at me, she said, "About my exam answers, we can do it at uni, if you like. Just let me know."

"Shola," I whined. "I told you, I can't ..."

She stood there with her handbag hanging by her side as if she had just walked in. She smiled. "Anyway, there's always next Saturday."

"No, there isn't," I said. "It's half-term – no Reiki class."

"Oh." She shrugged her shoulders. "Well, the week after."

Chapter 17

The girl sitting opposite me on the tube reminded me of Gwen when she was that age. Long brown hair, green eyes, prim and pretty. She was wearing a low-cut top under a corduroy jacket and stylish three-quarter length jeans. Gwen always liked to dress well, too. I almost expected her to look up from her *Metro* and, in a Welsh accent, say to me, *You should always leave the house as if you might meet the man of your dreams.* She carried on saying that even after marrying Roger.

Then I thought about Shola, perhaps to avoid thinking about Gwen's impending death. I wasn't sure if I felt relieved or disappointed about not seeing her the following day.

The William Tell Overture struck up and I felt my mobile vibrating against my thigh. I extracted it from my pocket. "Hello!"

"Owen? This is Professor Crawford." Dean Martin. The last person I wanted to speak to at that moment.

"Hi, Martin. What can I do you for?"

He hesitated, apparently deciding whether to pick up on my flippancy. Then he went on, "Where are you?"

"Somewhere between North Ealing and Park Royal, I think," I said, peering out of the window.

"I didn't mean exactly where you are," he snapped. "You're on your way home?"

"Wending my weary way."

"I need to see you as soon as possible."

"I won't be in again until next Wednesday. Marking at home."

"Ten o'clock Monday morning. My office."

My eyes narrowed. I was beginning to get a bad feeling about this. "What's it about?"

"Someone has made a complaint about your behaviour."

"Who?" I asked.

"I'd rather not say on the phone."

"Well, what sort of behaviour?" I was aware of my voice beginning to shake as I began to suspect what this was about.

"I'd rather not talk about it on the phone," he insisted. "It's a delicate matter."

I opened my mouth to ask another question, but he hung up. The train stopped at Park Royal. I couldn't just sit there now. I had to escape. I jumped up and grabbed my briefcase and the blue zipped bag containing thirty-one nursing care studies for marking. The young woman opposite looked up at me in alarm.

I rushed along the platform. I knew what this was about! It was about Shola! Out of breath, I stopped at the top of the stairs, looking around wildly. Where was I going? What was I doing? Should I get the next train back to the university and try to see Crawford straight away? Oh, how he'd love to see me panicking like this. And what if this was about something else, some nonsense that he was dramatising?

My mind shot back to when I first met him. It was part of my induction to Riverside University fourteen years before. During my hour's slot in his office he had an interview with a young nursing student who had failed an assessment for a second time without any mitigating circumstances. He told her she would have to leave the course. Was there no way she could have another chance, she pleaded.

"Absolutely not," he replied. He gazed at her impassively as she sat there with tears silently rolling down her cheeks.

She finally got up. Shoulders hunched and dabbing her eyes with a tissue, she left his office. To my amazement, he said nothing – no words of solace or encouragement.

"Just going to get a glass of water," I said.

A couple of minutes later he came out to hand his notes to his PA at her station just outside his office. He saw the student sobbing openly on my shoulder. I've never forgotten the look of hatred on his face as his eyes locked with mine.

Well, you won't see me collapse, you bastard! I was still breathing heavily, the extra stone I'd put on in recent years telling on me. A woman passing with a little girl drew her closer to her side. Without taking her eyes off me, she gave me a wide berth. A guard at the barrier turned and stared at me with narrowed eyes. This is how people might get picked up by the police and carted off to a "place of safety", I thought.

That last thought was like a bucket of cold water thrown in my face, an image reinforced by the sensation of sweat running down the back of my neck. I took a deep breath, smoothed down my grey hair, and walked back down to the platform as steadily as I could.

Chapter 18

All that remained of Susan was in a slender cardboard box. A few photos and a lock of auburn hair. I put it here nearly a quarter of a century ago so that Fiona, for whom the attic was a no-go area because of the spiders, would never come across it by chance. She didn't want any reminders of that tragic time and she had never mentioned the girl since. Throw it into that black bag for the rubbish dump, I told myself. Achieve closure once and for all! But I placed it on the to-keep pile instead.

Back aching from stooping down under dusty beams and sweat beading on my forehead, I wondered why Brad couldn't spend his break from the university lying around watching videos like other kids.

He held up a spaniel-eared copy of Abraham Maslow's *A Theory of Human Motivation.* "You want to keep this?"

"I'd better have a look –"

"When did you use it last?" he asked, flipping through it. "It looks really out of date."

"Perhaps it's got historical interest –"

"You've got to be ruthless, Dad, otherwise we'll never get this place tidied up." He tossed it into the black bag for the charity shop.

I watched him swing his muscular body around one of the attic supports and absent-mindedly flick a cobweb away from his dark, short cropped hair. Physically he was everything I'd never been. He showed the same disdain for authority as I did, but with him it was natural arrogance, whereas mine, I was beginning to believe, was a protective shell.

Reluctant as I was to do this physical work, I realised that it was keeping my anxiety at bay, although now and then the thought of facing Martin across his desk clasped my brain like a cold hand. When Brad wasn't looking, I retrieved Maslow's book and hid it in the to-keep pile. It mentioned the ability to tolerate ambiguity as being one of the characteristics of a self-actualised person. I certainly needed to cope with not being sure what Martin wanted to see me about until Monday.

"What's this?" asked Brad, rotating a padded package in his hand. "A video?"

"Let me see," I said, reaching for it. I opened one end and slid out a maroon book. The edges were worn and the spine had become loose. "It's not a video," I said, beginning to remember. "There were no such things as videos in those days. It's a diary."

"Yours?"

"Yes," I murmured.

"Why did you hide it?"

"I didn't hide it!" I was aware of sounding defensive.

"Well, it *was* under a floorboard." Squinting at the faded cover, he exclaimed, "1967!"

"I was in the Merchant Navy then."

"Cool. Can I read it?"

"No, it must be quite repetitive – scrubbing decks, keeping watch and, and ..."

"And what?"

"Well, you know, personal things."

"Like?" He drew the word out long.

"Well, you know ..."

"Not ... not sex?"

After a moment's hesitation, I shrugged.

Brad grinned. "I never thought you had it in you, Dad!"

"Lunch!" Fiona called from downstairs. I'd never been so glad to hear her voice. "We're eating *al fresco*."

"She means in the garden," said Brad.

"Yes, Brad. I know what *al fresco* means. But in April?"

"Just put your jumper on."

As Brad and I waited at the plastic table, I had to admit that the sun was quite warm. Fiona came out of the kitchen door with a cardigan thrown over her shoulders. She carried a large cooking pot across the grass.

"*Paella* with *fruits de mer*," she announced, setting it down on the table.

"Isn't *paella* Spanish and *fruits de mer* French?" said Brad.

Fiona began scooping the yellow contents onto the plates. "Yes, that's right. Very good, Bradley."

"So shouldn't you say it in Spanish – whatever seafood is?"

She slowed down and I could see she was struggling to remember what that was.

"Let's just call it a soup of languages," I chipped in.

She gave me a disapproving look as she thrust the plate under my nose. "Some people can't even speak English properly."

When Brad went inside to watch football on TV, Fiona and I carried on eating in silence. I supposed there wasn't much left to say after twenty-five years. I got up, stretched and said, perhaps too casually, "Just going to have a lie down before Brad drags me up to the attic again."

"That's right, dear," she intoned. "You don't want to exhaust yourself."

I turned to respond to her sarcasm, but she was not even looking at me.

Lying on the bed under my dressing gown, I leaned over and opened the bedside table drawer, taking out the diary from under my socks. Lying back, I began to read the words that I'd written thirty-eight years before. The blue ink was faint now. I'd written it with the Parker pen my mother had just given me for Christmas. A Parker pen with a gold nib. Only posh kids had Parker pens in those days – usually the ones who went to Grammar School.

Brad was right about it being a video because, as I read, long-forgotten images came flooding back ...

Chapter 19

Huge snowflakes were falling in slow motion out of the blackness, illuminated by the light on the mainmast. I paused to watch them landing on the port side navigation light, where they created a moving picture of white and red as they melted. They made me think of Christmas and home and my girlfriend, Megan.

I turned up the collar of my duffle coat against the cold. As I paced from one side of the monkey island to the other, peering through the white and black for the lights of other ships, I couldn't help feeling envious of the second mate. Toffee-nosed Stratton, I thought, he'll be holed up in the warmth of the bridge beneath my feet.

Was it snowing in the rest of the Norwegian Sea? Or was it just around the *Albatross*, like in one of those snow globe ornaments? I'd had the same feeling about ten years earlier when I'd ran out of the house into the snow with my two sisters, the eldest one, Gwen, still winding a scarf around my neck. As I looked back at the house, my mother opened a bedroom window, causing a thick wedge of snow to fall to the ground. "Be careful with the boy!" she called.

I hadn't stopped until I reached the top of the highest coal tip, now white instead of black. Gwen and Delyth were looking up at me. I looked all around – at the village on the top of the hill, at the other one in the valley, at our house across the common. Yes, as far as I could tell, it *was* snowing everywhere.

That started me thinking about when Merfyn and I were playing with my green plastic soldiers on the floor in my bedroom. He said he was going down to the toilet. I don't know what made me go and look for him – maybe it was because I didn't hear him galloping down the stairs as he usually did. I found him sitting on Gwen's bed watching her put on her makeup in front of her dressing mirror. I took a step backwards, but from where I could still see them. We were about twelve then, so Gwen must have been about seventeen. Finishing putting her lipstick on, she swung around to him and said, "That's it. What do you think?"

"You're lovely," he'd mumbled. "Gwen ..."

"What?"

Merfyn stared at her, then swallowed hard.

"What?" she asked again, louder.

"I'll give you a shilling."

"What are you talking about?" She half-closed those green eyes that everyone said were so beautiful. "What for?"

Looking down at the carpet, he tried to sound casual. "If you'll let me ..."

"Let you what? Oh, come on, Merfyn, out with it!"

"If you'll let me feel inside your knickers," he said all at once.

I bit the back of my hand to stop myself laughing out loud. I wondered what she was thinking during that half a minute that she stared at him, but then she said, "A shilling? Just for that? That's a week's pocket money for you, isn't it?"

He nodded.

"Are you sure about this?" she asked.

"Yes, I'm sure."

"But why?"

"Don't know. Just want to."

She was thinking again. "Have you got a shilling?"

"Yes." He dug deep into the pocket of his short trousers and brought out a shiny shilling.

"Okay, it's a deal," she said, holding her hand out.

He dropped the coin into her hand and then sat up straight, expectantly. His eyes followed her as she stood up.

"Okay," she said. "They're in the top drawer. Put them back tidy when you've finished."

She'd tossed the coin in the air and caught it with a clap as she walked out of the room.

Merfyn couldn't come to the cinema that Saturday. Gwen said it served him right, the attitude he had towards girls.

Hearing someone cough, I turned to see a hooded head, followed by a well-covered figure, ascending the port side ladder. Dai Jones, a can of beer in one hand and a cigarette in the other, trudged through the snow and stood beside me. "What have you done to the weather, *bach*?" he said.

"Beautiful, isn't it – the snow?"

"Huh! Wait until you've been here a dozen times and shovelled tons of it overboard."

I indicated the can in his hand. "Lager? Bit cold for that, yntê?"

"It warms you up here," he said, tapping the side of his head.

I laughed and turned back to the dark sea in front of us. "Well, there's nothing around."

"How do you know?" He grunted, squinting through the snow. "We'd better just hope the radar picks up anything that is out there."

I thought of the *Titanic* cruising through the night, passengers revelling in the luxury of the floating hotel, unaware of the sharp iceberg waiting in the darkness. Then I stamped my feet to make sure I could still feel them, reassuring myself that I didn't have frostbite. "I didn't know it could be this cold."

"Cold?" he laughed. "Mild this is, *myn*. Just wait until we've crossed the Arctic Circle."

"How cold does it get, then?"

"Well, you know what the grades on the Arctic thermometer are, don't you?"

I thought for a moment, then shook my head. "This is my first trip, remember."

"They're 'cold', 'very cold' and 'freeze the balls off of yer'."

I chuckled. "Is that what you do when you're here on lookout – make up things like that?"

"You've got to do something. Sometimes I sing." In deep baritone, he sang a few lines from a melancholy Welsh folksong, one that my mother often sang while doing the housework.

"That's really good," I said, surprised. "You should be an opera singer."

"Nearly was once."

I waited for him to go on, but when he didn't, I asked, "So what happened?"

"It's a long story. Oh, what the hell, if you haven't got time at sea, when have you? The truth is, Owen, I wasn't always the innocent, upstanding man you see before you now. Don't laugh ... Oh, you didn't. Anyway, I started drinking when I was very young – must've been fourteen or fifteen. In the local pubs and working men's clubs."

"They served you at that age?"

"They weren't as strict as they are now. Besides, I looked older than I was. You could take me for eighteen, at a push. But eventually I got done for underage drinking, so that put the mockers on that. No one in the village would serve me anymore. There was no way I could drink at home, my parents being chapel people. So I decided to go up to London, where the streets were supposed to be paved with gold. I was eighteen by then. Couldn't hold a job down. Started singing in the pubs. The English liked it. They gave me tips and bought me drinks. They said with my voice I should go to drama college."

"Really? So did you?"

"I got an interview. When I told my parents they were over the moon. They said they'd pay the fees and support me if I was accepted." Dai shook his head slowly. "Big mistake. It was the birthday of the bloke who was putting me up on the day of the interview, so we started drinking at breakfast time. I didn't get to the interview. But I told my parents I'd been accepted for a three-year course. They thought I'd finally made good, that it had only been a phase I was going through. They must have scrimped and saved to finance my life of debauchery in the West End. It was nearly two years later they found out I'd conned them."

"What happened then?"

"With no money, I had to go home. That's when I admitted I had a problem and went to a rehabilitation unit. In Carmarthen Hospital, the lunatic asylum."

"What did your parents say about sending you all that money?"

"Nothing. They never mentioned it. But whenever I sang after that they just turned the other way. Then I joined the Merchant Navy. Went to the *Vindi* in Gloucester, like you." He stared at the sea for a long time before continuing. "I wasn't proud of what I'd done. I always imagined I'd make it up to them somehow, some day. But first my father went, then my mother. And I never got the chance."

I didn't know how to respond to his sadness, so I kept quiet. Thankfully, he went on at last, "That's the thing about parents. You only miss them when they're gone."

"Well, you can't miss them before, can you?"

"But you can appreciate them." He tried to smile. Then he changed the subject. "So you've just come from the training school? How are things there?"

"It closed down. The *Vindicatrix* went to the breaker's yard."

Dai's jaw dropped. "I heard it was on the cards ... When ...?"

"Just now. In December. I was in the last intake."

"That's it, then. The end of an era."

We were silent for a while, then he said, "When I was there, we used to live on the ship."

"What, sleeping on board as well?"

"Oh, yes. In those long dormitories where the crew used to sleep when she was at sea. They only built the camp when there wasn't enough room on the *Vindi* for all the boys who came for training."

"Phew!"

"Yeah, it was a bit tight. Did they still wake you up with, 'Hands off cocks, on socks!'?"

I nodded. "Our instructor used to say, 'You're not with your mother now. You can go back to her if you like, but you won't have her forever ...'" My words trailed off as I thought about what Dai had just said about his parents.

But he laughed, *"I'm your mother now!* The boys on watch used to ring the fo'c'sle bell every hour during the night. Drove me nuts, it did."

"They still did that, at the entrance of the camp," I said. "You know how you're supposed to ring it in twos? Like *ding-ding, ding-ding* for 4 a.m.?"

Dai nodded.

"Well, the chap I was on watch with misunderstood and rang it twice for each hour at four o'clock: *ding-ding, ding-ding, ding-ding, ding-ding.* Instructors and boys came running out in their pyjamas or y-fronts, thinking there was a fire."

Dai laughed. "You always get some twat. Ours is Willy. Have you met him yet?"

"No. On the 12-4, isn't he?"

"Yes, that's the boy. He might relieve you at midnight. Either him or Mitch."

"Mitch?"

Even though I couldn't see Dai's face clearly, it felt as if a shadow had passed over it. "The less said about him, the better."

"Why? What's wrong with him?"

"You'll find out soon enough. But I advise you to keep out of his way as much as you can."

After a long silence, I said, "Mind you, it would be better if it was in English."

"What would?"

"That song you were singing."

"Oh, that. What's wrong with Welsh, then?"

"I'm not saying there's anything wrong with Welsh. Just who wants to hear it, that's all?"

"Yes, well ... What do you do to pass the time on lookout?"

"I just sort of daydream."

Dai gave a short laugh.

"What?" I said defensively.

"Shows the different stages of life we're at. I think about the past and you think about the future. What do you daydream about?"

"The usual sort of things – girls, money ..."

Dai laughed again. "I don't know about money, but you'll have plenty of girls in Norway, if the randy little bastards on this ship are to be believed."

"Yes," I grinned. "I can't wait to get to Narvik."

"Free love *started* there, you know – in Scandinavia."

I nodded, "But from what I've heard, the local boys don't bother much with the girls. That's weird."

"Know why?" he challenged.

"No."

"Well, I've got a theory about it." He took a drag of his cigarette and tilted his head back as he blew out the smoke. "I think prolonged exposure to the cold causes chronic contraction of the balls, making the males lose interest in sex. The cold doesn't affect females in that way, of course, and visitors from warmer climes are the obvious solution. That includes the UK, thanks to the Gulf Stream."

I waited for more, but he just said, "You'd better get below and warm up. Otherwise you won't be any use to the Norwegian girls either. Careful with the snow on the ladder."

"Yes," I said, turning to go.

"Hold on." He fished a can of lager out of his coat pocket. "This'll take your mind off those girls and help you sleep."

I took the can unsurely. "They say they used to put bromide in our cocoa at the sea training school for that."

He laughed. "That's what they used to say when I was on the *Vindi* twenty years ago. So there must be some truth in it."

"Thanks," I said, holding up the can awkwardly.

"*Croeso,*" he said.

The ladder and the port side boat deck were thick with snow. I turned the heavy metal handle and entered the crew's accommodation, pausing to scrape the snow off my boots on the bottom lip of the door.

In the warmth of my cabin I stared at the can of beer in my hands. I didn't have a can-opener. I clicked my tongue. Ah, well. But then I remembered the sheath with my knife and marline spike threaded through the belt of my jeans. I took out the spike and pierced two holes in the top of the can. Sipping from the can in my bunk, I smiled as I realised that was the first time I'd ever used the spike.

Chapter 20

As the doors of the lift began to close I saw Sophie in the refectory. Someone tutted behind me as I jammed my briefcase between the doors which, after a struggle, shuddered open again, allowing me to get out.

Rushing towards Sophie, I grabbed a packet of crisps from a display stand without slowing down or taking my eyes off her. I stood behind her in the queue for the till. Her black hair hung down her slender back almost to her jeans. She was holding a bar of chocolate.

Leaning forward, I whispered in her ear, "Chocolate, Sophie? Naughty!"

She turned and smiled. "That's your fault," she said. "You don't bring me Welsh cakes anymore."

I nodded. "Yes, it's time I got my pinny on again."

"If you'd give me the recipe I could have a go at making them myself."

"I told you, it's nothing to do with recipes – it's a matter of genetics. And you are clearly Jewish through and through." I glanced at the Star of David hanging from her neck on a silver chain. "Mind you," I added, "there is a theory that the Welsh are one of the lost tribes of Israel …"

"Why are you in so early, anyway? I bet you've never seen the building at this time before."

"I've got an audition with Dean Martin."

She raised an eyebrow. "What have you done now?"

"Nothing. I'm just checking up on him."

She giggled and nudged me with her elbow. "By the way, my mum asked if you cater for weddings and bar mitzvahs?"

"And did you ask her if she used to go dancing in the Hammersmith Palais in the early eighties?"

"I did," she said, with that mock-serious expression that always made me want to cuddle her. "She said she never went there. So there's no way you could be my dad after all."

"Well, she would say that, wouldn't she?" I said while paying for the crisps.

Then I was in the lift again, going up to see the dean. For the first time, it occurred to me that the word dean – *dyn* in Welsh – meant "man". I was going up to face the man who hated me. It was my *High Noon*. The only indication we were moving was the red light counting the floors, and as I stared up at it I began to feel sick.

"Is Dean Martin in?" I asked Lisa, who was typing at her computer outside the dean's office. It was a silly question because if he wasn't she'd be chatting on the phone and filing her fingernails. Her eyes flashed up to me, catching me gazing at her cleavage. Why dress like that if she didn't want men to look, I wondered.

"If you mean Professor Martin Crawford, yes he is. But he's got someone with him." Her eyes wandered down to my chest, then back to my face again and she said in fake disapproval, "Coming to see the dean without a tie, Mr Roberts? Tut-tut."

"Oh, I thought the invitation said smart casual."

She suppressed a smile. "I'll call you when he's ready."

Walking to my desk, I noticed that there were more lecturers in at this time than I would have expected. Even Charity was there. She had drawn a chair up to Les's desk and was waiting as he rummaged through piles of files and papers, muttering, "I know it's here somewhere."

Wencheng, isolated by his headset, sat at his desk conducting a podcast. Philip was downloading enough PowerPoint slides to bore his class for hours.

Sitting in front of my computer with its plastic Welsh flag stuck to the top of it, I started checking my emails. That was always a good time-filler. I muttered under my breath, *crap, crap, crap* as I deleted one after another. Then I came to one from the dean.

"Re your response to the vice chancellor's request for suggestions for a new logo for the university, I find it offensive." Even in my present state of mind I chuckled as I remembered my suggestion, which was a Reply to All: "How about Mickey Mouse?" Was that why he wanted to see me? I put my hands together in prayer. Oh, please God, let it be that!

From the corner of my eye I saw Audrey come out of the dean's office, walking briskly. I smiled at her as she passed me, but she just looked straight ahead. Perplexed, I swivelled around on my chair to face her desk, a little way behind me. She quickly turned her eyes away from me.

Lisa disappeared into the dean's office, reappearing a few minutes later. She sat down at her station and picked up the phone. Mine rang and I saluted her as I picked it up.

"Professor Crawford will see you now," she said into the phone, looking straight at me.

Crawford was sitting in his throne-like chair behind his mahogany desk. His catchphrase "Tidy desk, tidy mind" came to mind. Once he had added, "I have no doubt that your desk is like your mind, Owen – a heaving quagmire". I wondered how he would describe Les's mind.

"You'd better close the door behind you," he said, then looked down at the file in front of him. "Right. As I said, this is a delicate matter."

"I take it you didn't like my suggestion for the new logo, then?"

His hand froze in the act of opening the file, which had my name on it. "If we are a Mickey Mouse university, it's because of people like you. You and your touchy-feely nonsense."

"Well, we are supposed to be models for a caring profession."

"We should be models for professionalism." Flicking through the file, he went on, almost as if he were talking to himself, "I wouldn't give you the time of day for all that humanistic mumbo-jumbo."

He extracted a sheet of paper from the file. The light from the window behind him passed through it and I could see it was a printout of an email. "Anyway, this is far more serious. I've received a complaint about your inappropriate behaviour with one of the students."

I felt the blood drain from my face. He watched it happen with satisfaction, and it was then I remembered the dream I'd had the night before of vultures circling above me. One of them had Crawford's face.

"Who's it from?" I asked, trying to stay calm.

"I can't tell you that at this stage."

"Well, can you tell me what it's about?"

"I'm sure you know what it's about. It's about your sexual abuse of a student by the name of Shola ... Nod-love-you." With a short, disparaging laugh, he added, "Where do they get these names from?"

"I believe it's pronounced *Jlovee*."

"Well, I suppose you should know."

"Anyway," I shrugged, rather too energetically, "even if it were true, it wouldn't be the first time that a lecturer and a student ..."

"What makes this particularly serious is that she is one of your personal students," Crawford cut across me, "which means that you are responsible for marking her work."

I tried to get more comfortable in the chair. "Is there any evidence for this – this allegation, or is it just based on rumour?"

"Oh yes, there's evidence. The person who reported it overheard a friend of this student talking about you. Another black student, by the name of Princess – also your personal student."

I folded my arms to try to stop my hands from shaking.

"Apparently you told Princess that you didn't have time to go through her essay before she submitted it. Later one of your colleagues heard her saying to another student, 'If my name was Sheila he'd have time'."

"Shola," I corrected him.

"Whatever." His cold blue eyes drilled into mine as he went on, "Quite rightly, she – your colleague –" he corrected himself, "took this Princess aside and questioned her. In the end she confessed she was referring to you and the fact that you were, to put it mildly, over-generous with the help you were giving Sheila –"

"Shola."

"This Princess woman eventually told her – that is, told your colleague – about your intimate relationship with her friend."

Despite his contemptuous glare, I felt a glimmer of optimism. "Sorry, Dean. That's not enough."

"True," he said. He stared down at the desk, allowing me to feel, just for a few seconds, that I might be off the hook. Then he riveted me with his eyes. "I would agree with you. Except that Sheila confessed to everything. She also described the contents of your house in detail, right down to the defective retaining rings in your kitchen lighting."

We stared at each other across that desk and I realised this was the real thing. True hate. I swallowed hard. He leaned towards me. "We know all the sordid details, Mr Roberts."

The sunlight through the window behind him began to hurt my eyes.

"Looks like your hugging students isn't so innocent after all, doesn't it?" he observed, sitting back. "I've had my suspicions about you for a long time. Ever since we first met, in fact."

"You mean when you threw that poor student off the course?" I asked. "You were so heartless."

"The word is professional. You expect tears at a time like that."

I heard my voice getting louder. "Expecting them and enjoying them are two different things."

For a split second the muscles around his eyes twitched.

"That really made your day," I went on through clenched teeth.

"Mine?" He raised his eyebrows. "You were the one holding her trembling young body against you. Disgusting. I should have got rid of you there and then. But I didn't, and you've been an albatross around my neck ever since."

I saw the bow of the *Albatross* crashing down into the sea, driving a wall of water over the fo'c'sle and flooding the main deck.

The dean swivelled in his chair, just once, without taking his eyes off me. "You know, you should have applied for redundancy when you had the chance, instead of making inane remarks about us needing to let our best staff go to ensure we stay at the bottom of the University League Table. Now you'll go with nothing. And you'll lose your pension." He almost smiled as he added, "No other university will touch you after this."

I leaned across the desk and shouted, "You're nothing but a sexually repressed arsehole!"

"I just wonder," he said calmly, "how many other defenceless students you've abused. I have no doubt that this is just the tip of the iceberg. You're a predator. But the most despicable thing is your betrayal of the university by helping students cheat."

The door opened just wide enough for Lisa to pop her head around. "Everything all right, Professor Crawford? Do you need me to call someone?"

The dean shook his head. "No, no. Everything is fine. Mr Roberts is just leaving."

I glared at Lisa as I hurried out, thinking: and that's another thing, if he's not interested in women, how come he's got the PA with the biggest tits in the university?

Chapter 21

The sunrise was no more than a silver glow on the starboard side as I went out on deck. An icy wind flapped the collar of my jacket. Dai, Mitch, and Kirk were standing by the starboard rail down on the main deck. As I approached them, Mitch was saying, "There's nothing like fucking both the mother and the daughter."

Dai turned to me. "We're just waiting for the bosun. He went up to see the mate."

"Gives you a real perspective on life," Mitch went on. "You should know that, Dai, being a bit of a man of the world yourself."

Dai took a deep drag on his cigarette as he gazed out at the grey sea as if he hadn't heard him.

"It started when her mother asked me to call in to help her hang some curtains," Mitch continued. "It was pretty obvious what she wanted because her husband and Janet were at work and her son was at school. She didn't keep up the pretence for long. She was nothing to look at – but what the hell, I was only on leave for a couple of weeks so I wasn't going to let any opportunities pass me by. It was great while it lasted."

"So what happened?" asked Kirk.

"Janet started getting serious, that's what happened. Started talking about marriage. Saying things like, 'What'll happen if I get pregnant? I don't want my child to be a bastard'. Then she stopped my tap. I still had her mother, though. Silly cow thought I was depending on her for it. One night I went to her house after drinking all day. Told her I needed to talk to her. Must have thought I was going to propose to her or something." Mitch chuckled as he added, "Instead I told her I was poking her mother. She didn't believe me, but was furious with me for saying it. Chucked me out of the house."

"That's horrible," I blurted out.

"It was lovely," Mitch grinned. "Wouldn't have missed that look in her eyes for anything. It was almost as good as sex itself. I guess she must've confronted her mum afterwards, because the next thing I knew her father was divorcing her mother and Janet went to live with her married sister."

"*Ychafi!*" I exclaimed.

"What?" said Mitch.

"That's sickening," Dai translated, sounding even more disgusted than me.

"Hey, hold on a minute," Mitch objected. "You're forgetting something: it was her mother who seduced *me*. Anyway, I don't know what's wrong with people like you. It's only human nature. Everyone fucks."

Behind Mitch, I saw the bosun coming along the deck.

"Don't you think it's too windy to open the hatch, Jeremy?" Dai asked him when he reached us.

The bosun glanced at the sea rushing past us. "No, it's okay. I've just spoken to the mate. He said it's okay."

"Nice try, Dai," said Mitch.

"Well, it was worth having a go," said Dai, cupping his gloved hands around his mouth and blowing into them.

Kirk tied the wide end of the tapered shoot to a post attached to the starboard rail. The wind crossing the main deck immediately inflated it, blowing it over the grey sea like a paper party horn.

"That's to stop the iron ore blowing back on deck," the bosun explained to me. Then he turned to Mitch. "Will you be able to reach it with the full buckets there?"

"We will," said Mitch. He turned his eyes to me and added, "But I'm not sure about the boy."

Kirk laughed.

"Don't worry about him. He's coming below with me and Dai."

"Sure he'll be warm enough down there?" asked Mitch.

The bosun glared at him. "What?"

"What, what?" Mitch shot back at him. He smiled, but the edges of his mouth turned down in a sneer. "Didn't say anything, bosun."

Kirk laughed again, but this time it was cut short as the bosun turned his eyes to him.

"Okay," said the bosun after a moment's tense silence. "Let's get this hatch open."

We released the thick security clips from the top of number 2 hatch. Dai showed me how to use the long-handled wheel spanner to lower the small cast iron wheels along each side of it. The coldness of the tool crept through my canvas gloves.

"Make sure you put the retaining pin back in before taking the spanner out," said Dai. "If the wheel spins while the spanner is still in, you'll have an helluva clout on the nut."

The drum of the windlass on the fo'c'sle, a giant cotton reel with rust, turned in neutral as Mitch dragged a wire from it along the top of the hatch, his hobnailed boots clunking. He shackled the wire to the ring bolt at the after end of the hatch. Kirk crunched the windlass into gear and the hatch, grinding forward on its wheels, slowly opened.

"That's enough!" the bosun shouted, drawing his hand across his throat.

The windlass screeched as Kirk jerked the brake lever back.

"Careful as you go down," the bosun told me. "The steps are very narrow."

I stepped forward and looked over the rim of the hold. My heart beat faster at the sight of the metal steps disappearing into the darkness.

"I'll go first." Dai pushed in front of me. "That way, if you slip, I'll break your fall."

The bosun chuckled. "He'd certainly have a soft landing."

"But what about you, Dai?" I asked.

"Don't worry about me. I'm just about played out anyway." He pulled himself up over the coaming and, with a lamp attached to a long cable, began to go down as casually as if it were a stepladder in his house.

The bosun followed me down. I knew I was making him go very slowly, but he just paused from time to time without saying anything. With the stiff gloves, I was afraid that I would misjudge my grip. I imagined myself falling into the darkness in slow motion, my mouth open in a silent scream, my face turned up to the shrinking wedge of snow-filled sky. Dai reached the bottom before I was halfway down and clamped the lamp to a side batten. I felt a bit more confident as I moved into the pool of light.

I breathed a sigh of relief when my feet touched the bottom of the hold. The thin covering of iron ore powder, with drifts around the sides, looked like black snow.

"We'll brush it into piles," the bosun told me. His words echoed back to us. "Then we'll shovel it into buckets for those two tossers to heave up and dump over the side."

The light from the lamp made a sharp contrast between light and dark, exaggerating the men's features – the bosun's large nose and beady eyes; Dai's thick hair, white at the temples. Their faces looked ghostly. I must have appeared the same to them. Together with the blackness around us, the echo, the whistling of the wind through the hatch when the ship rolled a certain way, it was scary.

I jumped when something came clattering down the side of the hold. It was a couple of battered buckets attached to ropes. The bosun picked up one of them. "What knot is this supposed to be?"

"That must have been Harry," said Dai, and they both laughed. He turned to me and went on, "Harry signed on saying he was sixty-four, but it turned out he was seventy-four. He was sacked after one trip, but he caused havoc while he was here. Calling people for the wrong watch and God knows what else."

"But surely," I said, "his discharge book would have shown his age?"

"He wandered aboard in Port Talbot," said Dai. "Wanted a job as an AB. We were two deck hands down and wouldn't have been able to sail on that tide. So they probably didn't look that closely."

"I can't untie this," said the bosun. "Here, Dai, see if you can."

Dai struggled with the knot, swearing under his breath as he turned it one way then another.

"Such bad seamanship," said the bosun, shaking his head. "Just cut it off and do a proper knot."

"Anyone got a knife?" asked Dai.

I reached for the knife hanging at my side. At the same time, the bosun reached for his. It reminded me of a draw in the Westerns. The bosun let me win. I handed my new wooden-handled Green River to Dai.

"A sailor without a knife, Dai," the bosun tutted. "That's like a doctor without a stethoscope."

"You're lucky to see me on deck at all at this time," said Dai, cutting the rope just above the knot and tying the bucket back on with a clove hitch.

As we swept the surplus iron ore into piles, Dai said, "How about your dad, Owen? What does he do?"

"He died in a coal mining accident in 1956."

"You must have been very young?"

"Six years old."

"Do you remember him?" asked the bosun.

"I remember him coming home from work covered in coal dust. A muffler round his neck, a couple of logs under his arm for firewood. And my mother filling the tin bath in front of the fire for him."

"Must have been awful," said Dai, "losing your dad like that."

I shrugged my shoulders. The bosun touched my arm, then turned to carry on working. Dai cleared his throat and followed his example.

Chapter 22

Feeling queasy with the constant rolling of the ship, I went out on the poop for some fresh air before breakfast. When I entered the messroom, the sight of Dai tucking into a fried breakfast made my stomach turn. I went to the serving hatch and asked the cook for scrambled egg on toast and a glass of orange juice.

"Is that all, sweetie?" he asked. "You must keep your strength up, you know, working out there in this weather."

I studied his round face with his green eyes and long eyelashes. He stared back at me and pursed his lips. His name was Paul, but everyone called him Pussy.

I waited until the messman finished sprinkling water on the tablecloth next to Dai. I must have looked puzzled because he explained, "This is to stop the plates sliding onto the deck."

"Oh, right," I said, plonking my plate and glass down next to my watch-mate.

"*Bore da, bach,*" he said.

"*Bo –* good morning," I replied.

He chuckled. "Nearly caught you then. There's nothing wrong with being Welsh, you know."

"Never said there was."

"So why do you refuse to speak your own language?"

"English is my language."

"You were speaking it tidy enough while I was waiting for you to get out of that telephone kiosk in Port Talbot."

"Oh." I'd forgotten about that. "That was just to an old aunt of mine. Pretends she doesn't understand English."

"She's a bit like you, then, only the other way round."

"I hardly know any Welsh."

He shook his head sadly and carried on eating.

"What?" I said, raising my voice.

A man two or three years older than me put his plate down on the table next to mine. "Hello. You must be the new deck boy?"

I nodded.

"Welcome aboard." He held out his hand and I shook it. "I'm Marcos."

"Marcos?" I questioned. "Is that Italian or something?"

"Or something."

"So where *do* you come from?"

"Ladbroke Grove." He laughed at my blank expression. "My parents emigrated from Portugal about twenty years ago. I was born just after they arrived. And I mean just after – they took my mother straight from King George the Fifth dock to St. Charles Hospital."

"If you'd been born on the ship," said Dai, "would you have been Portuguese or English?"

Marcos shook his head, smiling. "Don't know. That's an interesting question. But things were difficult for immigrants in those days, you know. Pass the salt, Dai. I got called names in school because I looked different. It's not so bad these days, of course. There are a lot more immigrants now – especially in London."

"My mam was persecuted at school because she spoke Welsh," I said. "She moved from the Rhondda Valley to Swansea when she was five years old, and couldn't speak a word of English. If she said anything in Welsh in class – and that was all she knew – the teachers would hang a board around her neck that said 'Welsh-Not'."

"For speaking her own language in her own country?" queried Marcos. "That's incredible."

"That explains a lot, that does," said Dai.

I glared at him.

"So what did your parents do when they came to England?" I asked Marcos.

"My mother stayed at home – they already had three kids, besides me. My father got a job as a hospital porter and has been there ever since. Worked his way up to head porter. He's so proud of that. Don't know how he gets the other porters to listen to him," he chuckled, "being so little and with his strong accent."

"Could he speak English when he arrived in England?" I asked.

"Hardly. He learned mainly from nursing and medical journals he found hanging around. Read them during quiet times at work, and at home, too. He would come home and say things like, 'I had a man with a right extended hemicolectomy today'. My mother would laugh and say, 'What are you talking? You only push trolley that take him to theatre!'"

When Marcos stood up to take his plate away, he added sadly, "He always thought I'd do something in the hospital. He was disappointed when I wanted to go to sea."

"Come to my cabin for a couple of jars later," Dai called after him.

Marcos turned and gave him a look of fake disapproval. I looked at Dai, wondering what was going on.

"He doesn't smoke, drink, fuck or anything," Dai explained. "He's the sort who gives sailors a bad name."

The tall figure of the bosun appeared in the doorway. "When you've finished breakfast, start chipping the rust around number 3 hatch," he told us. "Then touch it up with red oxide. If the weather holds, we'll be able to put undercoat on this afternoon." He sounded gruff, but he smiled when his eyes settled on me.

Dai's deep voice quietly humming a Welsh hymn could just be heard above the din of our chipping hammers. 'Oh God,' I felt like saying, 'can't you choose something a bit more cheerful?' but I didn't want to get into a discussion about the Welsh language with him again. He just wouldn't admit that people who spoke Welsh were seen as second class citizens. Other kids in school, and even some teachers, had regularly poked fun at me for speaking Welsh.

When the *Albatross* rolled steeply I grasped the hatch to support myself.

"How did you ever manage to get the first two hatches finished?" I asked, pressing my hands together to warm them up.

"That was during the last trip – to Melilla," said Dai.

"Where's that?" Feeling embarrassed by my ignorance, I added, "Exactly?"

"In the Med – North Africa. No problem with the weather there. Sunshine every day." He looked up at the blotchy white sky with disgust. "These other two hatches will take yonks."

"That's the sort of place I wanted to go to."

"Why didn't you, then?"

"They told me at the Pool that this was just right for my first trip – just five days out and five back."

"Was that Gerry?"

"Yes."

He laughed, shaking his head. "Could sell sand to the Arabs, that one."

"Smoko!" the bosun called from the next deck up, just outside his cabin, leaning forward on the rail.

Dai's hammer clanged as he dropped it on the deck beside the hatch. "Grand. I could do with a livener. You fancy one?"

"Oh, no – a cup of coffee will do me."

As we walked aft, I said, "There seems to be a lot of alcohol about, Dai. I thought we were only allowed three cans of beer a night from the bond."

"Yes, that's right. But people bought loads of booze in Melilla, where it was dirt cheap. When we got back to Port Talbot you couldn't uncoil a rope or open a roll of canvas without finding a bottle of brandy or ouzo hidden in it."

I couldn't go into my cabin because Mitch and Willy were painting my porthole boxes. They were still scraping the rust marks off one and rubbing the white paint down with a pumice stone. The other one was ready for painting, the patches of red lead made it look like a psychedelic Dalmatian.

"Chucked out of my own home," I jokingly complained.

"You'll have to share the bosun's cabin, then," said Mitch, winking at Willy, who doubled up laughing.

I was still wondering what had been so funny about Mitch's comment as I made a cup of coffee in the pantry, next to the galley. Then I went along the starboard side passageway to Lisping Larry's cabin. The strumming of his guitar announced that he was in. It went silent when I knocked on the door. I knocked again. The door opened a crack and a pair of blue eyes peered out at me.

"Oh, it'th you," said Larry, relieved, opening the door fully.

"I'm homeless," I joked. "Can I have my smoko here?"

He looked at me questioningly.

"They're painting in my cabin," I explained.

"Sure – come in, come in," he said in his Cockney accent. "You gave me a fright – I thought it was Riley looking for me."

"Riley?"

"The thecond theward."

I stared at him for a moment, then said, "Oh, you mean the second steward."

"That's what I thaid – the thecond theward. Don't fuck with me, Taff, okay? You haven't met him yet?"

"No."

"That's not really his name, of courth."

"What is his real name?" I wrapped my hands around the coffee mug, enjoying the warmth.

Larry sat opposite me and put his head to one side in thought. "You know, I can't remember."

"So why do they call him Riley?"

Larry grinned. "You'll find out when you meet him." He positioned his guitar on his lap. "I'm rehearthing a thong," he went on.

"Another one of Tommy Steele's?"

"Who elth?"

At first I didn't understand him. "Oh, right," I said when I realised what he'd said. "Who *else*?"

He grinned and, as if to make a point, ran his fingers through his wavy blond hair.

"You know he wath in the Merchant Navy, catering department, too," he said.

"Yes, you mentioned it."

"Did I tell you a couple of girlth in a pub on the Isle of Grain came up to me and athked me for my autograph? I didn't have the heart to tell them I wathn't Tommy Thteele."

"Good heavens!"

"What can you do," he mused. "I'm often mithtaken for the Bermondthey Boy. You get uthed to it." He strummed a chord. "Being admired ith one thing, but what I really want ith a thsteady girlfriend. How about you, Taff? … You got any thisters?"

"Yes, two."

"Really? Maybe you can fix me up with one of them. What are they like?"

"The younger one, Delyth, is three years older than me. She's quiet. Ordinary looking. Not very bright, they say, but she's nice. The other one, Gwen, is twenty-two. She's very pretty. All the boys are after her. She went to work in the laundry when she left school, and the van driver, Roger, seems to have decided that she's going to marry him, even though he's a lot older than her."

"Roger the Dodger, eh?"

I gave a short laugh. "You wouldn't say that if you saw him. He's really big, like a bear, and moves very slowly. Like this." I swayed my shoulders from side to side. "Gwen says she wouldn't marry him if he was the last man on earth. He's always around, though. Even goes to pick her up in the laundry van if she misses the last bus home. Even when she's out with another bloke. Mam likes him. Says she feels Gwen is safe with him. So shall I try to fix you up with Delyth?"

Larry's head was bent forward over his guitar as he adjusted one of the strings. "You know what? I think it'll have to be Gwen."

"Gwen? I'm not sure if you'll like her."

"Why not?"

"Well, she's very headstrong. Always wants what she wants. Delyth is much more easy going."

"All the thame, I think it'll have to be Gwen. Only becauthe she'th more my age, not becauthe of anything elth."

"Oh, I don't know. I'll ask her, but –"

"Yeth, you do that." A music sheet rested between a large book and the bulkhead on his table. He picked it up and handed it to me. "Do me a favour and hold thith for me. It keepth falling down with the roll of the ship."

Strumming the guitar, he launched into *Singing the Blues.*
After a couple of minutes of trying not to laugh, I interrupted him. "That's
great, Larry. Great. But have you ever thought of picking a song with less
esses in it?"

"Why?" He sounded irritated.

"Well, you have got a slight lisp."

He smiled. "But you hardly hear it when I *thing*, do you? I think you're
being a bit too critical, Taff. Let'th try it again from the top. One, two,
three …" and he was off again.

This time the interruption was a knock on the door. Larry stared at me
with round eyes. The dreaded Riley? He crept to the door and opened it a
crack.

"Sorry to disturb the concert." It was the bosun. Looking at me over
Larry's shoulder, he went on, "Time to get back to work, Owen."

By the time I knocked off at midday and had lunch, they had finished
painting my portholes. The fresh paint around the portholes made the cabin
look much better. I couldn't put the curtains back up yet as the paint was
still wet, but I undressed and got into my bed, *cwtshing* up. Through the
portholes I watched the wispy clouds gently move up and down in the pale
blue sky until my eyes closed in sleep.

Chapter 23

I stopped reading when I heard the front door open and close, listening,
perfectly still, like a frightened rabbit. Then I heard Fiona running up the
stairs. It was her angry, no-nonsense, arms swinging run. I stuffed the diary
under the pillow and pretended to be asleep. Either things had not gone well
at her Reiki class or seeing the bedroom curtains closed from the street had
peeved her.

I felt her standing with her hands on her hips staring down at me. My
closed eyes began to twitch and I realised my mouth wouldn't be closed
tight if I were really asleep, but I dared not change it now. Then I heard one
of the floorboards squeak as she walked over to the window. As the curtains
rattled open I could see the bright sunlight through my eyelids. I opened my
eyes just as Fiona, in a yellow summer dress with a matching chiffon scarf,
turned to face me.

"I won't ask what you were doing," she said. "I don't think I want to know.
But I know you weren't sleeping – I've faked that often enough with you in
the past to recognise it when I see it."

I mumbled something incoherent, as if I were just waking up.

"What's wrong with you?" she demanded. Then softening her tone a little added, "Shall I do a *sei hei ki* for you?"

That was the Reiki symbol for peace and harmony.

"No, you're all right," I said.

"What are you waiting for," the tone was harsh again, "the fairies to come and mark that pile of assessments on the dining room table? All you do lately is sleep."

She folded her arms, waiting for an answer. "Well, are you going to talk about it or not?"

The light behind her made her dress semi-transparent. She would have been horrified if she knew. A few months earlier I'd said to her, "I had an erotic dream about you last night. Ridiculous, isn't it, having an erotic dream about your own wife?" I thought of folding back the sheet and asking her to get into bed with me. Fiona shook her head and walked out of the room. I heard her going back downstairs.

There seemed to be only one way to escape from her coldness. I retrieved the diary from under the pillow.

Chapter 24

Lookout was kept on the leeside wing of the bridge that night instead of on the monkey island because of the strong wind. As I made a mug of coffee in the pantry to take up with me, I heard *Albatross* by Fleetwood Mac playing in someone's cabin. I stopped stirring the coffee to listen until the haunting melody faded away.

When Dai came up to relieve me after my first hour, I watched him floundering about with his arms outstretched in front of him. He finally bumped into me and muttered, "Oh, by there you are, *myn*."

"Can't you see me?" I asked, amused.

"No. Black as the cobs of hell it is up here."

"At least we're down by here. It must be freezing on the monkey island."

"That's because we've got a lazy wind."

"*A lazy wind?*" I queried, thinking this must be some meteorological term I hadn't come across yet.

"Yes," he said, "it goes through you instead of around you."

I spent my hour below reading a James Bond novel and eating a cheese and pickle sandwich with a mug of tea in my cabin. Later I was the one floundering blindly on the wing of the bridge. Although I could hear Dai's deep-throated chuckle, I couldn't see him.

"This is incredible," I said.

"It's just that your eyes take time to adjust."

"I knew that," I said into the darkness.

"*Wrth gwrs* you did."

I stood beside him, looking out at the barely visible blackness of the sea.

"Did you see the bosun?" he asked.

"What, now?"

"Yes. It's his birthday. You must have heard the racket in his cabin."

"I heard someone singing *Candy and Cake*, and others laughing at him."

"That's Jeremy. He must be well gone now if he's singing that."

"How old is he today?"

"Forty-three."

"Good heavens. I didn't think he was that old!"

Dai laughed. "You must think I'm ancient, then."

I did, but I didn't say so. By now I could make out the outline of the portly figure beside me, the bulky jacket with the fur-lined hood, and several days' growth of dark stubble on his face.

"Right, *boyo*," he said, turning to go. "Better get back to the party before Jeremy reports me missing overboard."

I turned up the collar of my coat and scanned the dark sea. After about ten minutes I saw a flash of light which seemed to come from the front of the bridge. It was so brief that I thought I might have imagined it, but when it happened again I decided I should report it. I slid back the wheelhouse door just enough to poke my head inside. I could just make out the outline of Stratton on the opposite wing of the bridge.

I cleared my throat. "Excuse me, Second. A light flashed …"

He laughed as he turned to me and said, "It's just this." It was then I saw something hanging from his neck in front of him.

"A camera?" I queried.

"Yes."

He held it up so that I could see it.

"Wow!" I said.

"It's a Pentax Spotmatic. An SLR." Seeing that I didn't know what he meant, he went on, "Single-lens reflex. That means what you see is what is actually photographed. It's the first camera to have a built-in light meter, so I don't have to mess about with a handheld meter every time I want to take a photo. It's an incredible piece of technology."

"You seem to know a lot about photography."

"It's a hobby of mine. I'll take a photo of you, if you like." He stepped back and lifted the camera up to his face. "Keep still now."

I was momentarily blinded by the flash. "I'll look like a scared rabbit," I said.

"No, you won't. The photo was taken in the split second before you reacted to the flash."

"That's incredible."

"I'll show it to you when I get it developed," he said as he wound the film on.

"Back in Port Talbot?"

"Unless I finish the spool before we get to Narvik," he said. "You know, what I'd really like to do is develop and print the photos myself on board."

"Could you do that?"

"Oh, yes. In our bathroom. I've just got to convince the old man that it's safe and it won't inconvenience the other officers too much. Of course I'd only be able to print photos when the sea was calm. But think how great that would be. You could take a photo one day and see it the next!"

When Willy came up to relieve me at midnight, he did the arms outstretched in front of him routine. But in his case, it looked like he was sleepwalking.

"Owen ... Owen ...?" he murmured in his slightly high-pitched voice.

Wickedly, I stepped out of his way every time he approached me, just as we used to do as kids playing blind man's bluff. Then he stopped and, after a few seconds, turned to feel for the sliding door of the bridge. Assuming he was about to go in to ask the second mate where the lookout was, I grasped his arm. He swung around with a cry and a look of horror on his face.

"It's only me," I said.

"Oh, I couldn't see you."

"I know. I was just messing about. Sorry."

He laughed nervously. "Oh, good joke."

"There's nothing to report, Willy," I went on, feeling guilty about having startled him.

"Right you are." After a moment, he added, "I've just come from the bosun's cabin. It's his birthday."

"Yes, so I heard."

"He said for you to go there."

"Righto." I walked the few steps to the ladder. Then I turned around and said, "Are you all right now?"

"Me? Yes." The nervous laugh again. "I'm fine."

When I got to the bottom of the ladder, on the boat deck, I was surprised by a gust of wind blowing between the back of the bridge and the funnel. It sent me racing across the deck until I was able to grab the handle of an air vent. The wind rushed past me, howling. Holding onto whatever I could, I made my way to the ladder leading down to the crew's accommodation deck, where I was again sheltered from the wind.

As I stepped into the accommodation near the bosun's cabin and closed the heavy metal door behind me, I heard raucous voices singing *Maggie May*. I could distinguish the voices of Dai and the bosun. The words of the Liverpool folk song about a prostitute followed me down the stairway to my cabin. I took off my duffle coat, balaclava and gloves and threw them on the bed.

As I went back up the stairs to the bosun's cabin, haunted by the thought that I had almost paid with my life for teasing my feeble-minded shipmate. And that I still might.

I stood peering through the swirling smoke with my left hand on my hip, in a posture I later realised was effeminate, and tried to avoid. The air was thick with the smell of alcohol and tobacco, the wastepaper bin overflowing with empty beer cans and spirit bottles. I didn't know whether I should just walk in or wait to be invited. Feeling a bit intimidated, a third option popped into my mind: turn around and go back to my own cabin.

The bosun, in his easy chair, was leaning towards the others: "And he said 'What's in it for me?' and she goes, 'Sand, I should think!'" and they all burst out laughing.

Then he saw me. His laughter died away and he stared at me in the same way as when he first saw me a few days earlier when I joined the ship in Port Talbot. I had been on my hands and knees cleaning the inside of the starboard lifeboat, out of sight, when he called me from the boatdeck. I stood up and looked down at him from the lifeboat. The bosun had stared back at me, spellbound.

He beckoned and said, "Come and join the party."

As I was looking around for somewhere to sit, Kirk slapped his thigh. "Come and sit here. I'll smooth yer."

The bosun gave him a disapproving look.

I sat on the settee between Dai, who already looked the worse for wear since I'd seen him an hour ago and John, the Londoner. "What'll it be, lager or ..." Dai picked up a bottle and turned it so that he could squint at the label, "Scotch?"

"Oh, I don't know – lager, I think ..."

"You are old enough to drink, aren't you?" asked the bosun with pretend concern. Despite his efforts, his speech was slightly slurred.

"Who gives a cobbler's in the middle of the fucking Atlantic?" Dai blurted out.

John laughed. "Have you any idea where you are, Dai?"

"We're at sea, it's the bosun's birthday, it's brass monkey weather outside, it's warm by here and we've got booze. Who gives a toss about anything else? Here, Owen, start off with a lager. The night is young."

"Which is more than can be said for you," said the bosun.

Dai pulled a face. "How about you, John – a bit more Bacardi in your Coke?"

"No," replied John, covering his glass with his hand. "I wouldn't want to be you in the morning, Dai. You'll be looking like the wreck of the *Hesperus* again."

"And does it matter?" Callum, the Scottish steward put in. "I used to worry about the day after too. But not now. Okay, I'll feel like shite warmed up in the morning, but right now I'm having a great time. And that's all that counts. We might not even be alive tomorrow. *Carpe diem!*"

"Crap what?" asked Kirk.

"*Carpe diem*, you ignoramus," said Dai. "Seize the day. From the Roman philosopher Horace."

I glanced at Dai with my mouth open, amazed by his knowledge.

"How's our second mate getting on up there?" Mitch asked me.

"He's okay," I answered.

"He wouldn't be if he knew what happened at the back of the Red Lion on Christmas Eve," said Mitch, smiling smugly. "Would he, Dai?"

Dai tapped the ash from his cigarette into an empty beer can, as if he hadn't heard him.

"Why, what happened?" I asked.

"He introduced me to his wife, that's what happened. Big mistake! By the end of the night I was picking her pubic hairs out from between my teeth."

The bosun changed the subject. "What's it like out there, Owen?"

"It's cold ... and windy." As a sailor, I thought, I should be more precise about the weather. I glanced from one expectant face to another.

"Cold, windy ..." the bosun prompted.

"Yes," I shrugged. "Cold and windy."

"He's not obsessed with the weather yet," Dai laughed. "Not like us morons. He's still got other things to think about." A beer can hissed as he twisted the opener into it.

Light bounced off the gold medallion hanging from Mitch's neck by a silver chain. Noticing me looking at it, he grinned.

"This was my father's," he said. "What a man he was – a great man and a great sailor. It's solid gold. He bought it from someone who worked in a gold mine in Brazil." He held it in his hand and looked down at it lovingly. "Gave it to me just before he crossed the bar."

I must have looked puzzled, because he went on, "That's died, to you."

"Great party, bosun," said Paddy as he stood up. He stopped to steady himself on the way to the door, straightened up his spindly frame and belched. "Great."

The bosun continued staring at the doorway after he'd gone. "Looks like the stick insect had one too many," he said, amused.

"Why do you call him that?" I asked.

Everyone laughed. They obviously knew why.

"Well, look at him," said the bosun. "When he's up the mast, you can't see him. He looks like part of the rigging."

"Can't help the way he looks," I muttered.

"True," Dai conceded. "But it would help if he took his shirts off their hangers before wearing them."

After a while John glanced at his wristwatch. "I'm going to turn in." He knocked back the last bit of his whisky, put the glass down on the table and stood up. He looked at me uncertainly. "You'd better not stay too late either. You'll be back on watch at 4 a.m."

"I'm going now, after this," I said, raising my can a little higher.

John didn't look convinced, but he said goodnight and left.

Dai's eyelids seemed to be getting heavier and heavier, and the can in his hand was starting to tilt at a dangerous angle. Then he finally began to snore with his eyes half closed.

"Looks like it's past your bedtime as well, Dai," said the bosun.

Dai sat up almost straight. "Aye. Let's go, Owen."

"He doesn't have to go yet. He's as fresh as a daisy."

"He has to get up for the 4-8, same as me."

"I'll look after him."

"That's what I'm worried about," Dai mumbled.

"Eh?"

"I said good, there's nothing to worry about, then."

Dai walked unsteadily to the doorway.

"Close the door after you," said the bosun.

Dai's eyes narrowed with suspicion.

"It's late – hands are trying to sleep."

Dai's mouth tightened and he shook his head slowly before turning and disappearing from sight. The bosun was glaring at the open door. "I hate people like that!"

"I thought you were friends –"

"With friends like that, who needs enemies?" His face relaxed into a smile as he turned back to me. "No, he's all right, really. We go back a long way, me and Dai."

"Oh, how long?"

He didn't hear me as he stood up and went to the door. He unfastened the hook that kept it open and closed it with a thud that to me sounded like a bank's time vault.

I wasn't sure whether it was the roll of the ship or the effect of the alcohol, but as he came back to his chair he lurched towards me, putting his large hand on my knee to steady himself and looking straight into my eyes.

Chapter 25

"Good morning, Cozmin," I said to the young man with the Yogi Bear five o'clock shadow behind the refectory counter.

"Good morning, sir. What can I get you?"

"Coffee, please."

"And how does sir like his coffee?"

"Strong with cream and three sugars." As he turned to prepare it, I added, "But I'll have it weak and black with saccharin."

He laughed, but probably thought, what a *shmuck*, or whatever that was in Romanian.

Cardboard cup of coffee in hand, I looked around the refectory for Neville McEmery, the COHSE representative. Wencheng had suggested I arranged to see him. I had always imagined him being the type to use phrases like "grass roots", "at the end of the day", and "rank and file". He was a Practical Skills Centre technician in his late forties.

I spotted him sitting at a table near the window. I waved as he looked up from his laptop. He nodded once.

As I made my way between the tables towards him, I realised why the appearance of this tall, bony man had always repulsed me. With his slightly long canine teeth, glossy lips and pale skin he reminded me of Dracula. We'd always walked past each other without speaking.

He didn't stop jabbing the keyboard with two fingers until I was standing in front of him.

"I'm Owen Roberts," I said.

"I know." He closed the laptop and pushed it to one side, opening a folder in its place. "Sit down. Right, I've got copies of the student's statement, and her friend's. Now I need to hear your side of the story."

I'd never seen him this close before. I noticed that his ears stuck out a bit and the rims of his eyes were red.

"Right," he went on. "If I'm going to help you, you have to be honest with me. Is that clear?"

He waited until I nodded.

"First of all, did you have sex with this student?"

I moved my mouth, but nothing came out.

"You want to phone a friend?"

I was astounded to see he had a sense of humour.

"Yes, I did have sexual contact with her."

"I don't want any unpleasant surprises on the day of the hearing, so I have to ask you this: have there been any others?"

"You mean students?"

"Whatever you do with anyone else doesn't concern me."

I shook my head. "No, no others."

This was a nightmare.

"The next question is even more important. Did you help her fill in her answer booklet at your home after the exam?"

"No." This time I didn't hesitate.

"Final answer?"

I actually considered this for a moment before saying, "Definitely. I don't know why she's doing this."

"Never mind why she's doing it. You need to concentrate on the solution, not on the cause. To do otherwise would be futile." He handed me a few stapled pages. "This is her statement."

As I read it through, I said, "Look, she says herself that I didn't help her to cheat – look, right here."

"I wouldn't get too excited about that. She's not likely to admit it, is she?"

I had always had a vague contempt for this man who only appeared when someone was in trouble. Like some sort of vampire, the problems of others were his lifeblood. It had seemed to me that was what gave meaning to his life. Now he was looking at me as if he'd always known the moment would come when I would be squirming in front of him, pleading for help.

He took some more papers out of a plastic folder and handed them to me. "This is the statement of her friend, Princess. As you can see, she claims that Shola gave you sexual favours in return for exam answers."

"That's not true."

"Any idea why she would say it, then?"

"Because she felt I was helping Shola more than her."

"And were you?"

"Shola is a weak student. She needed extra help just to get through the course, whereas Princess was only after higher grades. And besides ..." I hesitated.

Neville tilted his head to one side inquisitively.

"Besides that," I went on, "she used to look at me in class."

"Lecturers usually get used to that."

"No, this was different. She used to stare – *provocatively.*"

"It must be difficult, having all these women throwing themselves at you."

I looked down at Princess's statement. My hands were trembling so much now that I couldn't read it, so I put it on the table in front of me. My mouth was dry. I reached for the cardboard cup.

"Careful," said Neville. "Don't spill coffee on it."

I looked at him, thinking he might have been joking. But he was already looking down, scribbling notes with a serious expression on his face.

"I wouldn't talk to your colleagues about this, if I were you," he said when I finished reading the statement.

"They all seem to know already."

"One more thing, I advise you to change your behaviour with female students – at least until after the hearing."

"Change? In what way?"

He looked impatient for a moment. "No more cuddling them and so on."

"I don't think I could be any other way."

"I know you nailed your colours to the mast a long time ago," he said. "But your career is on the line here."

Strange he should use a nautical metaphor, I thought.

"The boundary wall between friendly and over-friendly is quite low," he went on.

Two young black women on the road outside caught my attention. I don't know why – perhaps I needed to escape from the unpleasant situation I found myself in. They were both tall and slim. Probably students. They were dressed mainly in black, one with long plaited hair, the other with a ponytail. Long high-heeled boots over tight trousers made their legs look so long. Seeming to be waiting for someone, they criss-crossed each other, glancing around. They reminded me of wading birds.

Then I noticed Neville was staring at me as if I'd just confirmed everything he'd ever thought about me.

I expected him to make a comment, but instead he said, "Do you want to ask me anything?"

I paused for a moment, then asked, "What are the implications for my pension?"

He gave an ironic laugh. "That's the first question they always ask at your age. The bottom line is that if the charges are proven against you, you could lose it. Generally, sexual indiscretion with students is tolerated quite well. But helping them to cheat, now that's serious shit. The first is seen as a human failing, the second as outright dishonesty."

I swallowed hard. "What actually happens at these hearings?"

"It's like a tribunal, or a court case. There will be three people on the panel – one of them will be from human resources. Witnesses will give evidence and be cross-examined ..."

"Witnesses?"

"Yes. Like Shola, Princess ... you."

"Will you be there?"

"I can be, if you like. But given the seriousness of the matter, you might prefer to have a solicitor."

I intertwined my fingers to try to stop, or hide, the trembling. We'd never had time for each other, Neville and I. Now he was being magnanimous and enjoying it. He knew I'd never be able to walk past him again without acknowledging him and feeling humble.

"Where are they held?"

"In one of the small classrooms."

"Is there a chance it won't come to a disciplinary hearing?"

"Yes, it could be cancelled due to insufficient evidence."

For the first time, I felt there was a glimmer of hope.

"But would you want that?" Neville continued. "Some people in your position would want a hearing to clear their name."

Suddenly I was a little boy again, taking a short-cut home from school through the lane that ran behind the industrial laundry where later Gwen and Roger would work. I knew it was out of bounds for us, but that only added to its appeal. I saw the steam billowing out of pipes and smelt the starch and warm chemicals. I noticed the smashed window, but it didn't occur to me that I would be hauled before the headmaster, a policeman and my form teacher accused of throwing a stone at it. I broke down at the meeting and ran out in tears, followed by my mother. This was taken as confirmation of my guilt. My mother paid for the window and stopped my pocket money for three weeks.

"Not me," I said, coming back to the present. "I have nightmares about it."

"So you'd be happy if it were cancelled?"

"Yes, definitely. The thought of a hearing scares the shit out of me. I don't think I'd be able to stand it. What would happen if I didn't turn up?"

"It might be adjourned. Or a decision could be made in your absence. Either way, it wouldn't be good."

"I don't think I could go through with it."

"What are you afraid of?"

"Of breaking down. Of making a fool of myself."

Neville twisted his mouth one way, then the other. "How about if we have a mock hearing first, with people you know from the university? I'll get three people together and we'll make it as realistic as possible."

"Desensitisation?"

He smiled. He looked less like a vampire now.

"If you say so," he said. "Who do you think would agree to role-play panel members? Give me some names."

"I don't know … Wencheng would, I'm sure. And maybe Charity …"

He jotted the names down. "Who else?"

"I don't know …"

"How about Philip?"

"No, not him."

"Why not?"

"He'd have a field day attacking me."

"He'd be ideal, then." Neville added his name to the list. "I'll have to give them all the information, including copies of the statements. But they'll have to promise to maintain strict confidentiality."

I crossed my arms tightly over my chest to try to stop my heart pounding. Looking out the window again, I saw that the wading birds had flown. Now, like with those pictures of randomness that suddenly resolve themselves into a 3-D image, my eyes re-focused on the glass itself and I saw the reflection of an overweight man with white hair staring back at me. So different from the slim, tawny-haired teenager on the *Albatross* almost forty years earlier, feeling uncomfortable about being alone with the bosun.

Chapter 26

Feeling embarrassed by the bosun sitting there staring at me, I concentrated my attention on the snow falling outside the porthole.

After a while, he asked, "Are you counting them?"

"No." I blushed. "I was just watching how they fall slower when the ship rolls this way and faster when it rolls that way."

"Really? I never noticed that. Must be an optical illusion. Another drink?"

"No, I'm okay." I swished the beer around my can to show it wasn't empty.

"Don't worry, if you're not fit to go back to your cabin you can sleep here." And for a moment there was that spellbound expression again, before his face creased into a smile.

"All I'd have to do is fall down the stairs and I'd end up in my cabin."

He threw his head back with a loud laugh, and I could see that several back teeth were missing. I didn't think it was that funny.

"Tell me, Owen, have you got a girlfriend or ..."

"Yes. Megan."

"What's she like?"

"She's about as tall as me ..."

The bosun raised his eyebrows. "As *tall* as you?"

"Well, you know, my height, like. Short, wavy hair – brown, although she dyes it blonde sometimes."

"How old is she?"

"Same as me. Seventeen."

"Is she pretty?"

"Very pretty, Megan is." I hesitated. "Don't know if I'll carry on with her, though."

"Why not?"

"I don't know ... She only wrote to me once while I was away at sea training school and made up silly excuses ... and she went out with a couple of other boys."

"How do you know?"

"She told me."

"At least she told you."

"Well, yes, but she sort of rubbed it in. She sat by there and laughed as she told me, watching how I reacted, enjoying it, like."

"Women are strange creatures," he commented, opening another two cans of lager. He almost lost his balance as he leaned forward to hand one to me and put his hand on my shoulder to steady himself. He was so close I could smell the tobacco and alcohol on his breath.

Settling back in his chair he smiled and said, "You know, you're too nice to be at sea, Owen." There was a long pause while he seemed to wait to see what effect his words would have.

"You mean I need to be tougher?" I presumed. "So's not to be taken advantage of?"

"No, I think you're great as you are. No, it's just that I've been thinking of buying a flat." He went on, almost as if talking to himself, "twenty-five years I've been at sea, staying with my mum when I'm on leave ..."

"Your mother's still alive?"

"Oh, yes." He laughed. "She's alive, all right. Ask anyone who goes to the Mariner's Arms in Southampton. She runs it on her own since my dad died years ago. The thing is, I don't always have the same room when I go home. Depends on who else is staying there at the time. My sister and her husband, or their daughters ... I've even had to sleep on the sofa for the whole of my leave before now."

The only thing of interest to me was his nieces. I wondered if they might fall within my age range.

"You could share the flat with me," he continued. "Look after it while I'm at sea."

"What?"

I looked out of the porthole again, at the snow falling fast, then slow, then fast.

"I'll be good to you, Owen." His voice seemed to come from far away. "You'll want for nothing."

"I don't know what you mean."

"I mean, I need someone special to come home to."

I stared at him in disbelief.

"Someone to think about during difficult times. To be there for me ..." Tears welled up in his eyes.

This was beyond anything I'd ever experienced before – personally, in films or in any other way. What he was saying – so tenderly – would have been laughable if it weren't so outrageous. I wanted to be a sailor, not a housewife. An image of me welcoming him home in a pinny and with curlers in my hair flashed through my mind.

I stood up, putting the half-empty beer can down on the little table and turned to walk out of the cabin.

"Owen." I thought he was going to apologise or say he was joking. Instead he said, "You will at least think about it?"

Chapter 27

Monica dabbed her eyes with a tissue. Kamanu, the Nigerian student sitting next to her in the circle put his hand around her shoulder. She shrugged it away.

"Just trying to comfort you," he said.

"Why?" she demanded.

"Well ... because you're upset."

"I'm not upset! I'm fucking angry! Shows how much you know, doesn't it?"

"Yeah, man," said his friend Lovemore. "Right at the end of your Mental Health training and you still don't know the difference between upset and fucking angry."

"It's easy to confuse the two," I put in. "Even within yourself."

I was finding it difficult to concentrate on the supervision session. I'd always enjoyed them, ever since Wencheng had set them up years before. It felt good to use my counselling skills to help students reflect on their clinical placement. More recently, I'd also enjoyed Ewelina's admiration as she acted as my co-supervisor to gain experience. This pretty Polish woman had become my sidekick, just as I'd been Wencheng's previously. But the meeting with Crawford had changed everything. Now everything was difficult to cope with.

Monica was saying, "The doctor said he didn't want to take me on the home visit. In the ward round, in front of everyone. He wanted a social worker instead. But I was the one who'd been visiting her every week. I was the one writing a care study about her. It was me who'd said she needed the emergency visit, for goodness' sake!"

"Did he say why he didn't want to take you?" Kamanu asked.

"Perhaps we should explore Monica's feelings about it first," suggested Ewelina looking at me to see if I approved of her intervention.

The night before I'd dreamed about Susan. I was playing with her and talking to her, and I wondered how this was possible when she was dead. Did it mean that death didn't really exist?

Ewelina's eyes on me brought me back to the present.

"I felt humiliated." Monica stared down at the floor.

At that moment the classroom door opened and Princess burst in. "Sorry I'm late. The underground is murder, delays everywhere."

Feeling anxious about coming to this session and facing Shola and Princess, I'd been relieved to find they were not here. But then I was worried about what their absence might have meant.

"Where's Shola?" asked Lovemore.

"Not coming," replied Princess. "She's sick."

"Sick of what, I wonder?" said Lovemore, grinning, and looking at me from the corner of his eye.

"Maybe she ate something that disagreed with her," said his friend Kamanu.

"Or maybe it was the wrong colour!" Lovemore laughed, slapping his thigh with his hand.

"What's up with you two?" said Monica, looking up. "You're acting like a couple of idiots."

Princess didn't laugh either. She just sat there staring at me. I had become used to seeing anger and frustration in her eyes, but now I saw something that puzzled me – hurt.

"Should I confront him about it?" Monica went on. "If so, on his own or in the ward round?"

"You ain't got nothing to lose either way," said Kamanu.

Lovemore wasn't listening. He was staring at Ewelina's crossed legs. He muttered something in his own language. Kamanu glanced at me and sniggered. Ewelina looked tense as she tugged her short skirt down a bit.

I glanced at my wristwatch. "Okay, that'll do for today."

The students gathered up their things.

As soon as the last one was out of the door, Ewelina leapt to her feet and stood in front of me, anger and confusion in her eyes. "Damn! What's wrong with you? Why did you let them abuse you – and me – like that?"

I glanced up at her, but avoided eye contact.

"I don't understand," she said, glaring at me. "I've never seen you like this before."

She doesn't know, I thought as I rubbed my forehead. *She's one of the few who don't know.*

"Remember what you told me when I joined this group?" she said. "About being honest with each other at all times, no matter what?"

I nodded.

"Well …?"

"I'm sorry." I felt a scrawny deckboy on the *Albatross* again. "I'll explain everything to you, Ewelina. I promise. But not now, not now."

Chapter 28

"I'm taking my attendance registers down to Sophie. Shall I take yours as well?"

Wencheng gave me a sideways glance. He grinned. "No, I've already put mine in her pigeon-hole. It's just along the corridor, you know."

"Ah, but there's nothing like the personal touch."

He swivelled around from his computer to face me, moving his shoulders to relax them. "Got a good story for her?"

"Of course, I always spend about an hour making up a funny story for her. Then another hour figuring out how to make it sound spontaneous."

In contrast to the heaviness I'd felt over the previous few weeks, there was almost a spring in my step as I descended the stairs to the second floor. These brief exchanges with the Jewish woman of half my age never failed to raise my spirits. I observed her slim figure and her black hair in ringlets as I approached her.

"Registers, Sophie," I sang out as I stood in front of her desk.

"Just leave them in that box," she said without taking her eyes off the computer screen.

"Hey, you'll never guess what I found on my desk when I got in this morning."

"What?"

"A dead mouse!"

"Oh, God!" She screwed up her face in disgust.

"Yes, it was lying on its back like this." I curled my hands up in front of my chest and turned my eyes upwards with my mouth open, motionless.

"What did you do with it?"

"I called the IT department and they told me to just throw it in the bin and collect another one."

I smiled and waited for the penny to drop and for her to laugh, but she just said, "Gee, that's sick," and turned back to her computer.

My smile disintegrated, and *I* felt sick as I left the Registration Office. I slumped behind my own desk, stunned. Sophie had never reacted to me like that before. What had happened to our special relationship? She must have heard about the accusations against me. It felt like something beautiful had died. *Susan.* She would have been about Sophie's age by now if ...

If I hadn't taken her to the beach on that last day in Torremolinos on the Costa del Sol. Brad, a year older than her, was having swimming lessons in the hotel's pool.

"Just make sure you're back for lunch," Fiona had reminded me as we stood in the sun outside the hotel.

I gave her a lingering kiss.

Breaking away, she said, "You're only going to the beach!"

"Right. But I'm looking forward to one more *siesta* with you." I dropped my voice, "Know what I mean, nudge nudge wink wink?"

She was still laughing when I glanced back to wave at her. That was the last time she saw Susan alive, and the last time she looked at me like that.

As I draped a towel over a sun lounger under one of those straw canopies that look like the top of a giant coconut, Susan was jumping up and down. "Come on, Daddy, let's go in the water!"

"Put this on first," I said, taking her duck-shaped yellow and red life buoy out of the beach bag.

"It's silly," she complained as she lifted her arms. "None of the other children wear them."

"Well, you do," I insisted, slipping it on her.

The sea was warm. The sky cloudless. Susan and her holiday friends were splashing and chattering, each in their own language. It didn't matter that they couldn't understand each other. In the background was the drone of a distant motorboat.

"Back in a minute," I called to Susan. I don't think she heard me.

I hurried back to the sun lounger for my camera. As I rummaged through the beach bag, I was vaguely aware of the droning sound getting louder. I opened one zip after another, feeling sure I'd left the camera there the day before.

I froze when I heard the commotion behind me. People were yelling for their children, gathering them up, taking them out of the water. What was happening? Was there a shark? I ran back to the water's edge. I couldn't see Susan. I started calling for her. The motorboat was near the shore and a few bathers were struggling to lift its stern. As I threshed through the water towards them, I saw the water turning red.

Auburn hair was wrapped around the propeller. Susan looked as if she was asleep. Someone was wailing; I became aware that it was me. I held her beautiful face up out of the water, but I knew she wasn't breathing.

Then the people gathering around the boat were shouting at the two youngsters in the boat, and one man was held back from attacking them.

When the Cruz Roja arrived, they cut Susan's hair free from the propeller and allowed me to carry her to the ambulance. Through tears, I muttered over and over again, "How can I tell Fiona?"

Later, in the attic with Brad, I found a white sisal rope, a half inch in diameter, under an old blanket. Instinctively, I started coiling it up. I'd bought it in a yachting shop in Barnet soon after we moved into this house, some twenty-five years before, when I was stripping down and painting the upstairs wooden window frames. It was to tie around my waist as a lifeline as I reached out to do the outside of the frames.

I'd asked the woman in the shop for a strong rope and she showed me this one.

"Great," I'd said. "This will hold my weight."

She called a man from the back of the shop. They exchanged suspicious glances as they asked what I wanted it for, and only reluctantly sold it to me. While driving home from the shop with the rope on the passenger seat, I chuckled when I realised what they must have suspected.

Then my mind went back to just before I went to sea, to the sea training school in Gloucester. We were huddled in the corner of our accommodation hut where Scouse, who had been there a couple of months longer than us, was sitting with a length of rope draped over his lap.

"I shouldn't be showing yous this," he confided in his thick accent. "They'd chuck us out if they knew."

Someone threw another packet of five Woodbines onto the pile of cigarettes, biscuits and other items on the blanket by his side. They were mainly from food parcels received from home.

He bit his lower lip. "All right. Is someone watching the door?"

"It's covered," confirmed an Irish boy, whose name I can't remember.

"Sound," said Scouse.

There was absolute silence as he slowly formed the forbidden knot. We were mesmerised as he wound the rope around itself, one, two, three, four, five times. He finally held it up and looked at us defiantly.

"Is – is that really it?" asked one of the boys, wide-eyed.

Scouse answered by putting his hand inside the noose and bringing it down swiftly, causing the noose to snap tight around his wrist. There was a general gasp, and I noticed one boy's hand unconsciously shoot up to his throat.

As I coiled up the rope and hung it from one of the attic's struts, just as I'd done with heaving lines in the fo'c'sle of the *Albatross* almost forty years before, I couldn't help visualising how to do the knot Scouse had shown us. And I mused that those two people in the yachting shop might prove to be right, after all. Perhaps they knew something I didn't.

Chapter 29

I stood beside the overhead projector facing the ascending seats of the lecture theatre while students filed in. The keener ones sat near the front, while the ones who were just here to do their time or for the beer headed for the back. I'd often mused that I could probably predict how far back each student would sit just by the way they entered a theatre or classroom.

The lecture theatre was nearly half full. That was about as good as it would get. Normally I would start by saying something funny or unexpected to get everyone's attention. But this time there was hollowness in my voice as I began, "Does anyone know when the first theory of personality was formulated?"

I was aware of the monotony of my voice. I sounded timid. Okay, I said to myself, this won't be remembered as my best performance. This time I'll have to settle for mediocrity which, after all, was standard in many lecturers. And with that thought I began to relax.

But a little later I noticed two female students whispering to each other. Then one of them turned around and looked up and behind her. I followed her gaze ... to Shola. Arms folded, she was staring straight ahead, as if I wasn't there. For once, her friend Princess was not by her side.

My mouth was dry. As I moistened my lips with my tongue, students looked at me curiously, or turned and commented to each other.

"So personality is – is ..."

I froze. What was I going to say? Everyone could see I was like a scared rabbit. I opened my mouth, but nothing came out, just like in the dream of getting my foot caught in the railway tracks. Turning my eyes downwards, I stuffed the acetates back into my briefcase and hurried out of the lecture theatre.

Wencheng looked up at me as I put my teaching folder in the filing cabinet.

"You finished early," he said.

"Yes." I slammed the cabinet drawer closed with my hip.

"You okay?"

I shook my head. "No, not really."

"Want to talk?" He swivelled his chair towards me.

I hesitated before slumping into my chair and faced him. He waited. The way I'd seen him waiting so many times when a student came to him with a problem.

I glanced over my shoulder to make sure nobody could hear. "I suppose you know ...?"

"I heard something about you and a student."

"I'm going to lose everything because of it." I held my head in my hands. "My job, pension ... even my family, when Fiona finds out. There's going to be a disciplinary hearing. I can't face that."

"You can if you have to."

"I can't!"

"You've survived things in the past."

"Nothing as bad as this!"

Wencheng raised an eyebrow. "Are you sure? I remember you telling me the reason you went into psychiatric nursing, not long after we met. Do you remember?"

I nodded, feeling my eyes cloud over. "I suddenly realised it wasn't Susan I needed to let go of, but suffering."

"And you wanted to use that insight to help others."

"But it took me two years of therapy to realise that."

"So? Got anything better planned for the next couple of years?"

I stared at him for a moment, then cupped my hands over my face. "I just don't know what to do." I struggled to take a breath. "There's nothing I can do."

After sitting in silence for a while, Wencheng said, "Would consulting the *I Ching* help?"

I shook my head. "No, you know how I feel about that sort of thing. Why did you ask me that?"

Silence.

"When I tried it before, it told me nothing," I said.

"You weren't in a crisis then. You are now. Your normal coping mechanisms aren't working. I'm offering you something different. Do you want to try it?"

"How can it help?"

"You won't know unless you try."

"I don't believe in magic."

When Wencheng didn't respond I went on, "How can a book written thousands of years ago answer a question that I ask today?"

"I don't know. I only know it can."

After another silence, Wencheng opened the drawer of his desk and took out a book with Chinese characters on the front and underneath the words, *I Ching: Book of Changes.* He took three Chinese coins out of a little leather bag and handed them to me.

"I don't remember how ..."

"Just shake them like dice. Then drop them on this." He put an A4 writing block on the desk in front of me.

"Do I need to think of a question?"

"I think you've already got one."

I shook the copper coins once in my cupped hands, then looked at Wencheng. I shook them again vigorously and dropped them.

"Two tails and one head," I said.

"That's two *yin* and one *yang.*" He drew a small straight line on the pad in front of him.

"And again," he said. "Six times."

After I'd done it six times, he had drawn a pattern of six lines.

"Now what?" I asked.

"Now we look it up on the grid at the back ... Ah, here we are: Hexagram 58. *Tui/Joy.*"

He ignored my ironic laugh and flipped through the book. "Here, read this. As far as here, then this bit that says 'Nine in the second place'."

After reading it, I looked at him blankly.

"Does any of it seem to mean anything to you?" he asked.

"No, none of it."

"Nothing has any relevance to your life?"

"No. Except the name of this – what did you call it? – hexagram. *Tui.* That was the name of a place where Fiona and me stayed in a *parador* once."

"Tell me about it."

"It was a beautiful place in Spain. Portugal was on the other side of the wide river. Fiona was pregnant with Susan. Brad was a toddler. Everything seemed so perfect then."

"Does that seem to tell you something?"

"Not really." I scanned the couple of pages again. "It's funny the name is *Tui*, but that's just a coincidence."

"Jung used to say there are no such things as coincidences. Anything else seem significant?"

I shook my head.

"Shall I have a look?" offered Wencheng, and I handed him the book.

"... when two lakes are connected they are less likely to dry out because they restore each other."

"Me and Fiona ...?"

"Could be. So what's that telling you?"

I thought for a moment, then queried, "That I should tell her what's happening?"

"Sounds that way." He carried on reading silently. Then aloud, "... and not succumb to pleasures unbecoming for the superior man."

"Who is this superior man?"

"Could be you."

I gave a dismissive laugh.

He went on, "Engaging in such gratification results in regret; the superior man cannot derive true happiness from base pleasures."

"Me again?"

He nodded.

"Does it really say that?"

"In black and white. Look, right here."

I read it for myself. "But this could apply to so many people."

"Does that make it any the less true?"

"I wish I were half as wise as you, Wencheng," I commented, handing the book back to him.

"Do you think I'm wise because I use the oracle or I use the oracle because I'm wise?"

I thought for a moment, then said, "I don't know the answer to that one."

He grinned. "Perhaps you should ask the book."

Chapter 30

When I walked out onto the poop deck of the *Albatross* she was folding back the water of the Vest Fjord into a long wake. There were already a couple of sets of footprints in the snow. One led to Dai, standing by the ship's rail holding a steaming mug, the other to Sidney, sitting on a capstan, smoking. Sidney was an AB too, and with his white hair straggling across his forehead and around his ears, he made even Dai look young.

"Ever seen anything like this, Owen?" asked Sidney without taking his eyes off the horizon.

"It's beautiful," I said.

"Actually," put in Dai, "you should only use that word when describing a woman."

"Beautiful? Why's that?"

"It goes back to the origins of the word. It comes from the French *beau*, which means sweetheart, and the old English word 'titty-full', which means voluptuous. Originally it was pronounced 'bowtitiful'. So, strictly speaking, you can say your girlfriend is beautiful, but not that scenery is."

I laughed. "Where on earth do you get these things from, Dai?"

"I used to read a lot before."

"Before what?" asked Sidney.

"Before I became an alcofrolic." Dai threw the dregs of his coffee into the sea and went back inside.

Sidney took a drag of his cigarette and let the smoke out slowly. "An Arctic dawn," he said.

"I never thought the mountains would go straight down into the sea like that," I commented. Then, after studying them for a moment, added, "You'd think they were black."

"They are black."

I glanced at him, thinking he was joking. "No, they're not. They're covered in snow."

"Yes. And that snow is black."

"That's only because it's still dark there. What's wrong with you?"

He took another drag of his cigarette.

"They might look black, but I know they're white really," I insisted.

"They're made of granite. Granite is black."

"But snow is white."

"Sometimes," Sidney conceded.

I laughed. "Everyone knows snow is white."

"What colour is the snow further down? Around that cabin near the water's edge, for instance."

"Well, it looks … pale blue."

"So that's what it is. Pale blue."

I gestured towards the east, to the port side, and challenged, "So I suppose that water is red?"

"It's red there," he said. Then he nodded towards the other side of the ship. "Black there."

I shook my head, not believing his naivety. "But it's all the same water."

"Just goes to show, Owen, that things change according to how we see them."

"I don't quite get that," I said, "but it sounds very wise."

"You will one day, when you're older." He stuffed his cigarettes and matches into his pocket. "I'm going to turn in." Before going through the door to the crew's accommodation, he turned and said, "You have to learn to see things as they are, Owen, not as you suppose them to be."

I was still standing there gazing at the scene when the bosun came out through the door. "Oh, there you are," he said. "What are you doing?"

"Just looking."

"Yes, beautiful isn't it? A bit different from yesterday. We might as well start getting the mooring ropes up. Where's your watchmate?"

"Dai? He was here just now."

"I'll go and look for him. See you on the fo'c'sle in five minutes."

John was already on the fo'c'sle when I got there, shovelling snow over the side. I picked up the other shovel to help him.

"That'll do," said John after a while. "As long as we can get to the capstans and have space to coil the ropes down."

We heard Dai's smoker's cough on the main deck.

"Here he comes," grinned John. "Eyes like piss-holes in the snow again."

John unscrewed the wingnuts on the store hatch, pulled it open and dropped a heaving line down. Then he called out, "Just tie this to the first rope before you come up, Dai."

"Aye, aye," Dai called back and went straight on into the fore-peak.

"Heave away!" Dai's voice echoed from below and John wound the heaving line around the capstan a couple of times.

I switched the capstan on and it began to turn, pulling up the line and then the thick mooring rope. John untied the line in one swift movement and we began to coil the rope down on the deck.

"We don't usually do this until last minute up here in the winter," John commented.

"No?" I stood up straight for a moment to take the strain off my back.

"No. Weather's usually too bad. And when we do bring them up, we usually have to lash them down."

"You mean this weather's not bad?" I asked. "Last night I thought the ship was going to turn right over. When she rolled really steeply, I thought, this is it, she can't right herself this time. I ended up sleeping with my life-jacket on."

"Lot of good that'd do you if we turned turtle," said Dai, joining us. "What would you do, swim out of your cabin to an outer door like you were in your local swimming pool – in the dark and with everything upside down?"

"Stop scaring the boy," said John.

"I'd get out of the porthole. Then the life-jacket would float me up to the surface." I felt proud of the way I'd worked it out.

Dai laughed. "The water coming through your porthole would be like a water cannon. And even if you could get out, you'd be crushed by the water pressure at that depth."

John looked around without interrupting the hand-over-hand motion of coiling the rope. The mountains were changing from black to a celestial blue. "No," he said. "This is incredibly mild weather."

"The calm before the storm." Dai was suddenly serious.

We were coiling down the last mooring rope when the bosun came up onto the fo'c'sle. He stood next to me and held the rope with both hands, taking the strain off me. "How are you doing?" he asked.

"I'm okay."

"These ropes are heavy until you get used to them. Take a break."

"I'm okay," I repeated, despite the ache in the small of my back.

"When are we getting in, Jeremy?" asked Dai.

"We should get to Narvik early in this weather. We'll go alongside around six."

I stared at him in dread. "I'll be on the wheel then."

He smiled. "How many hours have you done now?"

"Six."

"Well, I'm sure you'll cope. You only have to do four more to get your certificate."

"It's okay on the open sea, going straight ahead," I said, "but, but –"

The bosun laughed. "You'll be okay. Just do exactly what the pilot tells you and remember to repeat every order clearly."

"Shouldn't I get my certificate before taking her alongside?"

"I wouldn't let you do it if I felt you weren't ready."

"But I heard that once, in Port Talbot, the pilot and the captain, they disagreed about something and what would I do then? I wouldn't know what to do."

"In that case, you do what the old man says. He's got the ultimate responsibility for the ship."

"But what if …?"

"Don't worry, Owen. You'll be fine."

Chapter 31

I got up just before midnight, after only three hours sleep. I wasn't sure if it was the excitement of arriving in Narvik soon or the anxiety about steering the ship alongside. I plonked a bar of soap and a bottle of shampoo on my towel. As I walked along the dimly lit passageway, I could hear the faint hum of the engine room behind the olive green bulkhead facing the cabins. I put my hand on it and felt the vibration.

The only sound in the shower was the splashing of the hot water. Enveloped in white steam, I couldn't resist looking behind me as I thought of the film *Psycho*. I chuckled as I imagined Pussy creeping in with his carving knife.

I dried myself in my cabin and put on some clean clothes before going up to the messroom to make some tea. There was a wedge of cheese in the fridge. I wondered if there'd be enough left for Mitch and Willy on the 12-4 watch if I had some.

I buttered a couple of pieces of bread and put a sharp knife to the cheese, calculating what would be a reasonable amount to take.

"Take as much as you like," said a voice behind me.

I spun around.

"I'll put some more there later," the man went on.

I'd never seen him before. He must have been about thirty. He was clean shaven, with dark hair and thick-rimmed black glasses. He reminded me of Hank Marvin in *The Shadows*.

"You scared me," I said. "I didn't expect anyone to be up this late."

"Ships can be pretty creepy at night. You must be the new deck boy?"

"Yes, I am."

"And do you have a name?"

"Of course I do."

"Well, what is it?"

"It's Owen Roberts."

He held out a hand. "Hi, Owen. I'm Graham." As we shook hands, he went on, "Come to my cabin. It's a bit cosier than here. Bring that with you," he pointed at my mug of tea. "It'll be nice to have someone sensible to talk to for a change."

"Sensible?"

He nodded. "If you've met the rest of the stewards, you'll know what I mean."

I picked up the mug, the bread and the cheese and followed him to his cabin. It was decorated with souvenirs from different parts of the world. There was a Persian carpet on the floor and a colourful cover on the bunk – a zigzag pattern – which he said he bought in Narvik. The ebony mask propped up on the bookshelf looked African. There were framed pictures of attractive women on his chest of drawers.

He took a pack of Embassy out of a drawer and offered me one.

"No, thanks. I don't smoke."

"Given up?"

"Never started."

"That's unusual."

He lit the cigarette with a silver lighter. "This is a Christmas present from my wife." He turned it in his hand lovingly before slipping it back into his pocket.

"See this," he went on, showing me the end of the cigarette. "This is a filter tip. Reduces the amount of tobacco you take in. They say smoking causes lung cancer. It's probably nonsense, but I always smoke these just in case."

He noticed me looking at the wooden-framed picture of a beautiful girl in a sexy pose. She had blonde hair that hung past her shoulders.

"How do you reckon her?" he asked.

"Is she a film star?"

He laughed. "No. She's my girlfriend in Narvik."

"She's amazing."

He picked up another photo of a dark-haired woman with two young children.

"And this is my wife and kids in Ipswich."

"Good heavens – she's quite pretty, too. Do they know about each other?"

"God, no. When I'm in Narvik, this one goes in the drawer –" he indicated the family portrait. "When I'm in the UK, that one goes in. Any other time – like now – they are both out. That way everyone is happy."

"It must be difficult to lead a double life like that. I mean, if you had to choose between them, which would you choose?"

He smiled. "I don't have to choose. Life isn't that cruel. As long as I'm careful, I can carry on living the life of Riley."

"The life of …? Are you the second steward?"

The question took him by surprise. "Yes. That's right."

"I'd give anything to have a girl like that."

"Like …?"

"Like her – the blonde one."

"Who says you won't?"

I munched on my sandwich and took a sip of tea. "Someone like that wouldn't even look at me."

"You never know. There's no accounting for taste. Is this your first trip?"

"Yes."

"It's a good company, McGowan Brothers. All their ships are named after sea birds, you know. The *Albatross, Seagull, Tern, Puffin, Shag* –"

"I'm glad I wasn't offered that one!"

He looked at me questioningly.

"That last one," I said, laughing. "Back in the village they would have teased me no end. 'Hey, look out, Owen's on the *shag*!'"

"It's just the name of a bird, Owen."

"I know." I suddenly felt silly and immature. Then, to change the subject, I said, "I'm really looking forward to getting to Norway tomorrow."

Riley grinned and gave me a knowing look. "Yes, I bet you are. Tell me something, Owen, have you ever been in love?"

"When I was a kid I used to go to the house of my two aunties to look after their dog when they went out sometimes. They were both ancient. They used to force-feed me, especially with their homemade *bara brith*."

"What the hell's that?"

"It's sort of Welsh bread, made with fruit and spices. *Bara brith* means speckled bread. That's what it looks like. I used to be so bored there. There was nothing to do. The tick of the grandfather clock sounded so loud it used to drive me bonkers. The seconds passed so slowly. Tick, tick, tick. And it chimed every quarter of an hour! Then they got a calendar with a picture of a girl with straw-coloured hair and blue eyes. Sitting on a bale of hay in a sunny field."

"How old were you?"

"I must have been eight or nine. They hung it on the wall next to the dining table. When my aunts forced yet another piece of cake on me, the girl on the calendar looked like she was smiling at me. When they went out, I'd take the calendar down and lie on the couch looking at it. If I half-closed my eyes it seemed like she was really there with me. I enjoyed sort of … touching myself, like. I never knew what her name was. I looked all over the calendar for it. In the end I called her June."

Riley nodded.

"Then one day I heard a sound and opened my eyes to see the two little old ladies looking down on me. They looked shocked. I couldn't believe I hadn't heard them come in. They'd come back early and caught me 'at it'. I didn't really know what 'at it' meant then, but later I realised they must've thought I was masturbating."

"You were."

"No, I wasn't!" My voice had gone up an octave. "I didn't even know what that was!"

"You might not have known what it was, but that doesn't mean you weren't doing it."

I didn't see any point in arguing the point, so I relaxed and went on, "They never mentioned it to me again, but I was afraid they'd tell my mam. I kept expecting Mam to bring it up, but she never did. Anyway, when I went to dogsit for their boxer the next Thursday, the calendar wasn't there. After they left, I looked everywhere for it, even in the drawers of the Welsh dresser, which I'd never have opened normally. I couldn't find it. I never saw her again."

"What an amazing love story," said Riley, lighting another cigarette.

Back in my cabin, I took the diary I'd bought in Port Talbot before boarding the *Albatross* out of a drawer. My intention had been to keep a record of my first sea voyage, but more than a week of the year had passed without me writing a word. *If I don't start now*, I told myself, *I never will.*

At that time I had no inkling about the incredible events, both magnificent and terrifying, that I would be recording.

I turned to 10th January 1967 and wrote:

The ship rolled like mad last night. I woke a few times wondering why we had not yet capsized. But today has been very calm. I can hardly feel the ship moving at all now. Just met Riley. That's not his real name. He's very sophisticated, has two women and smokes filtered cigarettes. Can't wait to get to Norway in a few hours' time. Can't wait to see the girls. Hope they like me.

Chapter 32

I lifted the rolled-up pilot ladder over the rail and let it go clattering down the ship's side. The pilot boat was manoeuvring alongside, its engine rapidly changing tone as it alternated between ahead and astern, thrashing the water white.

"Make sure there are no kinks in it," ordered the mate.

I leaned over the rail to look down. The hull was illuminated by the plankton in the water, and I could see that all the wooden steps on the rope ladder had separated successfully. I smiled at the thought of *The Kinks* rock band. As I straightened out, I said, "No, no Kinks."

The mate looked as if he was going to ask me what I found amusing, but instead he said, "Don't forget his bag."

I had forgotten. There was so much to remember. I picked up the coiled heaving line and waited until the boat was almost alongside us, then threw the end of it a little way out from the ship's side. It landed on the boat's deck. One of the crew tied it to the handle of the pilot's bag, which I then pulled up and put on the deck beside me.

Another held on to the pilot as he reached out for the ropes on each side of the short steps. I breathed a sigh of relief as he stepped safely onto the ladder and then began to climb up the side of the *Albatross*.

White steam was billowing from his mouth by the time he climbed over the rail. Standing on the deck next to us, he smoothed down his thick black overcoat. By the warm greeting, I could see he and the mate had met before. I picked up his bag and as the three of us walked back to the bridge I noticed the pilot glancing at me a couple of times.

"First time in Norway?" he asked in a fascinating Norwegian accent.

"First time anywhere," I replied.

"I think so." He smiled. "You look too young."

"Good to see you again," Captain Frazer said to the pilot as we entered the dark wheelhouse, and they shook hands.

"Shall I take the wheel now?" I asked the mate.

He nodded curtly, as if I should have known. I stood behind the helm and waited for him to disconnect the automatic steering.

"What is the course now?" the pilot asked.

"Zero eight five," Frazer replied.

"Okay, she's all yours," the mate told me, turning to join the others.

I nervously put both my hands on the helm.

"Steady as she goes," said the pilot.

"Steady as she goes!" He gave me a sideways glance. Did he think I was taking the piss out of his accent?

After about half an hour the pilot said, "Steer zero six five."

"Zero six five," I said, turning the helm to port.

Brian, in his white catering uniform, brought in a tray of coffee and toast for the three of them.

"Would you like some cheese?" Brian asked the pilot.

The pilot eyed him suspiciously. "As long as it is not Scotland Yard cheese like last time."

Brian looked puzzled. "Oh?"

"The one with the fingerprints on it."

The tiny cluster of lights on the quay were growing bigger. I could now make out the giant hoppers that would be used to pour iron ore into our holds.

"Stand by fore and aft, Mr Whitby," said Frazer.

"Aye, aye, sir." The mate wound his thick scarf around his neck before leaving the bridge.

Now I could see two shadowy figures on the main deck. One of them attached a wire to number one hatch, while the other operated the winch that slowly pulled forward the heavy slab of metal until it stuck up into the cold air, exposing the blackness of the hold. They went up onto the fo'c'sle and waited. When the weak light from the east became a little brighter I could see it was the bosun and John.

The mate strode along the main deck, seemingly oblivious to its treacherous covering of snow. He climbed the ladder up to the fo'c'sle and walked around its perimeter, moving his head as he looked this way and that. He leaned over the bow to inspect the front of the ship, then turned and looked up at the bridge, hands clasped behind his back. I smiled as I remembered the bosun saying this was a ritual of his.

Next came Willy, taking short, careful steps with his head down and hands held out from his sides in case he slipped. The last one to appear was Dai, the Michelin Man in his super-insulated jacket. He was carrying a steaming mug of coffee. As soon as he got to the fo'c'sle, he set the mug down on top of a capstan and took something out of his jacket pocket. His face, framed by black hair, white at the temples, was illuminated for a second by the flame of a cigarette lighter.

"Now that's what I call a motley crew," the Captain observed, as if to himself.

Despite my anxiety about steering the ship into port, I was glad to be in the warm wheelhouse rather than on the freezing fo'c'sle.

"Port easy," the pilot shouted from the opposite side of the bridge.

"Port easy," I echoed, putting the wheel a quarter turn to the left and holding it there. I glanced at the pilot as we approached the quay at what seemed a considerable speed to me.

"Hard a-starboard," he said at last, and I could hear the relief in my voice as I repeated the order.

Now I could see the stevedores waiting on the quay.

"Stop engines, Captain," said the pilot.

"Stop engines." The telegraph bell rang as Frazer pulled back the brass handle to that position to inform the engine room.

"Midships."

"Midships." I brought the wheel back to the central position.

The *Albatross* was now parallel to the quay.

"Finished with engines," said the pilot.

Frazer repeated the order and the telegraph sounded again.

Leaning over the port wing of the bridge, Frazer held a megaphone to his mouth and pointed it aft. "We're in position, Second."

On the fo'c'sle Dai bowled a heaving line ashore and the stevedores began pulling down the first mooring rope. The bosun turned and gave me the thumbs-up with a grin. In that moment, all tension left me and I felt a warm glow from within.

"You can stand down now," said Frazer and he smiled.

As I turned to leave, the pilot asked, "You go ashore?"

"Oh yes, soon as it gets light."

He laughed, looked at the sky, then at me again. "This is about as light as it gets here in winter."

I grinned. Maybe so, but that won't stop this being the greatest adventure of my life.

Chapter 33

After breakfast I put on the multi-coloured woollen hat with a bobble that my mother had knitted for me. "You'll need this in the North Pole," she'd said. Examining myself in the mirror, I felt it looked ridiculous, but at least it was warm. It was also clean, unlike the grey one I'd been wearing on deck.

I had to wait while Sidney and Mitch finished securing the gangway before I could go ashore. When Mitch went down to check that the platform was safe on the quay, I said to Sidney, "I can't believe I'm here."

"You've never been abroad before?" asked Sidney.

"Oh, yes – I went to England once."

"Have a good time," Sidney called as I went down the gangway. "But be careful – it's fifteen below."

"Below what?" When I saw his face drop, I added, "Joke, *myn.*"

"He's joking, *myn,*" Mitch mocked me.

Then I stepped onto Norway for the first time. The snow was more than a foot deep. I began to collect it up and in no time I had a ball as big as a snowman's head. I looked around for someone to throw it at. There were only the stevedores, and I didn't know how they would take it. Probably so used to snow, they wouldn't see the fun of it. I threw it against the ship's side. It disintegrated into powdery pieces, leaving a round white mark on the black hull.

Trudging through the snow, I found my way out of the docks and onto Konengs Gate, which led up the sloop to the town. I was a bit disappointed that the road's name had an English word in it. Here the coloured houses and shops, all made of wood, looked unreal, like façades in a Western film.

It was then I noticed a young girl hurrying along behind me. When I slowed down to let her pass, she turned and smiled. This is indeed the land of milk and honey, I thought.

"Excuse me, do you speak English?"

"*Ja* – a little."

"Can you tell me …" I had to think quickly, "where I can get a cup of coffee?" I cringed inwardly. God, was that the best I could do?

"Coffee? Sure. The *Kafeteria Nordstjernon* is near. Come, I show you."

I noticed that she seemed to have all the time in the world now, as she walked along by my side. A dark fringe hung below her fur-lined hood and shadowed soft brown eyes, a broad nose and a few freckles. A Norwegian girl, I thought, smiling.

"You're out very early," I said.

"Oh, *ja.* I go to work walking. I like it walking in the snow. Also the exercise it is good for me. You work on ship?" she asked.

"Yes, the *Albatross.* I just brought her in."

She didn't seem to be impressed, though she might not have understood what I meant. She just went on, "And your name?"

"Owen."

"Owen? I never heard that before."

"It's Welsh."

"What is Welsh, please?"

"That means I'm from Wales."

"Ah, in England."

"Well, not exactly ...."

"Part of *Kongeriket Storbritannia!*"

"Does that mean United Kingdom?"

"*Ja* ... We turn here."

She stopped outside a large, square building. "Here is *Nordsjernon.* I meet you here at twelve, *ja?*"

She smiled, waiting for my answer.

"What, you come here for lunch?" I asked, taken aback by her suggestion.

"For coffee. I bring my special lunch." She indicated the bag hanging at her side.

"Yes, okay ... see you at twelve, then."

She carried on walking.

"*Aros,*" I said, then cursed myself for slipping into Welsh in my confusion. "Wait – what's your name?"

"Torruld," she called back.

Even the coffee tasted different in this country. Quite bitter. I went to ask the tall man behind the counter to add more milk and sugar. It was warm in there. The man watched as I took off my outer layer of clothes and put it on the chair next to me. Besides as many wooden tables and chairs as could be crammed in, the large room was quite bare. There were a number of hand-painted cupboards. A few photographs of mountains, bears and wolves adorned the wooden walls.

When I left the cafeteria I looked for the name of the street so that I could find my way back there at lunchtime. I found it on the house on the corner. *Hareks Gate.* I carried on walking along Konengs Gate and noted that the next street to branch off to the right was Tore Hunds Gate ... and then the penny dropped. Gate didn't mean gate at all! It meant street. The Norwegians hadn't taken the word from English, it was the other way around.

I paused to look into the shop windows where there were witches and trolls made out of bits of wood and moss, postcards of the Northern Lights, salted fish, and sealskin purses.

I recognised the name *Torvet Plass.* This was where the Norwegian teenagers met, according to my shipmates. I sat on a bench on the side of the square, taking in the atmosphere.

My eyes wandered from the *Kriegsminnemuseum* at the far end of the square to the huge shop windows on the other two sides. I hunched my shoulders and tucked my chin in to keep warm. Then I noticed the first-floor restaurant on the side of the square facing me. They had told me about that as well: one of the few places in Narvik where you could get an alcoholic drink.

Dai's words came back to me: "How can Norway call itself a civilised country when it's got no pubs!"

The waitress in the restaurant smiled when I asked for a bottle of beer. She went to speak to a colleague, who looked at me with an amused expression. I spent an hour sitting in the warm by the window and watching people in coloured woollen hats and scarves passing in the snow, sipping my beer.

Torruld was already at the *Nordstjernon* when I got there, and she had someone with her.

"This is my cousin Marit." I couldn't believe my eyes when Marit curtseyed.

Neither could I believe how beautiful she was with her blue eyes and her honey-blonde hair flowing halfway down her back.

"What will you eat?" asked Torruld. She had a small bowl of salad in front of her.

"Oh, I don't know." I looked at Marit's plate. "That looks nice. What is it?"

"*Kjøttkaker,*" said Torruld.

"Really? I'll take your word for it."

"Meatballs. And we call this," Marit indicated the brown sauce on top, "Spanish sauce."

"And is that stewed cabbage?"

"*Ja,*" said Torruld. "And potatoes. I order you some."

She made her way through the maze of tables and chairs to the counter.

"You like Norway?" asked Marit.

"I love it."

"I suppose you've seen many countries?"

"Not at all. This is my first trip. The only time I left Wales before was to go to London on a weekend trip with the factory I was working in. But not everyone sees that as going abroad because you don't cross the sea and they speak the same language."

Torruld put a steaming plate in front of me. "You worked in a fish factory?"

Marit smiled. "There are other types of factory, Torruld."

"I know that," said Torruld. "But Wales is by the sea, too. I looked it up in one atlas today."

"It was a toy factory," I said.

I popped one of the meat balls into my mouth. "Oh, this is delicious!"

"Is it?" asked Torruld. "Let me try!" She reached over with her fork. "Marit works in a bookshop."

"That's interesting," I said.

"No, it's not," Marit disagreed. "It's boring. But at least I can sit and read books."

"What do you read?"

"English romantic novels," Torruld replied for her. "Mills and Boon, I love you, darling! That is why the English of her is better than mine."

Marit blushed. "English novels when we have them, otherwise Norwegian books." She looked at her watch. "Talking about work, I must get back. It's been nice meeting with you, Mr Owen."

"Owen, just Owen."

"Owen." She tried to say it exactly as I did and we both smiled. Through the corner of my eye I could see Torruld watching.

"When does the ship leave?" asked Torruld.

"On the morning tide tomorrow. About six o'clock."

"So we see you here tonight? Around seven?"

Chapter 34

Although it was only two-thirty p.m. when I got back to the *Albatross*, it was almost dark. The black iron ore powder was pouring out of the hopper into number 3 hatch and the ship was now much lower in the water. As I climbed up the gangway I noticed that it was now at much less of an angle. Black water occasionally slapped against the hull of the still ship.

I had the strange sensation that I was coming home. Just six days on the ship, and this was my floating home. And Norway was my country. At least for now.

There was an unfamiliar white shape on the poop deck, silhouetted against the grey sky. What structure, covered in snow, was this? I felt compelled to pass the entrance to the accommodation and carry on to the poop to check it out. It was a large snowman.

A cold missile hit me on the side of the head. It came from above, from the boat deck. As I looked up I saw Larry diving for cover behind a wire reel. I quickly made a snowball and returned fire.

Later, I made a cup of coffee in the pantry and took it along to the recreation room.

"Double top," came John's voice, and when I got to the door I saw him poised, standing sideways, a dart between his fingers. He brought his hand back to his ear to throw the dart through the air.

He shook his head sadly as he retrieved the darts from the board and handed them to Dai.

"Tough shit," said Dai. His shirt sleeves were rolled up, revealing the red, black and blue tattoos that covered his forearms.

"Oh, you're back," said John as he saw me in the doorway. "How did you get on?"

"You look pleased with yourself," commented Dai. "Don't tell me you've dipped your wick already?"

John gave me a knowing smile as I sat on an easy chair next to Brian and Willy.

"Well?" Brian asked when I didn't reply to Dai's question.

"Well what?"

"Something must have happened. You look like the cat who got the cream."

I told them about Torruld and Marit, and I realised that I was lingering on my description of Marit, especially her hair and eyes.

"How can you pick up a girl like that and I can't?" Brian complained. "I'm better-looking than you. Look at my hair compared with yours. And I'm taller."

"You know what they say," Dai grinned. "Big man, small cock. Small man, all cock."

"I haven't got time to sit around listening to this nonsense." Brian stubbed out his cigarette and left.

"You lucky blighter," said Willy.

"Lucky?"

"Having a girl back home and now another one here. Just like Riley."

"I wouldn't call that lucky," I said. "Anyway, I'm sure Megan's going to give me the bum's rush soon."

Sidney was lying on his bunk reading when I went into his cabin.

"You're back," he said, peering over the top of his reading glasses. "How did you get on? Can I get you a coffee?"

"No, thanks. I've just had one."

I sat down under the poster of a boy, wearing nothing but underpants, throwing a javelin.

"How did you get on ashore?"

"I met two smashing girls."

"*Two* girls?"

"Yes. One of them I really fell for. She seems to feel the same way about me, even though we've just met. Do you think that's crazy?"

Sidney laughed. "Maybe. But if you can't be crazy at your age, when can you?"

"You remember what it's like to be seventeen, then?"

"I am seventeen."

I laughed, but quickly stopped when he added, "And sixty."

"You can't be both."

"Can't I? When you get to my age you realise that time is just nature's way of stopping everything happening at once."

"You mean you can remember what it was like to be a teenager?"

"What it *is* like to be a teenager. But it's more than that. I also know now what it's like to be eighty, even though I might not even reach that age."

"I never thought of that before."

"No reason why you should have. And you might not think of it again until you're much older."

I grinned. "In the next century. I don't really understand all this, but somehow it makes me feel better." I stood up. "I'm going to change for the girls. I want them to see just how snazzy I can be."

"But you know there's no shore leave this evening? We're moving ship."

"No! From what time?"

"I don't know. There should be a notice by the gangway."

I grabbed my coat and gloves and dashed out to the main deck. The bosun's bare hands were red and trembling as he tied the black noticeboard to the rail next to the ladder. He turned and smiled at me.

"Feel that," he said, putting the palm of his hand on my flushed cheek. He kept it there, staring at me, for a few seconds longer than I thought was necessary to get his message across.

I stepped around him to read the words chalked on the board, and he must have seen the desperation in my face.

"What's wrong?" he asked, slipping his thick canvas gloves back on.

"Nothing. It's just that I was going to meet someone ashore tonight."

"A girl?"

"Yes."

"Don't worry, we'll probably come back here again next trip."

I nodded. A feeling of sadness came over me as I retraced my footsteps along the deck.

"Owen," the bosun called.

He must have been standing there watching me. I could feel tears stinging my eyes.

"It's okay, you can go ashore. There's enough of us to shift the ship a couple of hundred yards without you. I'll clear it with the mate – he owes me one."

"Are you sure?"

"I'm sure. Just make sure you're back by 5 a.m., ready to sail at six."

"I won't be that late!"

He winked. "You never know! We don't want to stifle true love, do we?" He added under his breath, "There's been enough of that this trip already."

Chapter 35

It was the Cuban Crisis all over again! Kennedy and Khrushchev stood eyeball to eyeball, shouting at each other. Then the Russian leader turned on his heel and strode away. Behind the Kremlin, which looked suspiciously like our back garden in Wales, he put a rocket in an empty milk bottle and lit the blue fuse paper with a match. It shot up into the air, heading for America. Then he did the same with another, then another ... Kennedy was doing the same thing in the White House's backyard. The whole world was being destroyed.

We were in the middle of the Atlantic.

"We'll head for Rangoon," said the captain. "It's our last chance."

Rangoon had been spared the destruction suffered by the rest of the world. But as we approached the port there was a blinding flash in the sky and the city went up in a mushroom cloud.

"That was our last chance!" I moaned, staring up at the light that had just been switched on in my cabin.

Mick glowered at me. "Last chance for what?"

I rubbed my eyes. "Nothing. I must have been dreaming."

"I've never known you to do anything else." Narrowing his eyes, he added, "I didn't see you coming on board."

"I think you were checking the forward ropes." Snug under the bedclothes, I felt his being there was an intrusion.

"You must've been creeping around like a cat burglar to get past me. Anyway, it's a quarter to eight. In case you want breakfast before going gallivanting again. We're not sailing this morning."

Although I hated the underlying sarcasm in his voice, I just said, "Okay, thanks."

He continued to observe me for a moment. "Why weren't you here to shift ship last night? What did you do for the bosun for that? I'll make sure *you* are night-watchman next time we're here."

But nothing could stop that feeling of excitement as I got ready to go ashore to look for Marit and Torruld. First I went up to the messroom.

"What'll it be, sweetie?" asked Pussy, gazing at me through the serving hatch.

"Everything you've got," I said.

"Oooh! That's the best offer I've had so far today."

He swung around with a flourish and started preparing my breakfast.

"Can't wait to get ashore to see the lucky lady, eh?" he called from the galley. Then he began singing in what sounded to me like Italian.

My mouth watered as the combined aroma of egg, bacon, tomatoes, sausages and bubble and squeak reached me.

"Here you are, darling," he winked as he handed me the plate. "That'll put lead in your pencil."

I walked into a conversation between Riley, who was standing up leaning against the bulkhead, and Larry, seated at a table, eating.

"I'm getting fed up with hearing you moaning about the Ice Maiden," Riley was saying.

"I wish you wouldn't call her that," Larry objected.

"Well, what's her name?"

"I can't remember – it'th Norwegian. But the point ith it'th not fair that you can bring your girlfriend on board and the retht of uth can't."

"Two things: first, she's not your girlfriend. You can't even remember her name! Second, it's one of the perks of being a petty officer. When you're a second steward like me you can live the life of Riley too. Until then, you'll just have to lump it."

"Well, it'th not right that you can uthe a nithe warm cabin while the old man thtopped me bringing my girl aboard." The angrier Larry got, the more noticeable his lisp became. "We had to go and have it in the thnow, dammit!"

"Poor girl," said Paddy, munching. "Her arse must've been blue."

"It'th jutht a big joke to you lot, ithn't it?" Larry slammed down his knife and fork.

A big man with tattooed arms and chest, who I'd never seen before, appeared at the messroom door, a steaming kettle at his side. His belly was trying to escape from his boiler suit, from which hung an oil rag. There were streaks of black grease on his face.

"What's up, Ivor?" asked John.

"The nineteen bloody sixties," he complained with a Welsh accent, "and we can't even boil water to make a cup of bloody coffee down in the engine room. So Christ knows how we're going to make it back to Port Talbot."

"What happened?"

"Everything's kaput. We blew a gasifier while moving ship last night. I've been up all night trying to fix the bloody thing. But the gasket is smashed to smithereens."

"Lucky it didn't happen while we were at sea," said Paddy. "We'd really have been in the shit without a paddle."

"What's a *gasifier*?" I whispered to Dai.

"Don't you know?" he boomed. "It's the spring they wind up in the engine room that makes the ship go."

"We're going to be stuck here for days waiting for the bloody spare part," Ivor went on. "Looks like I'll miss my daughter's wedding. The wife will bloody kill me!"

A few more days in Narvik. With Marit. And it was the weekend.

"Who did you say is the patron saint of sailors?" I asked Dai.

"Erasmus. St Erasmus."

I put my hands together in prayer. "Thank you, St Erasmus. Thank you!"

As I scraped the remains of my breakfast into the bin in the pantry, I glanced out of the window and noticed that the snowman on the poop had acquired a carrot as a nose and two plums for eyes.

Chapter 36

I met the girls in Torvet Plass and told them the good news.

"So you'll be here all weekend!" enthused Torruld, clapping her gloved hands. "So what shall we do today?"

"You know what I'd love to do?" I said. "Go skiing."

"Skiing?" Repeated Torruld, and the two girls looked at each other. "You've done so before?"

"No. We don't have skiing in Britain. That's why I'd love to try it while I'm here."

"You can't go skiing just like that," said Marit. "You must have schooling first."

"Can you ski?"

She laughed. "I've been on the *piste* since I was three years old."

"Good heavens, that's longer than Dai!"

"Pardon?"

"Nothing. Joke." I didn't fancy trying to explain that one to them. But I was glad I'd known what a *piste* was – and that was only because Dai found it so funny.

"It's dangerous if you don't know what to do," cautioned Torruld.

"Okay, forget skiing," I said. "Plan B: let's just climb the mountain."

"Fagernesfjell?" Torruld looked shocked.

"If that's what it's called, yes. The one above Narvik."

"We could take the *taubane* as far as the restaurant ..." said Marit, looking at Torruld.

I assumed she meant the cable car.

"And walk the rest of the way," I said.

Torruld turned and looked up at the mountain. "Okay," she agreed, turning back to us. "But first we go home to change."

We walked through the snow to their house on the outskirts of the town. It must have been towards the northwest, I figured. It was a bungalow, like most of the residences around, with concrete steps leading up to an ornately carved porch. To the right of the porch was a large alcove stacked ten feet high with firewood. There were skis and skiing boots in the entrance, which seemed to be as normal as umbrellas and wellies for us in Wales. I followed their example, taking my shoes off.

"Sorry about the smell," I apologised, "but I forgot to bring another pair of socks when I joined the ship."

I laughed at my own joke.

A woman with a bob of dark hair hurried to meet us, cleaning her hands on her apron. She was slim and quite pretty for her age. She must have been over forty.

"This is my mother," said Torruld.

She offered me her hand. "*Welcomen!*"

"Thank you, Mrs ..." I felt a bit foolish not even knowing how to address someone formally in Norwegian.

"Larsen. But you call me Inger. All Torruld's friends call me so."

She picked up a box of matches and lit the fattest, reddest candle I'd ever seen. Several others, of different colours, were burning in different parts of the room.

"I've never seen so many candles lit at once," I murmured. "Except on a birthday cake."

"It is to welcome visitors," explained Torruld.

"Oh." I thought for a moment. "Is that because of the climate – a symbolic offering of light and warmth?"

She shrugged. "I don't know. We just do it."

The girls went to change, and Mrs Larsen carried on talking to me as she peeled potatoes in the kitchen area, which was in a corner of the large living room. There was also a dining area with a heavy pine table and a sitting area with leather sofas and armchairs. I'd never seen a room like that before.

"It's much warmer in here than I expected," I commented.

"It's all from that," said Mrs Larsen, pointing to a wood-burning stove near the armchairs. "We burn it all day and night. You stay for lunch, *nei?*"

"That's nice of you, but we are going to go up that mountain ... Fagernesfjell."

Her hands froze for a second, and I didn't think it was because of my pronunciation. Then, when the girls came back, wearing trousers, she spoke to them in Norwegian and I noticed the anxiety in her voice. She mentioned Fagernesfjell a couple of times. Torruld laughed, said something in her own language, then touched her mother's arm reassuringly.

As we were leaving, Mrs Larsen said something to her daughter in Norwegian, to which she replied, "*Ja.*" Then she seemed to have an idea. "Is it okay that Owen comes, too?"

The woman looked at me and smiled. I could see that she liked me. "It's okay," she said, then added, "Next time you come to Norway, Owen, I make

you traditional Norwegian dish."
  Torruld wrinkled her nose, "Not *lutefisk?*"
  "What's wrong with *lutefisk?*"
  "It's not everyone's taste."
  "You come to Norway, you try *lutefisk*. Let him decide if it pleases or no."
She turned to me and raised her eyebrows.
  "Yes, sure," I gushed. "I'd love to try it."

As we walked to the cable car station, I asked Torruld, "What was that all
about? Can I come where?"
  "Here. To baby-sit with us tomorrow night."
  "Who are we baby-sitting?"
  "The son of my sister," said Torruld. "My sister and my mother they go to
theatre in Narvik to hear music of Grieg."
  "How old is he?"
  "Grieg?"
  "No, your nephew."
  The three of us burst out laughing.
  "Nearly … three years," Marit managed to say at last.
  "And what's his name?"
  "Per Eirike."
  "Per … Oh, right. John or Fred would've been too easy, I suppose?"
  "I beg your pardon?"
  "Nothing. Joke." I shook my head, smiling.

Chapter 37

At the cable car station I watched a carriage full of people ascending the
mountain in the distance. The carriages hung from a cable, while another
one pulled it up. It looked pretty dodgy.
  "How do they haul it up?" I asked.
  "It's electric," said Torruld. "The cable goes round a big – what do you call
it?"
  "A drum," Marit answered.
  "Oh, like a windlass," I said.
  Marit pulled a face. "If you say so."
  A carriage was coming down slowly. I glanced at the people waiting
around us. Almost everyone had skis on their shoulders, even the children.
  "Perhaps we should have brought skis just in case," I said.
  Torruld gave a polite nod. Marit smiled.

The carriage swayed from side to side as we began to ascend the mountain, like the roll of the ship. But this must have been more like being on a plane, I imagined. From above, the little wooden buildings and the vehicles looked more like the Matchbox toys we used to make in the factory.

And then the landscape was completely white.

"This makes me think of the abominable snowman," I said.

The girls looked at each other and then at me.

"In the Himalayas," I explained.

"We have a lot of snowmen here," said Torruld.

"Really? I thought there was only one – in the Himalayas."

They stared at me blankly.

"Some reputable people claim to have seen him," I went on. "Others say they have seen his footprints. But he always runs away if anyone tries to get close to him."

At this point the two girls burst out laughing.

"It's true," I said. "I'm not joking."

This only made them laugh more.

"I never saw a snowman run away!" Torruld managed to say.

"We – we –," Marit spluttered, "we will have to see if our snowman is still in the garden!"

"We learn about the Yeti in school," I insisted.

"That's his name? Yeti?"

"Yeti!" Torruld's laughter was uncontrollable. She put her hands between her legs as if she was afraid she would wet herself.

The thick cables came to a halt and we got out by the semi-circular restaurant overlooking the port. Then we began walking the rest of the way up the mountain. I soon found it was much more difficult than I'd expected. Very different from a stroll in the Brecon Beacons, that was for sure. We made our way up through the snow sideways, holding each other's hands. It soon became obvious that Marit was the fittest and most competent. She went first, followed by me, and then Torruld.

Torruld suddenly stopped, gasping for breath, and let go of my hand. "Go on without me," she gasped. "I wait in the restaurant."

Marit hesitated before saying, "Okay, if you are sure."

"I am." Torruld smiled.

So we carried on, quicker now. Soon we were both panting, sending out plumes of white steam.

"You need to rest?"

"No," she said. "But we can if you want."

"No, no. I'm okay if you are." I wasn't going to give in before a girl.

"Look!" Marit came to a stop. "A skiers' hut."

I followed her gaze but could see nothing but white on white right up to the top of the mountain. I managed to make out the little brown hut.

"How could you not see it?" she asked.

"Perhaps it's because I'm not Norwegian." I made a mental note to mention it to Sidney. He'd be able to explain it.

When we reached the wooden structure, Marit knocked on the door and then opened it a crack to peep inside.

"No one is here," she said, opening it fully.

I followed her in. It was completely bare. Everything was made from wood, including the floor. There was no glass in the two window frames, but shutters which were closed. I opened one of the shutters and looked out at the landscape of snow. We might just as well have been on Mount Everest. Sheltered from the icy breeze, Marit took off her gloves and hat, shaking her blonde hair loose.

"I wonder how long this has been here," she said, touching the wood with her slender fingers. "How many lives it might have saved ...?"

I sat on a sort of shelf that stuck out from three of the walls as a bench, and unzipped my jacket. Marit continued walking around the hut examining the wood. When she came back to me, she just stood looking down at me. I reached up and pulled her down until she was squatting on my lap, facing me. Then we kissed for the first time, her hair flowing down onto my shoulders. Her mouth moist and warm.

I slipped my gloves off and unbuttoned her coat, which fell open, and warmed my hands inside. She ran her fingers through my hair.

"It's long," she commented.

"It's the fashion back home."

"I know. The boys here begin to do the same."

I just wanted her to press her lips against mine again. She touched my face in the same way as she'd touched the wood of the hut.

"You're so pretty," she said. "Especially your mouth."

"You don't say that."

Her eyes questioned me.

"Girls are pretty," I explained.

I slid my hands down her back to her waist and pulled her closer towards me. She put her hands on my shoulders and drew away.

"What's wrong?"

"I don't think that this is right. Torruld likes you."

"And I like her. But the way I feel about you –"

She put a finger on my mouth.

"Tell Torruld," she said.

She got up and put her gloves and hat back on.

"I think she'll understand," I murmured, standing up and zipping my jacket right up to my chin.

She pulled a face as if to say, you don't know her! "All the same, perhaps you could bring someone else from the ship. A nice boy to meet her ... Shall we go back down? She waits for us."

I nodded. "Getting to the top would be an anti-climax now, anyway."

"What is anti-climax?"

"It means nothing could be better than being here with you."

To my surprise, going down was more difficult than coming up, but *much* quicker. Instead of going sideways, we went down more directly, tumbling over a few times. Now I knew why they had changed into trousers. Again Marit took the lead. At one point we slid down at a tremendous speed and, embarrassingly, I was screaming while holding onto her shoulders like a girl on a rollercoaster. I was skiing after all, but without skis!

Near the restaurant, we shot off a snowbank and glided some fifteen feet through the air. Now she was screaming as well. We landed on soft snow, cutting a crater through it until we came to a stop with me lying on her back.

"Are you okay?" I gasped.

She was laughing as she turned to face me. As we lay in each other's arms, her soft blue eyes gazing at me, there was a hint of a smile on her parted lips. I could feel her warm breath on my face.

"Perhaps we should have gone all the way," she said at last.

"I don't think we should rush things. And you were worried about Torruld," I replied, glowing inside.

She looked puzzled for a moment. Then she jokingly punched me on the chest. "I meant to the top of the mountain!"

We found Torruld sitting by a coffee table in the reception, reading one of the glossy magazines which were scattered on it. In front of her was an empty coffee cup and the wrappers of two or three chocolate bars. She looked up and smiled with a questioning glint in her eyes.

"So you go to the top?" she asked.

"No, it was much harder than I expected," I said, sitting opposite her.

Marit stayed on her feet.

"Sit, Marit." She tapped the seat next to her.

"I'm going to the lavatory," said Marit. Then, after a moment's hesitation, "I think Owen wants to talk to you."

We both watched her walk away, head bowed. I couldn't believe it when Torruld looked down and started flipping through another magazine. Looking back on it, I think she knew what was coming.

She finally threw the magazine down and fixed her eyes on me. "Well, what is it?"

I cleared my throat. "We felt it was only fair to tell you ..."

As she stared and waited, a shadow seemed to descend over her eyes like a rain cloud coming down the mountain.

"It's just that me and Marit ..." my voice trailed off.

"You love her?"

I nodded, supporting my chin with my hand and trying to keep eye contact with her.

"I will never have a boyfriend – once they see her, they want her."

"But that won't happen again, will it?"

"*Ja*, it will."

"It won't because, don't you see, now she's got me."

"It's because of her hair," she wailed. "Why can't I have blonde parents like everyone else? It's the sins of my parents passing down on me!"

"Torruld, you've got *personality*."

"The boys don't want personality! They want blonde hair!"

The rain cloud burst. Marit, who was now standing beside her, took a handkerchief out of her handbag and handed it to her cousin. Then she sat down and we exchanged a nervous glance.

"It's not fair," said Torruld, her mouth turning down like a child's. "I saw him first!"

Tears were welling up in Marit's eyes as she said, "Oh, Torruld, you can have him if you really want."

"Hey, wait a minute," I protested, moving to the edge of my seat. "What do you think I am – a stray dog?"

"I'll never have a boyfriend because of my hair," moaned Torruld. She wiped her nose. "I will dye my hair!"

Marit put her hand on her cousin's and said, "Come, let's go home."

Chapter 38

"I'll get a taxi to your place later," I told the girls when we were back in the town.

"You have the address safe?" asked Marit.

I tapped my jacket pocket, which contained the serviette she had written the address on at the restaurant. "Safe as houses."

I watched them walk away in the snow, Marit supporting Torruld as she leaned into her. A confusing mixture of emotions welled up in me as I turned and headed back to the ship.

Before going down to my cabin, I went to see if the snowman was still on the poop. It hadn't run away or been demolished. In fact, it now had a bowler hat and an umbrella.

Making myself a cup of coffee in the pantry, through the serving hatch I saw Brian in the galley. He had his white uniform on and was loading some trays.

"Brian!" I called.

He looked all around with a blank expression on his face before seeing my head protruding through the hatch. "Oh, it's you, Taff. Thought you'd be ashore with your bit of fluff."

"That's what I wanted to talk to you about. Do you fancy coming to her house to meet her cousin tonight?"

He looked suspicious. "Is this a case of 'don't care much for yours'?"

"No! She's a lovely girl."

"So why don't you have her, and I'll have the one you've got?"

"Well, if you're not interested ..."

"I didn't say that," he said. "But I can't make it tonight. Officers are having a bit of a do."

I raised my voice above the clattering of the plates and cutlery he was dropping on trays. "That's a pity because we're baby-sitting tomorrow night."

There was silence as he slowly turned his head and looked at me sideways with a glint in his eye. "Baby-sitting? In their house?"

"Yes. I'm going there tonight, too."

"Wow! That's something that doesn't happen every day. Look, jot their address down here in case I can get away early tonight."

I took the serviette out of my pocket and copied the address in the notebook Brian took from his chest pocket, not forgetting to put a line through the o in Strømmengate.

Then I went below to see Marcos. He was sitting on his settee with his feet up on his bunk reading a book about marine biology.

He lowered the book. "How's it going, Owen?"

"Okay," I said, sitting on his chair.

He observed me for a moment before saying, "You've got something to tell me?"

"No, no." I was beginning to smile. I put my hand to my mouth to hide it. "Come on, what is it?"

"Well, I met this girl."

"Uh-huh." He closed the book. "Okay, I'm listening."

As I told him about Marit and her cousin Torruld, I had the impression he was trying to gauge my feelings, trying to see beyond the words I was saying.

"And I was wondering if you could, you know, advise me."

"On what?"

"You know, on the sexual side of it. I haven't had much experience in that way."

"Neither have I."

I was confused. "I thought you were engaged."

"I am. Have been for over a year. But we decided right from the beginning that we wouldn't do anything until we got married. That'll be when we've saved enough to buy a house. I'll stay at sea until then."

"Isn't that hard – not even seeing her?"

"Sometimes. But look at the money I save by not paying for accommodation and food. It all goes towards our future house."

I gave a short laugh. "Not many men on the ship think like that!"

"No, and that's their choice. As for me, I believe in clean living. As it happens, saving money is compatible with that. You could do the same with this girl – you could build a great future with her. But you'd have to discuss it with each other at the beginning, not after you've started messing about. Yes, clean living. You can't beat it."

"But doesn't it make you feel, I don't know – different?"

Marcos opened his eyes wider. "I *am* different. Sure, they try to get me to conform to the sailor stereotype – especially when I join a new ship. But why should I? I'm not in this world for their benefit."

"I don't think I'd have the nerve."

"You don't know if you don't try. Look, they will reap the consequences of their actions and I will reap the consequences of mine. Mine will be having a wife, two children and a Dulux dog on the carpet."

I got a taxi from the town centre and it stopped at the short road that led up to the bungalow.

"You walk from here," said the driver. "It's difficult in car."

"How much?" I asked.

"One kronor."

As I handed him the note I quickly calculated that I could have had a good night out in Swansea for that – a couple of pints, Top Rank dancing and a curry.

I walked up to the wooden building. The snow was nearly two feet deep, even though there was a bank of it piled up on each side of the road where it had been cleared away. I couldn't resist drawing my hand along the wooden rail beside the steps leading up to the front door and squeezing the snow between my hands. I threw it into the maple tree beside the house, causing a shimmering cascade from its branches.

The doorbell rang, and I had to step back a little as Marit opened the door. I'd forgotten that the doors open outwards here. She was wearing a blue silk blouse and a black skirt and she looked stunning.

She laughed. "Come in."

I stepped in and made to kiss her, but she lifted her hand up to my face.

"You're so cold," she said.

I took off my gloves and stuffed them in my coat pocket.

"I remembered to change my socks this time," I said, taking my shoes off. As I fumbled to undo the buttons of my coat, Marit helped me.

"Hi." Torruld came into the hall. She took the woolly hat off my head and began to unwind my scarf.

Torruld's mother popped her head round the door. "Hallo! Oh, you are still undressing him."

The two girls looked at each other and laughed.

"Come meet my sister Frida," said Torruld, taking me by the hand. "She is school teacher in Narvik."

Frida was sitting cross-legged on an armchair in front of a low table with a pot of scarlet heather in the middle of it. Short hair with glasses, a black blouse and a silver necklace. A jag of a mouth, like a letter box, I thought, and when she smiled she seemed to be inviting me to pop a letter in. I shook her hand and sat next to her. The toddler with the unpronounceable name was using the sofa opposite her as a trampoline until Torruld picked him up and set him down on one side so she could sit there herself. He was big and strong with white-blond hair – a baby Viking. Marit sat next to her cousin.

Mrs Larsen set a tray down on the table and I could smell the freshly ground coffee. There were some sort of pancakes, cream and raspberry sauce too. She paused to light a crimson candle in a glass bowl.

"Coffee?" she asked me, lifting the pot.

"Oh, yes. With milk, please."

"Milk?" She looked puzzled.

"We always take it black," Frida explained.

"Cream okay?" Suggested Torruld.

"Yes ..."

She scooped up a dollop from the dish with a teaspoon and stirred it into my coffee.

"It's soured cream," she said. "But try it."

That's an order, not a suggestion. I stared down at the brown liquid with white bits floating on the top. Coffee with sour milk. Right. I reluctantly put the cup to my lips.

"Mmm. It tastes good."

"You see," affirmed Torruld. "You can't always tell by looks."

Marit pulled a face. "Don't know how you can drink it like that."

"You like waffles?" asked Mrs Larsen.

"Never really tried them," I said, feeling a little foolish.

"What does that mean?" demanded Torruld. "Either you have tried or you haven't."

"I haven't, then. But I know what they are."

Frida spread cream and raspberry sauce on one and handed it to me on a plate. The four women watched as I tasted it. They all seemed to let out a sigh of relief as I said, "Delicious!"

"Is that your father?" I asked Torruld, indicating a photo of a man in a smart military uniform hanging on the wall.

"It's my grandfather," she said, getting up to bring the photo to me.

"He's a soldier?"

"He was. He died fighting on land during the famous battle between your Royal Navy and the German *Kriegsmarine* in the Ofotfjord, near Narvik."

"Oh, when was that?"

She looked at me incredulously. "You don't know about the battle?"

"No. History was never my best subject."

She snatched the photo off me and replaced it on the wall.

"That was in 1940," her sister came to my rescue. "When the Germans occupied Narvik."

"Oh, yes, I remember now."

Torruld dropped down on the sofa, glaring at me with her heavy-lidded eyes. I decided I should change the subject before I started World War Three.

"Is your husband a fisherman, too?" I asked Frida, lifting my cup and saucer.

"Who?"

"Your husband. As he's away, I thought perhaps –"

"I'm not married."

"Oh, I thought this was your child." I indicated the toddler.

"He is."

I could feel myself beginning to blush. I'd managed to get out of a hole only to fall headlong into a crater. "I'm sorry – I –"

"I met his father doing teacher training in Trømso. He was a student also. But later we decided to each go our separate way."

Marit was smiling at me. I could see she knew how I felt, which made everything all right. I wanted to take her in my arms and feel her softness pressing against me. For her to take my hand and lead me to her bed – wherever that was. As vividly as I imagined it, I knew it wasn't possible now. But tomorrow night, when we were baby-sitting and whatsisname was fast asleep … Marit's aunt was gazing at me with a curious expression.

"Have you seen the rest of the house?"

"No …" Was she reading my mind?

"Why don't you show him around?" she suggested to her sister.

"Sure! Come, Marit, let's show him."

I followed them to a corridor.

"This is Mum and Dad's bedroom," chirped Torruld.

I looked inside. There was a large bed with an elaborately embroidered cover. A wooden chest decorated with roses and tendrils caught my eye.

"That was my grandmother's," she explained. "A travelling rose painter was in town and he painted it for her."

"Opposite is the study," said Marit.

The walls of the little room were lined with books which, I guessed, were in Norwegian, although an English title did stand out here and there.

"This is Frida's room," said Torruld, stopping at the next door, which was closed. "She keeps it closed because it's so tidy it scares people. Next door is the room of Per Eirike."

"And here is the most important room in the house," announced Marit, opening the door of the toilet.

"But where's yours?"

"Downstairs."

"Downstairs? I thought this was downstairs."

Torruld laughed. "Don't you have cellars in your country?"

"Yes, of course. Although I've never really seen one."

"All the houses here have cellars with rooms. Come, we show you."

She opened a door off the passage and I looked down a narrow staircase that led to complete darkness. She flipped a switch just inside and the lights came on.

"This is our private apartment," said Torruld. "No other person comes down here."

"Oh," I began to draw back.

"But you can, silly!"

I heard a metallic sound behind my back as I touched the wall. Looking around I saw a large key on a hook.

Torruld laughed. "Our uncle put it there when he remodelled the cellar, as a joke. It's never been used. We never even lock the front door of the house."

"Not even at night?"

She shrugged. "Nothing ever happens here."

At the bottom of the stairs was a sitting room. A coffee table stood on a wool carpet with a zig-zag design and was surrounded by two armchairs and a sofa, over which were thrown girls' clothes. In the corner was a single bed, unmade. Scattered all over the dressing table were powders, creams, lipstick and jewellery, mostly made of wood and beads and leather. I was assailed by the smell of perfume and saw three images of myself in the mirror.

"I sleep here," said Torruld. "And Marit through there."

We went into the smaller room, where there was another single bed and clothes thrown over a small armchair. A laughing cloth reindeer was sitting in front of the pillows. The poster of the Beatles sticky-taped to a wooden wall looked out of place somehow.

"I didn't expect there to be windows," I commented, looking up at the narrow horizontal panes near the ceiling.

"They don't let any light in now because the snow goes over them," said Marit. "But in the summer they do. And you can see the mountains."

When we went back up to ground level, Norwegian classical music was playing on the radiogram. For me it conjured up images of forests and trolls. Frida was stretched out on the sofa, posing.

"This is from Grieg," she purred. "It is what we will hear in the theatre tomorrow night."

Now there was a silver tray with a bottle and a number of liquor glasses on the coffee table. Frida came and sat down with us. "Did you try *aquavit*, Owen?"

"No. What is it?"

"It is distilled from potatoes, like vodka," she said, pouring the amber liquid into one of the little glasses and handing it to me. "Flavoured with herbs." She sniffed her own glass. "You can smell the – what is it called? – caraway?"

I put my nose to the glass. "Oh, yes, caraway."

"I don't think he's old enough for that," said Mrs Larsen.

"I'm sure one tiny glass won't harm," Frida replied.

"Water of life," put in Marit.

"Why do they call it that?"

"That's what it means in Latin," said Marit. "*Aqua vitae.*"

"You see, Torruld?" Mrs Larsen laughed. "Your cousin doesn't spend all day just reading the soppy novels."

"Come and dance." Torruld grabbed me and swirled me around the floor.

"Torruld!" her mother admonished her. "He's not *your* boyfriend."

Chapter 39

Ewelina rushed into the office with a stack of exam booklets in her hands, blonde ponytail swishing. "Have they started already?"

"Who? What?" I imitated her panicky tone.

"The moderation. The memo said nine-thirty."

"Haven't you learned yet that nine-thirty here means ten plus?"

"Oh, thank goodness!" She dropped the booklets on her desk. "I thought I was late. He called me, my husband – or ex-husband – I don't know what to call him now I've got the *decree nisi* but not the absolute."

I know what I would call him, I thought. *The dickhead.*

"I just couldn't get him off the phone. He's still insisting I sell the house and find something cheaper. But it's not fair to the girls. They're used to a nice house in a nice area …"

I decided that I loved that squeaky Polish accent.

"But doesn't he care about his children?"

"Yes, of course! No, not really. That's the problem. Anil is so disappointed that I've had two girls and no boys."

"Well, he can try again."

"That's what he wants to do. But with someone else."

"They're so beautiful." I remembered a photo she had showed me of them. "I can't understand anyone not wanting them."

For a moment, as she gazed at me, that permanently startled expression left her eyes. Then she shrugged. "It's a cultural thing."

I glanced at the clock on the wall. "We'd better get down there."

"I'm still seeing Wencheng once a week for counselling," she went on as if she hadn't heard me. "Unofficially. Lunchtime. He helped Brenda, the librarian, you know. When she was having her divorce. Now she's going to Canada on her own to visit her daughter and grandchildren. It's so good of him. Everything is confidential, of course. Much better than talking to everyone at work about your personal problems."

I gathered up my marked exam booklets, then asked, "You need a hand with that lot?"

"Yes, if you don't mind. My arms are killing me."

I picked up as many of her marked booklets as I could carry.

As the lift doors closed behind us, the new automated female voice filled the muted space: "Doors closing. Going down."

I looked at the pretty young woman in front of me. I imagined her smiling as she took the band out of her ponytail and shook her hair loose around her shoulders. She knelt in front of me and opened my zip ... Then her head was moving up and down ...

"Are you all right?" she asked.

"Yes, fine." How could such a fantasy pop into my mind at a time when I was being accused of sexual misconduct – and about Ewelina of all people?

"It's just that you were sort of moaning ... with your eyes shut."

"Oh, it's nothing. Up late marking, that's all."

Several of the classroom tables had been put together, with chairs around them, in the form of a board meeting. Philip glanced at his watch as we walked in. I had forgotten that he was leading the moderation. While we gave him our booklets and took our seats, Audrey and Sanjay came in and did the same. Then came Les, puffing and blowing, his treble chin making him look like a bullfrog.

"Lucky we're only on the second floor," quipped Audrey.

Les gave out a jolly laugh.

"Okay, let's make a start," said Philip, frowning as he glanced at his watch again.

We all picked up a booklet marked by someone else and started reading.

"This student made a huge leap," observed Sanjay after a while. "From 35% in the third attempt to 57% in this one."

"Who marked it?" asked Philip.

Sanjay turned to the front of the answer booklet. "Owen Roberts."

"Which student is that?" I asked, looking up from the booklet I was reading.

Sanjay read out the student number.

Philip ran his finger down his list. "That's Shola D – Dlov –oo –" He had problems with her surname.

"Ndlovu," I helped out. "The n and d sounds like our j, and the u like ee. Ndlovu."

"If you say so." He didn't look impressed.

Les cupped his hand around the side of his mouth and stage whispered, "The one with the big arse."

Audrey gave him a shrivelling look.

"Let me see that," said Philip, reaching out his hand.

He scrutinised the booklet. I felt myself getting hot.

"What do you think, Philip?" I asked when he'd finished. "If you don't think it's worth that, we can lower it. But it is a pass, isn't it?"

"Oh, it's definitely a pass. I'm not disputing that. What I'm questioning is the difference between the third and fourth attempt."

"She improved."

"But how could she improve so dramatically?"

"The fact that she was granted a third and then a fourth attempt means that she had problems during those periods that prevented her from doing her best ..." my words trailed off under his cold stare.

"What were the mitigating circumstances?"

"I can't remember off the top of my head ..."

"Dog ate her key text?" Philip suggested. "Left her notes on the bus?"

I raised a hand to loosen my open-neck collar even more.

"No," Philip went on. "Someone helped her with this."

"Of course. I helped her. I *am* her personal tutor."

"No, I mean someone actually gave her the answers to these questions."

"Impossible. It was an invigilated exam," I objected

"Exactly." Philip looked at the others. "Anyone know who invigilated?"

"Me and Wencheng," said Les.

"And nothing untoward happened?"

"No."

"Do you remember this student being there?"

"Yes," said Les. "She sat near the front, middle of the row."

"Gosh," said Philip, "do you remember where every student sits?"

Sanjay cupped his hand around the side of his mouth and imitated Les: "*I remember this one because of her arse.*"

I tried to laugh, knowing that Sanjay was trying to defuse the situation. Philip gave him a piercing look. Ewelina's face was like stone, while Audrey was engrossed in sifting through the evidence on the desk in front of her.

"So if nothing happened then, it must have been afterwards," said Philip.

"Did you see the student again after the exam?" Audrey asked me.

"Yes, of course. She's in my tutorial group."

"I mean," she dropped her voice, "on her own."

"Well, I –" I looked around at the others. All eyes were on me. I was beginning to panic. "I might have – well, she is one of my personal students."

"Did you see other students alone?"

"When necessary, yes. Some need more help than others."

"She needed more help than others?" asked Audrey.

Philip's head was moving between her and me as we spoke, as if he were at Wimbledon. He believed he had stumbled onto something. "There seems to be something fishy here," he said finally.

"For heaven's sake!" I realised I was raising my voice. "It's just that she worked hard and, and ..."

"Had a lot of extra help," Audrey finished for me.

"Yes, I gave her extra help. That's what we're paid for, isn't it?"

"The question is how we are paid," Audrey mumbled, looking away.

"What do you mean by that?" I challenged her.

Les was listening intently. I could see it was beginning to dawn on him that Shola's physical attributes might have something to do with this.

"Look, can we move on," said Sanjay. "I'm teaching at one o'clock and I'd like to get some lunch."

"That's right," said Les, adding, "seeing as they don't provide coffee and sandwiches for us anymore."

"We can't let this go," Philip asserted. "If there's been any irregularity ..."

"All this shows is what a good job Owen has done with this student," said Ewelina.

"I for one," said Audrey, "am not convinced this is all her own work."

Philip turned to me. "Didn't you question that when you marked it?"

"No ..."

"Why not?"

"Because ... students can improve."

"With extra help from you?" Audrey was keeping the pressure on.

"I don't know what went on here," said Philip, "but I think we should refer this for further investigation."

"I agree," said Audrey.

"Okay?" Philip checked with me.

"I don't think it's really necessary," I said.

"The reputation of the university is at stake," stated Audrey.

"That's a bit melodramatic!" My attempted laugh strangled itself.

"Students cheating is serious shit," said Philip. "Staff helping them cheat is even more serious."

"Well, if you want to waste the university's time ..." I tried to sound casual, but could feel my voice beginning to fail me. They didn't need my permission anyway.

Philip hesitated, the hand holding Shola's four attempts hovering between the pile of moderated booklets and the plastic tray marked For Investigation. It was touch and go ... They finally dropped into the tray with a loud thud.

Chapter 40

On the *Albatross*, a single set of footprints was faintly visible under the fresh snow. The thought of Mitch brought a bad taste to my mouth. The only sound was the crunch-crunch under my boots as I made my way aft. Instead of going straight down to my cabin, I continued on to the poop deck to see if the snowman was still there. It was, and it had acquired an erect white penis.

With a cup of hot chocolate from the pantry, I stepped into the messroom, stopping dead upon seeing the hooded figure of Mitch, sitting with his hobnailed boots up on a table.

"We're sailing tonight," he said. "That'll put a stop to your antics."

I stared at him in shock.

"Watches are back on," he continued. "So I'll be hauling your arse out at three-thirty. You'll be lucky to get two hours in your pit."

I turned and went down the stairs to our accommodation. I stared at Sidney through his open door.

He looked up from his book. "What's wrong?"

"I didn't expect to see you up ..."

He shrugged. "12-4 watch."

"I've just heard we're sailing tonight."

"That's right. That's what ships do."

"I can't go. I'm babysitting with the girls."

"Well, a quick call to the ship owners should fix it. I'm sure they won't mind us staying another day, just for you."

"I'm going to propose to Marit tonight."

His tone changed. "Sorry I was flippant. But we're not sailing until about eleven pm, so perhaps you can still go, if Dai agrees to cover for you. You've covered for him often enough when he's been drunk."

I entered his cabin and sat down, feeling dazed. "Has anything like this ever happened to you, Sidney?"

He sat back and entwined his fingers together thoughtfully. "Yes. With a girl I met in Rio. I hadn't been at sea long. I was just a little older than you are."

"What happened?" As I looked at his weathered face and wispy white hair, I realised he must have been good-looking many years before.

"After we put to sea I missed her terribly, but I told myself there would be others. And there were. All over the world. But I never forgot her. Sometimes I still feel sad when I think about what might have been."

"Do you think you'd have been happier now – with her, I mean?"

"I don't know."

"I don't know why they call you Professor. You don't seem to know much."

"At least I know that."

"Yet at the same time, you seem to know a lot."

"Maybe." He smiled as he added, "I don't know."

"Dai will cover for me and the bosun won't mind, knowing how much it means to me," I went on as if in a dream.

"Talking about the bosun ..."

"Yes?" There was something about Sidney's hesitation that worried me.

"Sorry, perhaps this isn't the best time to bring it up."

I felt myself tensing up. "What are you getting at?"

"Well, it's just that some of the crew are talking."

"About what?"

"About you and him."

"And?"

Sidney looked straight into my eyes. "They think there's something going on between you."

"*What?* That's not what you think, is it?"

"It wouldn't bother me ..."

"You think I'm a homo! How can you think that? I've got a girlfriend!"

Sidney gave me an ironic look. Then he shrugged. "They're probably just angry because he gives you special treatment. They call you his blue-eyed boy."

"What!"

Sidney sighed. "It's just an expression, Owen."

"I'm going to turn in," I sprang to my feet. "You won't stop me from seeing Marit tonight!"

"Me?"

"None of you. I'll jump ship if I have to!"

Back in the passageway, my hands shook as I fumbled in my jacket for the key to my cabin. I vaguely wondered whether it was fear or anger. Opening the door, I recognised the piece of paper on the deck as coming from Brian's pocket notebook. 'What time are we babysitting with the Norwegian birds?' it read.

Looks like we might not be, I thought, feeling my jaw tighten as the reality seeped into my consciousness. *I should get some sleep,* I told myself. But how could I sleep when my mind was in such turmoil? I decided to talk to Brian straight away. To avoid passing the messroom where Mitch was, I walked round to the starboard side before going up to the catering department's passageway. I put my ear against Brian's door. There was no sound.

I knocked on the door. "Brian," I said in a loud whisper. "Brian!"

Eventually I heard a stirring inside, then, "Fucking hell, Taff. Do you know what time it is?"

"I need to talk to you about tonight."

"Oh, come in, then."

He was now sitting up in his bunk, lighting a cigarette. "What's up?"

"We might not be able to go to the girls' house tonight."

"Why? You haven't messed it up by trying to grope them too soon, have you?"

"No!"

"So?"

"We're sailing tonight."

"I know, but not till late."

"But the watches are back on. When I come off at eight it'll be too late."

"Oh." He thought for a moment, then said, "Can't you swing it with the bosun? I heard that you and him were – you know ..."

"What?"

"Well, close."

"Why is everyone talking about me and the bosun?" My voice bristled with indignation.

"Maybe it's the way he looks at you ... Oh, let's face it, Taff, it's general knowledge."

"What is?"

Brian laughed.

"No, come on," I insisted. "I want to get to the bottom of this once and for all."

"Why are you getting so angry?"

"Because I don't like everyone saying we're close and all that." I took a deep breath before adding, "Brian, I think he's homosexual."

Brian stared at me with his mouth open. "You *think* he is?"

I nodded somberly. "That's why I don't want any more favours from him."

"Oh." His eyes half closed as he concentrated. "But that doesn't mean *I* can't go. Watches don't affect me."

"You can't go without me!"

"Why not?" There was a hint of triumph in his voice as he added, "I've got their address."

I glanced around his cabin. "Where?"

He knew what I was thinking. "Don't worry. It's safe."

For a crazy moment I thought of ransacking his cabin to find the slip of paper with the address and destroying it. But instead I tried to reason with him. "You don't know them."

"But you told them about me, right?"

"Yes, but –"

"Listen, Taff. This is too good an opportunity to miss."

"Brian, you have to understand that it's not like that."

"They're expecting us, right?"

I nodded.

"So what'll they think if we don't turn up?"

I hesitated. There was no way I could get a message to them.

"I'll tell you what they'll think: that we stood them up. At least if I go I'll be able to tell them why you couldn't make it."

He had a point.

"I can give them a message from you," he went on. "What's the name of yours again?"

"Marit."

"Right. What do you want me say to Marit?"

I turned my eyes up to the deckhead as if I would see it written there.

"You're blushing, Taff," he said after a minute, amused. "You're blushing! Go on, tell me – what do you want me to say to her?"

I couldn't help smiling. "Tell her I'll come back and see her as soon as I can."

"And ...?"

I looked down at the deck and murmured, "And I love her."

"That's better. I'll tell her, and everything will be fine, you'll see. Now stop worrying and try to get some sleep. I'll take care of it for you."

Chapter 41

I became aware of someone gently shaking my shoulder. Opening my eyes, I turned my head and saw the bosun sitting on the bunk staring down at me.

"What?" I mumbled, rubbing my eyes.

"It's three-thirty."

Through the porthole behind him I could see a dark grey sky over snow-covered mountains.

"Morning or afternoon?"

He smiled. "Afternoon."

Yes, of course. Now I remembered being shaken for the morning watch by Mitch. How different that was – loud and rough, more like a physical assault. Besides checking the mooring ropes every hour, Dai and I had just sat in the messroom on standby. My dozing on an aluminium chair was disrupted periodically by the *clank* of one of Dai's empty beer cans landing in the rubbish bin; *clank clank clank* if he missed, as he did more often as time went on. I had turned in straight after breakfast. Willy called me for lunch but, loathe as I normally was to ever miss a meal, I just went back to sleep.

"I sometimes wonder what would happen if no one called you," said the bosun, appearing to enjoy just sitting there. "Would you just carry on sleeping day after day, week after week? And in the end, when someone remembered about you, would he find just a skeleton in your bunk? Anyway, it's minus eighteen out there, but don't worry, I've got a job for you to do inside."

As I made myself a cup of coffee in the pantry, I looked at the snow-covered mountains through the porthole. The randy snowman glistened as if sprinkled with diamond dust.

"Are you fit?" asked the bosun, appearing at the door.

"Yes," I replied, snapping out of my reverie and stirring the coffee more vigorously.

"You can bring that with you."

I followed him along the stewards' passageway on the starboard side, stopping at the foremost point.

"See how grimy she's got after being laid up for a few days," he said, drawing a damp cloth along the bulkhead. "Iron ore powder gets everywhere and sticks to everything."

I set my mug down on top of a fire alarm box.

"Do the deckhead first," he went on, "then the bulkheads. When you finish here, come round and do our passageway. Can you reach the deckhead with this box?"

"Of course I can!"

He didn't look convinced. "Well, there's a stepladder in the fo'c'sle head if you need it. Be careful carrying it, though, with the condition of the deck." He hesitated. "Perhaps I should get it, in case –"

"I don't need it. I can reach."

He gave me a doubtful sideways glance. "Okay. Ask Pussy if you can fill the bucket with hot water from the galley."

He began walking down the passageway, then turned and said, "Another thing, try not to get too much soapy water on the deck. We don't want one of those poncey stewards going arse over tit and suing the company."

I rolled up my shirt sleeves, then poured some concentrated soap into the shiny metal bucket before walking aft to the galley, the handle of the bucket squeaking as it swung by my side.

Pussy was chopping vegetables on a large wooden block.

"Hello, gorgeous!" he greeted me. "Going a-milking?"

"What?"

"You look like a little milkmaid."

I looked down at the bucket. "Oh, this. I need some water."

Soap suds frothed up while I filled the bucket with boiling water. Pussy sat on a stool next to me, one leg crossed over the other and his fingertips primly on his knee.

"How is your Norwegian lady?"

"That's a sore point."

"Oh?"

I hesitated, not sure if I wanted to talk about it. "It's just that I can't go ashore to see her before we sail."

"Jeremy won't let you go? The bitch!"

"No, it's not that. He said I can go –"

"So go!"

"I can't. It's the rest of the crew – well, some of them – they think I'm – I'm his lover or something. They're angry –"

"Jealous."

I gave him a look.

"You heard me. You're a rose amongst thorns, a sparrow surrounded by crows. And they're jealous. If I were in your position," he leaned towards me and put his hand on my shoulder, "I'd ignore the buggers and milk Jeremy dry."

I stared back at him for a few seconds, then looked down at the overflowing bucket. Turning the tap off, I said, "So you think I should go ashore?"

"Well, how will you feel this time tomorrow if you don't?"

"It's just that I'm scared," I said. "They might do something to me at sea ..."

"Oh, don't be such a gooney!"

"*A gooney?*"

"Yes, an albatross."

"Why do you say that?"

He clasped his hands together, rendering a quick high-pitched laugh. "Don't know, darling! I've never said that before."

"I'm nothing like an albatross," I said, puzzled, remembering the flying bird in the poster above Marco's bunk. "They are big and powerful."

"They might look impressive, but they have a reputation with sailors as being stupid. They're a walkover. So docile and easy to kill, like the one in the *Ancient Mariner*."

"What's that? A film?"

"A poem, but don't worry about it. If Jeremy says you can go ashore –" he opened his hands as if appealing to common sense.

"No, I don't want any more favours from him."

"Why not, pray?"

"Because people talk."

"Huh! If I worried about people talking, I'd never get laid."

"Well, it's different for you."

Pussy cocked an eyebrow.

"What do you know about women, anyway?" I went on, lifting the full bucket out of the porcelain sink.

"Oh, I've had women."

Surprise must have shown on my face, because he corrected himself. "Well, *a* woman."

"Have you?"

"Uh-huh."

"And ...?"

"*And?*" he repeated, imitating my wide-eyed expression.

"Well, what did you think of it?"

"Oh, it was all right, I suppose. But I preferred the real thing."

Still thinking about the last thing Pussy had said, I stood on the box and began washing the deckhead with the hot soapy water. Was it true or was it a joke? I had to stand on my toes to reach, but I didn't want to go for the stepladder after insisting that I didn't need it.

I was about a third of the way along the passageway when a voice behind me boomed, "Look, here's the *boyo!*"

Balancing on the box, I turned my head to see Paddy in the doorway to the accommodation with an expression of feigned delight. Kirk leaned around the door and grinned at me. "Put some elbow grease into it, son!" he said.

"He hasn't got any," said Paddy, putting one hand on his hip and holding the other out, fingers hanging downwards. "He's one of the limp wrist brigade!"

They both laughed as they stepped into the passageway and came towards me.

"Careful," I cautioned.

That must have sounded like a threat because they stopped and looked at each other.

"The deck might be slippery," I explained.

"Water warm enough for your little hands?" asked Paddy. It was then I noticed that their faces were red with cold. "We must keep them nice and soft for the bosun, mustn't we?"

"Well, let's see." Kirk grabbed one of my hands and rubbed it between his, which were cold and rough. "Ahhh, lovely."

"Tell me something, *boyo*," said Paddy. "Why aren't you working outside with the men?"

Tears came to my eyes and I felt like punching him. I stepped down from the box and picked up the bucket, tilting it towards them threateningly.

Paddy took his watchmate's arm. "Let's go, Kirk, before he goes crying to the bosun."

Paddy carried on facing me with his thumbs hooked into his belt. Then he gave a short laugh before following the other man out through the door, glaring at me over his shoulder.

The bucket clanged as I let it drop back onto the deck. I ran down to my cabin and took out my diary. Hunched tensely over the chest of drawers, I wrote down what was happening to me and how I was feeling. I didn't know how this could help, but I had the feeling I was doing it for my future self. Then I sat back, breathing rapidly. It was the bosun's fault that some of the crew hated me, because he mollycoddled me. I put on my jumper and duffle coat. Pulling my gloves on, I thought, *I'll show them I'm not his fucking mistress!*

The icy breeze crept under my woolly hat as soon as I stepped outside. A spotlight guided me to where Sidney, Dai, Paddy and Kirk were working on the boat deck. As I approached them I could hear the scratching of the brooms with heavy bristle brushes on the wooden deck. Water sloshed onto the deck from the hose Paddy was using. He straightened himself up as he saw me, as if he expected trouble. Kirk leaned on his broom and watched.

"Is there a spare broom?" I asked.

"You can have this one," said Dai, handing me his. "I need to take a piss."

As he hurried below, I began scrubbing the wooden deck furiously. Sidney poured White Atlas cleaning solution onto the deck in front of us, and

Paddy hosed away the resulting black sludge. I worked so quickly that we were soon outside the spotlight's range.

"I'll go up and move the light," Sidney announced, leaning his broom against a davit.

"I'll help you," I said, following him up the ladder to the small deck on top of the housing. I didn't really think he needed any help, but I didn't want to be alone with Paddy and Kirk again. As Sidney took the handles of the spotlight and began to manoeuvre it into a new position, the bosun appeared on the deck below next to the two other men. He shielded his eyes as he squinted up at me in surprise. Then he came up the ladder two steps at a time.

"What are you doing here?" he demanded.

"The others said I should be here," I murmured.

"I tell you where you should be, not them."

I stared back at him, shaking. Sidney turned his head away.

The bosun's tone softened. "You know, if anyone else did this there'd be ructions."

I still said nothing. He looked at his wristwatch. "You'd better go and start getting ready to go ashore, anyway."

"I'm not going."

He was taken aback. "I thought you were going to the girl's house ..."

"I can't. I'm on watch."

"Listen, Owen," he said softly, putting his hand on my arm.

"Don't touch me!" I shouted, pulling my arm back. "Don't you ever touch me!"

Sidney turned back to us. Even with the little light there was, I could see that his face was white and taut. The bosun raised his right hand and I thought he was going to slap me. Later I realised that it was a pleading gesture. He turned and went back down the ladder and walked quickly aft, disappearing into the shadows.

"Oh, dear," said Paddy. "Who's after upsetting her, then?" He looked up at us. "Are you going to adjust that light or not?"

Sidney sighed and took the handles of the spotlight. Over the top of it, faintly illuminated by the lights of the gangway, I saw Brian going down to the quay with ...

"That's not Mitch, is it?" I queried, my heart thumping.

"Where?" Sidney turned to look behind him. "Yeah, looks like him. With that officers' steward."

"But how can he go ashore at this time?"

"Well, he has been night watchman since we've been in Narvik."

"Oh, no! Brian's taking him to the girls' house!"

Hearing the despair in my voice, Sidney said, "Perhaps they're just walking up to the town together."

My eyes squinted as I tried to see the hooded figure with Brian more clearly. He was certainly taller and broader than Brian. I grabbed the handles of the spotlight and swung it round until it shone on the two men walking along the quay.

"Hey, stop fucking about up there!" yelled Paddy.

Brian looked sideways towards the light, as if caught with his fingers in the honeypot.

Chapter 42

I was cleaning my teeth to go to bed when the phone rang. Fiona called, "It's Roger." She was standing at the bottom of the stairs with her hand over the receiver. I rinsed my mouth and went down to take the call, fearful of what news I might hear.

"How's Gwen?" I asked him.

"Not good," he said. "Not good. Perhaps you'd better come down and see her soon."

Roger was a master of understatement, so I said without hesitation, "I'll come tomorrow."

"That's fine, but I wouldn't leave it too late if I were you."

"Okay," I murmured. "I'll be there early."

Fiona came out of the kitchen as I hung up, wearing an apron and drying her hands. "What is it?" she asked when she saw my face.

"Gwen's taken a turn for the worse," I said. "I have to go there as soon as I can."

She put a hand to her chest. "Oh, no."

"I knew this day would come. I hoped I'd be ready for it, but ..." I hesitated before asking, "Do you want to come?"

"When are you going?"

"First light in the morning, before the M4 starts filling up."

She looked panicky. I knew what was going through her mind: three hours trapped in the car with me. So I went on, "You don't have to. You've got your Reiki teaching tomorrow."

"It's not that," she said. "It's just that I haven't seen your family for years. Even though I've always admired Gwen."

I took a deep breath. "You could come later, by train ..."

She looked relieved. "Yes, that's it. That way you can let me know if I need to come or not."

I packed a holdall with a couple of changes of clothes, but hesitated about putting the black tie in. It seemed a bit morbid. On the other hand, I wouldn't be in a fit state to go and look for one if anything did happen. Too stressed and tired to think anymore, I dropped it into the bag. Then I set the alarm clock for 5 a.m.

The sound of a baby crying woke me up. I lifted my head off the pillow to listen. I thought it might have been from next door, until I remembered they'd moved away. I became aware of being curled up in bed in the foetal position with wet eyes and cheeks. To my horror, I realised that it had been me, weeping in my sleep.

It was getting light by the time I reached the Severn Bridge, the half-moon to the west gradually becoming fainter, the sun an orange glow in the dark clouds behind me. As always, I scanned the banks of the Severn Estuary, trying to figure out where the *Vindicatrix* and its camp used to be but, once again, I failed to pinpoint it. As I drove off the bridge, the sight of the rolling hills and the greeting *Croeso i Gymru* seemed to give me strength to carry on.

Roger was already up when I knocked on their door. His ears seemed to be protruding more than ever and the red blotches on his face were more noticeable.

"The door was open," he grumbled. "We never lock it during the day."

"Sorry. I forgot."

Instead of offering his hand as he usually did, he hugged me. As we separated, after patting each other's back, I asked, "How is she?"

"Oh, you know …"

"Can I go up to see her?"

"She's in the parlour. She's been finding it hard to go up and down the stairs lately, so we had a bed put in there for her." He sat in his armchair, and I sat in Gwen's, next to him.

"Siân's coming back from Auckland as soon as she can get someone to look after her kids," he continued. "Should be here in a couple of days. I just hope she's in time – Mrs Jones opposite has already started making Welsh cakes."

For many years Mrs Jones had only made Welsh cakes for funerals. She'd made them for my mother's.

Roger massaged his temple with his fingertips. I waited for him to carry on speaking, but he didn't. He just stared into the coal fire, not even reacting when I got up.

I paused outside the parlour, taking a deep breath before opening the door. Gwen was asleep, her hair and face merging in with the whiteness of the pillow. If I'd come across her in a hospital bed, I wouldn't have recognised her. Gwen, who used to radiate such strength. The image of her as a gladiator in a school play when she was eleven years old flashed through my mind.

Her eyes fluttered open when I held her hand. She raised her head slightly to look behind me. "You came on your own?"

I tried to smile. "Yes, Gwen."

"How is Fiona?" Her voice was weak.

"She's okay."

"Okay? But still giving you hell about the death of your little girl?"

"I can't blame her, after what she went through."

"Well, it's time she stopped blaming you. It wasn't your fault." She stopped to catch her breath.

I felt tears brimming up in my eyes, and to hide them I leaned forward and rested my head on my sister's chest. "Oh, Gwen," I moaned.

"It's all right," she said, stroking my hair.

"No, it's not. It's all wrong. *I* should be comforting *you*, not – not ..." I sat up and took a tissue from the box on her bedside table. "Aren't you afraid?"

She looked surprised. "What is there to be afraid of?"

"It's just like you to be brave. Even about this."

"The only thing I'm worried about is Delyth. She needs someone to look out for her. Roger says he will, but she needs you, too. Come to see her more often when I'm not here, Owen."

"When you're not here?" My voice shook as I repeated her words.

"Promise me."

"Yes, I will. I promise." I took another tissue and blew my nose. "It should have been me instead of you."

"Don't say that."

"So many people need you."

"And you." She examined my face. "Owen, what's wrong? ... There's something else, isn't there?"

I tried to smile again, but this time it must have appeared even more grotesque. I wanted to tell her what was happening at the university. If she had been well, I would have. But I couldn't burden her with it the way she was. As she waited for me to answer, her eyes kept closing and I knew it was because of the morphine.

"You know something?" she said, her eyelids drooping. "I'm ready to go."

I held her hand and leaned towards her. "I wish I could go with you, Gwen."

"Oh no, Owen, no ..." Her voice trailed off as she closed her eyes.

"I'm going for a walk down to the village," I told Roger late in the afternoon.

"What for? There's nothing there, *myn.*"

Wrong you are, I thought. The village was packed with memories for me.

The brisk walk made me feel a bit better. For once I wasn't thinking about the university problem. In the park next to the bus terminus, I sat on a secluded bench. This was the exact spot where I'd kissed the prettiest girl in Wales – in a game of 'truth, dare, kiss or promise' – when I was eight years old.

Walking back through the village, I stopped to look at the industrial laundry on the opposite side of the road. That brought back only unpleasant memories. The incident with the window; the interview with the headmaster and the police; my bursting into tears.

A couple of weeks later the police sergeant had turned up at our house.

"You need to speak to Owen, is it?" my mother asked.

"No," he replied. "It's you I've come to speak to."

As he sat down in the kitchen, he said, "First of all, I'm pleased to tell you that the laundry is not pressing charges."

My mother sighed. "So the matter is over, thank goodness."

"Yes, but I feel I should warn you that simple acts of vandalism at a young age can lead to serious criminal behaviour later on," he said. "I've seen it so often."

Although my mother seemed quite old to me, in fact she must have been about thirty-five. Everyone said that Gwen had inherited her looks, which I supposed must have meant my mother was attractive.

As he was leaving, he said, "Your son, unfortunately, doesn't have a father figure. No one to discipline him. There's a danger of him running wild. Is there no one who can ...?"

My mother thought for a moment, then replied, "There is my brother, Bryn, I suppose."

He looked disappointed. "Well, if there's anything *I* can do for you, you know where to find me."

"That's very kind of you, Sergeant," said my mother, but I had the feeling she just wanted him to go.

When I told Gwen about it afterwards, she wanted to know everything, including how he kept adjusting his metal-framed glasses and clearing his throat.

"He only came to see her," she concluded, tightening her mouth.

"But why?"

"Oh, Owen. Don't you know *anything*?"

A week later my sisters and I had been getting ready to go to the Saturday matinee to see *One Hundred and One Dalmatians* when my mother told me, "You can't go. Uncle Bryn is coming to talk to you."

When he arrived, he put his arm on my shoulder. "Right, young man, we'd better go up to your room."

He locked the door behind us. Until then I didn't even know there was a key for that door. Then he turned to me and said, "So you think it's clever to smash other people's windows, do you?"

"I didn't ..." I stopped with the sight of him taking off his leather belt.

"Owen, *bach*," he said, smiling, "I'm going to make you wish you'd never been born."

Besides using the belt, he also used his fists a few times. He played cat and mouse with me, knowing I couldn't get out of the room. Whenever I could get to the door, I shook and tried to turn the knob and screamed for my mother. She didn't come.

The Dansette record player, a beloved Christmas present, was swept off a table and cracked as it hit the floor. Several of my 78s were broken too.

I didn't know what was worse – the physical pain or the fear, helplessness and outrage. Strangely, I also felt guilty for something I hadn't done.

At last Uncle Bryn stopped his onslaught. Putting his belt back on, he smiled at me whimpering in the corner. As he unlocked the door, he said, "Now you know what to expect if you don't keep your nose clean in the future."

A few weeks later I overheard my mother saying, "I wonder why Uncle Bryn doesn't come around anymore."

I entered the Indian takeaway that used to be a knitting shop, which I'd often gone into with my mother.

"Chicken curry and rice for two, please," I said to the young Indian man behind the counter.

"And chips?"

"No, just rice."

He looked confused. "You mean half and half? Rice and chips?"

"No, just rice."

He still didn't look convinced. Then I remembered that it was the custom in Wales to have chips with curry. When I got back to the house, I found that he had put a small portion of chips in the bag as well as the rice, anyway.

While Roger and I were eating in the kitchen, there was a knock on the door. As he went to answer it, I noticed he was moving even more slowly than usual now. At first I didn't recognise the person who came back with him. I had always thought I would be filled with uncontrollable rage upon seeing Uncle Bryn again, but all I saw now was a pathetic old man with no front teeth. Roger told him, "I'll just go and tell her you're here."

"Owen," he murmured, taking his flat cap off. "How are you?"

I looked away and carried on eating.

Roger returned and said, "I'm sorry, Bryn, but she says she doesn't want to see you."

My uncle fiddled with the cap in his hands. "I just wanted to see her for the last time. If she changes her mind ..."

"Sure," said Roger, as he let him out. "I'll let you know if she does."

When I went in to see Gwen again, I asked why she had turned Uncle Bryn away.

"I never wanted to see him again after what he did to you," she replied.

"You knew about that?"

"Of course I did. Mam shouldn't have allowed it."

"I suppose she just wanted someone to play the role of a father."

She nodded. "But he went too far."

"I often wondered why he never came round again ..."

For a moment the former wicked twinkle was back in her eyes. "I had a little word with him. He knew it wouldn't have been good for his health."

"You never told me."

She reached for my hand. "Owen, there's a song I want at my funeral service. I've tried to tell Roger, but he won't listen. He gets too emotional."

"Which one?"

"Can't you guess?"

I looked up at the ceiling as I mentally ran through the music she used to like. "*That'll Be the Day?*" I said. She'd played that over and over again on our radiogram when she had a crush on a boy at school.

She smiled. "No. But that's not a bad idea. No, it's *Suo Cân.* 'Lullaby'."

"You don't have to translate."

"Oh, I thought you'd become English by now." That wicked glint again. "That's what Mam used to sing to us, *Suo Cân.* Do you remember?"

I could hear the haunting lullaby being sung by our mother as I said, "Yes, I remember."

She closed her eyes with a smile on her lips, and I knew she could hear it too. After gazing at her for a minute with tears in my eyes, I slipped my shoes off and lay on the bed, my face close to hers, and soon I was asleep. When I awoke, I found her asleep and was dismayed by the slight rattling sound in her breathing. I kissed her on the forehead and went up to the bedroom Roger had prepared for me.

As I buttoned up my shirt next morning, I became aware of the absolute silence in the house. I glanced through Roger's open bedroom door; he wasn't there. I crept downstairs, fearful of what I might find. Roger wasn't in the sitting room, nor the kitchen, nor out the back.

As I came back into the house, I heard Gwen say, "He's gone to the shop."

Entering the parlour, I was amazed to see Gwen sitting up in bed with a cup of tea in her hand. "You're okay?" I asked.

She smiled. "I'm still here, anyway. Fancied a bit of blackberry jam on toast, so he's gone to look for some."

I phoned Fiona and told her that she needn't come, and that I would be returning to London that evening. She was extremely happy. I couldn't help thinking the main reason was because she didn't have to come to Wales.

It was getting dark when I took my holdall out to the car and found Roger leaning on the garden gate, absorbed in his own thoughts.

"You're off, then?" he said.

"Yes, I'd better make a move."

"Well, thanks for coming. Sorry it was a false alarm."

At first I didn't know what to say to that. "I'm just glad she's okay."

He put a hand up to his face. I couldn't see why, but I imagined it was to wipe away a tear. He sighed as he brought it down again. "Yes, for now."

We both leaned on the gate then, in silence, looking across the darkening common where the coal tips used to be.

Chapter 43

It was 7 a.m. when I relieved Dai on the port side wing of the bridge for the last hour of lookout. It was here instead of on the monkey island because it was so windy. He stayed to chat with me for a while, both of us leaning on the gunwale looking out at the restless sea. Glancing down, I saw that someone had made a path through the snow on each side of the main deck up to the fo'c'sle.

"So you've heard about Riley's little problem?" he asked me.

"Yes, I have." I was surprised *he* knew. "Have you? He asked me not to tell anyone."

"That's what he said to me, and apparently to everyone else on the ship."

"Poor *dab*. He doesn't know how he's going to tell his wife."

"Well, he'll have to. There's no two ways about it."

"He wants to die. He told me if he could get the keys for the controlled drugs cabinet he'd kill himself."

"Bullshit."

"That's what he told me, honest."

"I don't doubt he told you that," Dai chuckled. "But he wouldn't do it. Still, it's not the life of Riley for him anymore, that's for sure."

"I couldn't believe he caught it here, off a girl like that. Have you seen her? She's beautiful."

"Yes, I've seen her aboard a couple of times. But it looks like she wasn't just sitting around waiting for him after all. Just shows that you don't have to go to some knocking shop in Caracas to catch guns."

"*Guns?*"

"Gonorrhoea. You've never heard of it?"

"Sure I have. We had a lecture on VD at sea training school. They didn't call it *guns*, though."

"What else did they tell you?"

"They said gonorrhoea – *guns* – is curable with an injection of antibiotics in the bum. Imagine – an injection in the bum! Syphilis is much more serious, though, and you have to have injections and check-ups for at least six months. That can have terrible effects – can even make you crazy."

Dai looked sideways at me for a moment, then said, "Did they tell you about vaginismus?"

I turned my eyes up to the darkness above us, thinking hard. "No, I don't think so. What is this *vegi* – *vagi* – *nis* –. Oh, I can't get it out."

"Ha ha, that's a good one." Dai laughed. "Wish I'd said that."

I looked at him quizzically.

"It's a medical condition," Dai went on, sounding like a school teacher, "where contraction of the woman's vagina grips your dick and you can't get it out until she relaxes. Trouble is, when it happens it makes her even more tense, so it grips you even tighter, which makes her more tense ..." He glanced at me to make sure I was still following him. "There was a case in the newspapers recently, where firemen had to cut the roof off a car and lift the couple out with a hoist. It was only when she fell asleep in hospital that they were able to separate them."

"Good heavens! That couldn't happen to me, though."

"Why not?"

"I don't drive."

Dai laughed and punched my arm before turning to go down the ladder, leaving me to daydream about Marit and our future life together. From time to time the wonderful images were spoilt by the thought that Mitch might have gone to their house.

"I thought I'd better call you, sir," I heard the second mate saying inside the wheelhouse.

I could just make out the outline of the captain standing next to him, looking at the long barometer on the bulkhead.

"You were quite right," said Captain Frazer. "How long has it been falling?"

"Over the last half-hour. It's been very steep."

Frazer studied the barometer for a moment longer, then said, "Make sure Mr Clements is aware of it when he takes over from you. The bosun should know, too, so he can have everything on deck double checked." He glanced at the ship's clock. "But leave it till he comes on duty at nine o'clock. It's going to be pretty rough for him without being called out early."

The second mate stood looking out of the front of the wheelhouse. Raising his binoculars, he said, "There's a light two points on the starboard beam."

"The lookout hasn't even seen it yet," said the captain, turning to me. Although I couldn't see his face, I knew it was disapproving.

"Sorry, sir," I mumbled.

To my relief, he turned away without saying anything else.

"Call me if anything develops," he said to the second mate as he left the wheelhouse via the chart room at the back.

"Try to stay awake, there's a good lad," said the second mate in a sarcastic monotone, while scanning the horizon with his binoculars.

During the last twenty minutes before being relieved by Mitch on the 8-12, I tried to concentrate and not daydream. It wasn't easy when thoughts and images of Marit were so delicious. I never looked forward to seeing Mitch, but this time I was also nervous about what I might hear. A cold chill ran down my spine as he approached me, his face hidden by the shadow of his hood.

"What have you got?" he asked, pressing his gloved hands together for warmth.

"There's a light on the starboard beam."

Mitch squinted into the distance. "Yep, I see it. Probably a fishing boat."

"The second mate called the old man because the barometer was falling."

"Oh, fuck. That means trouble."

After a few seconds of staring ahead, Mitch turned to me. I guessed he was wondering why I was still there. Normally I couldn't wait to get away from him.

I cleared my throat. "How did you get on ashore in Narvik?"

He chuckled. "I got on very well."

I knew that if I could see his face it would be smirking.

"Oh, right ... Went for a drink, did you?"

"Nope. Didn't you notice there are no pubs in Norway?"

"I know ... but I was thinking, in a restaurant or –"

"Don't try to be cute with me, son. You know where I went."

So that was it. I couldn't avoid the truth any longer. Now I needed reassurance.

"You – met my girlfriend, then?"

"The blonde one? Yeah, I met her all right."

"Well, what did you think ...?" I hated to be asking him this.

"Lovely." Now I could just make out the grin under his hood. "A bit immature, maybe."

"She's only seventeen."

"But what the hell – any port in a storm, eh?"

I could feel my jaw tightening. "What do you mean by that?"

"It's not like you to stay and chat with me. Do you want something?"

"I just want to be sure that nothing happened ..." I sounded as if I was pleading with him!

He grinned again. "You don't go babysitting with a couple of girls like that with nothing happening." He added pointedly, "Unless you're queer, that is. Now you'd better go and turn in. We might have to haul your arse out again when the weather changes."

"Mitch, please – I need to know ..."

He turned his back on me to show the conversation was finished.

Chapter 44

My heart was pounding as I clattered down the ladder and went to the catering accommodation on the starboard side to look for Brian. His cabin was empty. Maybe he was in with the second steward. I rushed up to the catering petty officers' passageway, where I saw Brian walking ahead of me. He glanced over his shoulder at me, but carried on until he went around a corner.

"Brian!" I called, running after him.

When I turned the corner, he was nowhere to be seen. I tried the next deck up, where I found Lisping Larry loading a food lift. After greeting me with a smile, he said, "Thorry to hear about your girl."

"What about her?"

"Well, I heard about her and Mitch. But don't take it to heart. Thome young girlth like older men, that'th all. Mitch might be a brute, but he ith good-looking."

"What did you hear?"

He paused. "Oh, you didn't know? Look, maybe it wath only Mitch showing off. You know what he'th like."

"What did he say?"

"Look, it'th nothing to do with me. I can't help wondering why you didn't athk me to go on that date inthtead of Brian, though. I wouldn't have taken that thycho with me – then nothing would have happened."

"No, you would have just bored them to death!"

"Hey, there'th no need to get perthonal."

"So what happened?" I could feel the tension in my jaw.

Larry slammed the hatch closed. "Athk your friend Brian!"

He turned to go.

"Where is he?" I pleaded.

He turned back to me and his expression softened as he saw the anguish in my face. He glanced at his wristwatch. "He should be therving the officerth their breakfatht now."

He hadn't finished speaking before I was racing up to the officers' dining room. From the circular window of the serving area I could see Brian attending the tables. He was quiet and subdued. I waited for him to come back, carrying a tray of used dishes.

"Brian!"

"Jesus, Taff!" He almost dropped the tray. "Come like yourself, will you."

Despite looking half-asleep, he was obviously on edge.

I grabbed his arm. "What happened between Mitch and Marit?"

"I don't know – I wasn't with them all the time."

"Not with them? So where were you?"

"I was with the other one – with what's-her-name."

"But you do know what happened – you told Larry. Where were Mitch and Marit?"

"They were down in the bunker."

"The basement?"

"Looked more like a bunker to me. I was on the ground floor with the other one, with – what's her name again?"

"Just get on with it!"

"Yes, well, we were making the coffee. That was Mitch's idea. He wanted us to separate them. Anyway, we suddenly heard Marit scream. My one – Torruld, isn't it? – rushed down to the bunker, but the door was locked. She said that door was never locked, and I said well, perhaps they don't want to be disturbed. After all, Mitch is a handsome bloke, muscular and all that.

"But then we heard her scream again – and she was going no, no, noooo! Torruld started banging the door and calling to Marit. She tried to push the door open with her shoulder, but it didn't budge. Then she went outside – I didn't know why. I thought she just panicked. After a while I went to look for her, concerned, like. I found her clearing away snow from one of those horizontal windows at the top of the bunker. I kneeled down beside her at the window and looked down into the girl's bedroom." He nervously licked his lips with the tip of his tongue. "Jesus, Taff, you won't believe what I saw."

"What?"

Brian shook his head, as if he still couldn't believe it himself. His tongue flicked out nervously.

"What?" I shouted. "What did you see?"

"I don't know how to tell you."

"Just tell me!"

Brian took a deep breath. His tongue flicked out again as he said, "Mitch was shagging your girlfriend."

My hands tightened into fists.

"On her bed," he went on. "Don't blame me, I had nothing to do with it. She was crying, but I wasn't sure whether she wanted it or not. I mean she wasn't struggling or anything. She was just lying there with Mitch on top of her. When he rolled her over onto her stomach, I could see that the sheet was covered in blood and I thought, fuck me, she must have been a virgin!

"It was freezing in the snow, but I stayed there and watched, mesmerised, like. It's not that I enjoyed it or anything but, well, you know – it's not something you see every day." The tongue again, and this time it appeared to be forked, like a snake's. "Say what you will about Mitch, you've got to admire his stamina. He keeps himself in good shape. He didn't miss a beat, no matter how much she sobbed."

"I shouldn't have given you their address!"

The heat in my face and head was becoming unbearable. By the cautious way Brian was looking at me I knew it was visible. He went on anyway.

"Then there was this God almighty crash from inside the house, like splintering of wood. What now? I thought, and I went back in to have a butcher's. I found Torruld wielding a dirty big axe. She must have got it from the woodshed just outside. The door to the bunker was in a right mess. She was frantic, I mean really crazy. When I went up to her she turned and took a swipe at me. Scared the shit out of me, I can tell you. 'Don't come near me!' she screamed.

"Well, I wanted to take it off her before she hurt someone. She could have chopped someone's head off the way she was swinging that thing around. With her mascara streaming down her face and her hair all over the place she looked like some sort of demon. I tell you, she's a very violent person. I thanked my lucky stars I hadn't tried anything with her –"

"Never mind about your lucky stars! What about Marit?"

"I'm coming to it, Taff. I'm coming to it. Don't get excited. Anyway, without getting too close to her, I persuaded her to let me try talking to Mitch. With one eye on her, I knocked on the door and told Mitch we had a problem and had to get out of there fast.

"I don't know how well you know Mitch, but there was no way he'd finish until he finished, if you get what I mean. Torruld was slumped in a chair now, just staring, as if in a trance. I opened her fingers and took the axe off her. She didn't even seem to notice. From the veranda I tossed it into the bushes, out of sight in the snow. I didn't want her getting her hands on it again.

"When I put my ear against the bunker door again I could hear water running in the shower and Mitch whistling. Jesus, can you believe that? He's such a cool customer!

"I heard the inside of the door being unlocked at last. He came out, buckling his belt, his shirt still unbuttoned to below that big medallion of his, his hair still damp. And do you know what he said to me? He said, Where's the coffee? Can you believe that? Where's the coffee! I told him it was in the pot, but that it must have been stone-cold by then.

"Never mind, he goes, I could do with something stronger now. He turned to Torruld and asked her where they kept the booze. She didn't answer – I don't know if she heard him.

"Mitch, I says, we'd better go before someone comes home, and he goes okay, have you phoned for the taxi? Taxi? You want to wait for a taxi? I says. He goes, how else are we going to get back to the ship? If you want to walk in this weather, go ahead.

"So while I was ordering the taxi, Torruld seemed to wake up. She jumped up and rushed down to the bunker. As soon as I put the receiver down, I followed her."

"Why did you do that?"

"Why do you think? To make sure they were all right. I stood at the bedroom door looking in. Torruld had draped a dressing gown over her cousin's naked body and they were both sitting on the bed, forehead to forehead, crying. They didn't even notice me. There was nothing I could do, Taff. So I just turned and came back up the stairs.

"Mitch had found a bottle of something and was sitting as comfortable as you like in an armchair, a glass in one hand and a cigarette in the other. In the taxi later he just smiled to himself now and again, as if remembering, and saying, 'Lovely!' under his breath."

"I'll kill the bastard!"

Brian's eyes narrowed. "Don't let him hear you talking like that. Better just forget about it, Taff. He'd have you for breakfast."

Chapter 45

"Haven't seen you for a while, Owen," said the receptionist. "Where have you been?"

"Oh, you know, Julie," I replied. "Here and there."

She obviously didn't know that I'd been suspended. She looked back down at the work she was doing. When she looked up again I was still standing there.

"Are you waiting for someone?" she asked.

"Yes," I said. I didn't really want to tell her who in case she asked more questions. But as she carried on staring at me, waiting for me to tell her, I added, "For Neville."

"Count Dracula?"

I was taken aback for a moment. I'd thought I was the only one who made that comparison. "Yes, that's him," I said with a thin smile.

"Well, why don't you go up? He is in."

"No, it's okay. I – arranged to meet him here."

"I'll ring his extension." She was already dialling it before I could tell her not to bother.

Cupping her hand over the receiver, she said, "No answer. I'll try his cupboard for you." A few seconds later she said, "It's engaged."

"Don't worry," I said. "I can see you're busy."

She put the phone down. "At least you know where he is now. Why don't you just go up?"

The security man, seated behind his window, looked up as I approached him. I thought he was going to challenge me, if only because I was not wearing my ID card, but all he said was, "Good morning."

I stopped dead when I realised that there was a woman waiting for a lift, and that it was Princess. I glanced back at the reception desk and saw that Julie was still looking at me. It would look odd if I left this lift go and waited for another one, I thought. Anyway, why should I?

I stepped in after her. She swung around to face me, folding her arms, and we stared at each other. I was the first to look away. I took out my mobile phone and checked my recent text messages. From the corner of my eye I could see her still staring at me. I felt my hand begin to tremble. I wished someone else would get into the lift. Normally the lifts are overcrowded, but now that I wanted someone to get in, no one did.

I felt vulnerable, and my imagination began to do somersaults. What if she reported me for being in the building unescorted when I was suspended? What if she accused me of doing or saying something inappropriate to her while we were alone in the lift? I'd be starting off from a position of culpability as I had no right to be there. Princess got out on the third floor, walking past me as if I didn't exist.

I knocked on Neville's door and went in. Still on the phone, he looked surprised to see me. He indicated for me to sit down while he finished the phone conversation.

When he hung up, he said, "You should have waited until I came to fetch you."

"I know."

"Someone has to sign you in," he persisted.

"I know. But it seems so strange not to be able to just walk in."

"Well, what did you think being suspended meant? You're only a visitor now."

He observed me for a moment. "Sleepless night?"

I nodded. "How did you guess?"

"No guesswork involved. It's obvious just to look at you."

He picked up a pen and scribbled on a piece of paper. "Let me just make a note of this before I forget it," he said. "We're having another redundancy meeting next week. You didn't apply for redundancy the first time round?"

"No. But I would now, if I could ..."

Neville pulled a face. "You can't now, not with this going on. While it would be illegal for the university to try to get rid of you like this instead of paying you redundancy, it would save them big bucks." He glanced at his watch. "We'd better get up there."

A student in her early twenties smiled at me as we got into the lift. "You've lost weight, Owen," she beamed. "What's your secret?"

"Unbearable stress," I said. "Best diet known to man."

"Awww." She laughed and reached out to cuddle me, but I stiffened up. She drew her arms back to her sides, looking down at the floor.

"Bye," she murmured as she got out at the next floor.

"I feel awful about that," I said to Neville.

"About what?"

"Making her feel like that – rejected."

He shrugged. "It's a matter of protecting yourself. Remember you're fighting for your future."

We stopped outside a classroom and Neville looked through the little window in the door. "Charity's not here yet. She's so laidback it's not true. You can wait in here," he said, opening the door of the classroom next door, and as I went in he added, "I'll go and see what's going on."

When he came back a minute later, he said, "We'll start as soon as Charity arrives."

I perched on a chair and Neville sat on a desk looking down at me, making me feel even more intimidated.

"Okay so far?" he asked.

I shook my head. "I feel sick to my stomach."

"Better you feel it now and get it over with before the real thing. How's your wife taking your suspension?"

I hesitated. I hadn't wanted to talk about this to anyone. Finally I said, "I haven't told her yet."

His eyes widened. "I know you mental health lecturers have it cushy, but hasn't she noticed any difference?"

"No. I still leave the house about the same time every morning. Walk up to the underground station. Pick up my free copy of the *Metro* and read it while having a coffee in Nero's. Then I make out my Things Not to Do List." I could feel bitterness creeping into my voice. "You know, don't go to the staff business meeting, don't hold tutorials for personal students, don't take Group B for psychology. That sort of thing."

He was sitting there looking at me with his head to one side. "She's got to know sooner or later."

"I know. Unless ..."

"Unless?"

"Unless the case is dropped. I mean, there's still a chance of that, isn't there?"

"I suppose there's always a chance they might decide there's not enough evidence." He shook his head as he added, "But frankly, I think it's unlikely."

After staring at me for a little longer, he said, "A word of advice, Owen. Don't keep putting your hand over your mouth like that. Makes you look as if you have something to hide."

"It's just that this," I touched my scar with my middle finger, "gets more prominent with stress."

I put my hand down and turned my head to one side so he could see it more clearly. "You see."

After studying it for a moment, he said, "Turn to me again ... now the other way ... No," he concluded. "It looks exactly the same as always."

We heard a sound outside the door and saw Charity peering in through the window.

"At last," said Neville, getting up and opening the door for her.

She was carrying a cup of coffee and a packet of sandwiches. "Is it here?"

"No," replied Neville. "It's next door. The other two are ready. You want to leave those things here?"

"No, this is my breakfast."

"You can't have it during the hearing. "

"Why not? It's only a pretend hearing, isn't it?"

"It's a simulation," said Neville. "We need to make it as realistic as possible."

"Well, I've got to have my breakfast," Charity insisted.

"You can have it when we debrief afterwards," said Neville, reaching out his hands.

She reluctantly surrendered her provisions to him and went next door.

"We'll give her a couple of minutes to settle down." Neville glanced at his wristwatch.

"Who's chairing?" I asked.

"I don't know," Neville shrugged. "Let's go and have a look."

We looked through the pane at the three people who were waiting to judge me. Wencheng, wearing a suit and tie, was sitting in the middle, which meant he was chairing the mock hearing. His face was motionless, like stone. On his left, Charity was shuffling papers, trying to get them into some sort of order. Philip sat on the other side, his arms folded. I imagined myself sitting facing them – very small, sweating, trembling, squirming, inarticulate.

Seeing us outside the door, Wencheng had a quick word with each of the people at his side. Then Charity got up and came to the door. "You can come in now," she said.

"Okay, let's go for it," said Neville.

"No," I breathed.

"What?"

"No," I repeated, moving to one side of the door, out of the view of the others.

I wanted to turn and run, but I was frozen. Just like in the dream of having my foot trapped in the railway line.

Neville's eye twitched. "What do you mean?"

"I can't."

"Listen, you – you –" I wondered what he was going to call me. But I supposed I would never know, because instead he went on, controlling his anger the best he could, "You know how long it took me to arrange this for you? How many hours?"

"I'm sorry," I managed to say.

He grabbed my arm and the strength of his grip surprised me. Bringing his face close to mine, he snarled, "I'm warning you. Don't do this to me."

I stared back at him, horrified. When he released my arm, I turned and darted down the passageway, my mind in turmoil.

Chapter 46

The snow must have been settling on my woolly hat and Beatle-style fringe as I stood on the poop deck gazing at the *Albatross*'s creamy wake. It was so peaceful, yet inside me was a sickening turmoil. I knew I had to confront the man who had destroyed my greatest promise of happiness.

I stepped into Mitch's cabin, closing the door after me. He was sitting on his chair with a mug of coffee in his hand, one foot supported by the knee of the other leg. I stared at him.

"I didn't hear you knock," he said.

"What did you do?" I asked.

He smiled. "What are you talking about?"

"To Marit. What did you do to her?"

"Marit?"

"You know who I mean. You went to her house with Brian."

"Oh, was that her name?" Then he looked annoyed, as if it was an intrusion. "What's it got to do with you?"

"She's my girlfriend."

"What, that ship's moll? Don't make me laugh!"

"Watch what you say about her!" It was supposed to be a threat, but it came out as a squeak.

He sipped his coffee. "You need to learn to mind your own business, son."

"This is my business. We're engaged."

He laughed, nearly spilling his coffee.

I pointed a finger at him. "If it's true –"

"I'll tell you what's true," he interrupted, raising his voice. "You've only been at sea five minutes and you think you know everything. Well, you don't know jack shit. That's what's true."

"If you've hurt her ..." I could feel tears of rage welling up in my eyes.

"Oh, I get it now. You're pissed off because I had her and you didn't. You got out of your depth with her, son. You should have stuck with Mrs Palm and her five daughters." Seeing that I didn't understand what he meant, he made an up and down motion with his curled fingers.

"She didn't want you!" I yelled.

He looked at me with false sympathy. "It's hard to accept, isn't it? But don't you think you're making a fuss about nothing? She's just another tart."

"Brian heard her shouting 'no'!"

"Don't you know anything, you little brat? Don't you know that when a woman says no she means yes?" Mitch smiled coyly as he brought the mug up to his lips again. "You should've seen her. Maybe what Brian heard was her screaming for me not to stop. 'Don't stop – no, no, no!' She knew what she wanted all right."

"The bed was covered in blood!"

He shook his head. "You and Brian, you're just a couple of kids."

"You bastard!"

"She wanted a man with balls, not a miserable little sheep shagger."

"You're not a man – you're a rat!"

He put his mug down. "You're beginning to try my patience."

"Her father will kill you when he finds out!"

He laughed. "You don't think I'll be going back to that frost-bitten hole again? Let him come and look for me! He'll find me in a little beach bar in Port of Spain. Now, I suggest you get out of my cabin before *I* get angry."

"You raped her!"

His left eye twitched. That was the first sign of tension I'd ever seen in him, and it made me feel a little more confident.

"You're out of order, son. I wouldn't say things like that, if I were you."

"You won't get away with it!"

Mitch stood up slowly. "I told you to get out. I won't tell you again."

I stayed where I was. I couldn't say anything because my jaws were clenched so tightly. I could feel my legs shaking. Mitch looked down at them. "That's about the nearest you'll ever get to a knee-trembler," he smirked.

As he reached past me to open the door, I hit him as hard as I could on the side of the head. His hand shot up and covered his ear, while he looked at me in astonishment. He kicked shut the partially open door.

He pushed me across the cabin. I crashed against the outer bulkhead, crumpling to the deck. Even at this moment I marvelled at his strength – I was like a ragdoll in his hands. He flexed and extended his hands as he walked towards me. Then he stood in front of me, his hands hanging by his sides, as if inviting me to hit him again. Even if I had the nerve, I knew it was pointless.

I got up. My head bowed, my shoulders slumped, my eyes averted. The punch came to my stomach, an uppercut from his hip with such force that he turned sideways delivering it. I let out a cry as I reeled forward and collapsed onto my knees.

"That's enough," I panted, holding my abdomen with both hands, saliva dribbling from my mouth.

"No, it's not," he said, lifting me to my feet by the front of my shirt. He slammed me back against the bulkhead. He held me there, his nose two inches away from mine. "Just remember who started this," he said, before head-butting me.

For a moment there was nothing but blackness. Then I was looking up at him from the deck. I felt something running from my nose.

"Here's the deal," he said, looking down and gloating. "I won't kick seven colours of shit out of you this time. In return you promise never to breathe a word about that whore again."

He pulled me to my feet.

"Now," he said in a friendly tone, flicking imaginary fluff from my shoulder. "Have we got a deal?" He gazed into my eyes, the left one half-closed by the trauma.

When I shook my head he grasped the front of my throat with his hand.

"Let's try again," he said. "Have we got a deal?"

Not being able to breathe, I couldn't answer. I shook my head.

Squeezing harder, he lifted me upwards until I was on tip-toe. My Adam's apple was being crushed and felt like it was going to burst. My hands clasped the big hand that was choking me, but they were powerless to pull it away.

He drew me closer, his lips curling up at the edges. His mouth, smelling of stale tobacco, was almost touching mine. As he pressed against me I could feel his leather belt and its large buckle, and I thought of the knife hanging at his side.

About to black out, I knew I had to do something, even if it meant killing him. I felt for his waist, then ran my hand backwards along his belt. His expression softened and he looked bewildered. "You want to dance?"

I released the retaining loop on the knife. It scraped the inside of the leather sheath as I drew it out. Mitch cried out in pain as I plunged it into his belly. He took his hand from my throat and put it on the wound, leaving me gasping for air.

When he removed his hand, it looked as if it had been dipped in a tin of red paint. He grabbed a shirt from his bunk. He wrapped it round his abdomen, tying it on one side. Even before he'd finished, the shirt was turning red. That might have been my chance to escape, but he was between me and the door and I was struggling to fill my lungs.

"Right," he growled, taking my head under his arm. "Outside!"

Grimacing with pain, he dragged me out of the door and up the stairs. He stopped twice, grunting as he doubled over, but he didn't loosen his hold on me. On the poop deck, he threw me across the snow. I slid and spun, ending up in a heap next to the gunwale. He's going to throw me over the side, I thought – but I felt it didn't really matter now that I'd lost Marit. The sound of his hobnailed boots crunching in the snow got closer. The last thing I was aware of was trying to protect my head from them.

Chapter 47

"My God!" The cry brought me back to consciousness and, bit by bit, my eyes focused on the bosun. He was kneeling down beside me, a horrified expression on his face. "What happened to you?"

"He must've had an accident," another voice said. My eyes moved to the other man. I could just make out Willy's features in the dim light.

I was lying on my back. My hand closed around something cold and powdery. I gradually realised it was snow.

"You did a First Aid course last year, Willy," said the bosun. "What do we do?"

Willy's eyes darted from me to the bosun, then to me again. "The first thing is – we mustn't move him."

"Why not?"

"I don't know. But that's what they told us. In case he's done his neck in or something."

"But if we don't get him inside, he'll freeze to death."

"Right," said Willy, nodding.

"What's else?" asked the bosun.

"Next – no, wait, right – next we check that the casualty is not in any further danger. Like from oncoming traffic."

The bosun stared at him with his mouth open. "I don't think he's going to be run over by a double-decker bus in the middle of the Norwegian Sea."

"That was just an example," Willy whined. He looked up at the boat deck. "Perhaps he fell from somewhere . . ."

Willy leaned forward to look at my face more closely. "What's that on his mouth?"

"I don't know." The bosun tried to brush it away.

"Aaaah!" I cried out. It felt like my lower lip was being torn from my face.

"Oh, God," said the bosun. "Let's get him inside."

My teeth were chattering and my hands were numb. I saw the dark shape of a capstan and the curved gunwale behind it, and I realised I was on the poop deck. I groaned as I remembered how I had got there.

"Can you stand up?" asked the bosun in a shaky voice.

"We shouldn't move him."

The bosun glared at Willy. "So what's the correct procedure? Leave him freeze to death?"

With their help, I pulled myself up. The snow where my head had laid was stained red, like raspberry ripple ice cream. I couldn't keep my balance. I didn't know if it was the roll of the *Albatross* or because my head was spinning.

"Is he drunk?" asked Willy.

"No, of course not," said the bosun. But he put his nose near my mouth and sniffed, anyway. "Let's get him to my cabin."

They lay me on his settee. The bosun took a thick blanket out of the top shelf of his cupboard and put it over me. Then he held both my hands between his.

"Take his shoes off and hold his feet," he said. When Willy looked puzzled, he added, "To warm them up."

Willy reached under the blanket. "Looks like he's lost one of them."

"*What?*"

"His shoes. There's one missing."

"Oh." The bosun sounded relieved.

"And his feet, they're like blocks of ice," said Willy.

"I just hope he hasn't got frostbite." The bosun put his hands on my head and at last the chattering of my teeth began to lessen.

"Sorry I woke you up, bosun," Willy said. "I didn't know what to do. I was coming down off lookout when I saw him lying there. At first I thought it was a heap of rags or something. But I thought I'd better check what it was."

"You were right to call me, Willy. Thank God you found him in time."

I felt thick fluid trickling down my throat, which I guessed was blood. Now it was beginning to come back to me in detail. Being choked, the knife in my hand, being dragged up to the poop deck, the hobnailed boots ... I raised my hands to look at them. They were bruised and swollen.

"Who did this to you, Owen?" asked the bosun as he wiped the blood away from my face with a damp cloth.

I managed to shake my head.

"Who?" he insisted.

"I slipped. On the ladder."

"I said he might have fallen."

"Shut up, Willy." He turned back to me. "Why are you protecting him? This isn't just a scrap in the school yard, you know. Look what he's done to you."

"The ladder," I murmured. "It was slippery."

When he took the blood-soaked cloth away from my mouth, the bosun leaned closer, squinting as if he couldn't believe his eyes. Willy stared with his mouth open.

"We'd better get him up to the medical room," said the bosun. "Go and tell Osborne to meet us there."

Willy blinked. "Osborne? ... Oh, yes – the chief steward."

He carried on staring at me for a few seconds. Then he turned and hurried out.

"Okay, let's get you up there," said the bosun. "Shall I carry you?"

I knew he could have quite easily, but I rejected the indignity of being carried like a child. "I can walk," I replied, struggling to my feet.

"Lean on me. That's it. Nice and slow."

By the time we got to the medical room, at the back of the bridge, the bosun's shirt glistened with my blood. The chief steward was already there. He tried not to react when he saw my injuries.

"Sit him down there," he said, indicating a narrow wooden couch. "How did it happen?"

"Says he fell down a ladder."

Osborne looked at the bosun's bloodied shirt. "And what about you?"

"Me?" He looked down at his shirt. "No, this is from him."

Osborne sighed with relief.

"Well, let's get him cleaned up. These things often look worse than they are."

He began to wash my face with warm water. It smelt of antiseptic, and it stung.

After cleaning my eyes, he commented, "He's certainly going to have a couple of prize shiners."

A minute later he went on, "I'm not sure, but I think his nose is broken."

When he finished cleaning my mouth, the water in the sink was bright red. He turned his head away, as if there was something he couldn't bear the sight of. He took a deep breath before looking at me again and saying, "This needs stitching."

I looked at him questioningly.

"Your bottom lip. It's ... torn."

"Stitches?" said the bosun, alarmed. "Are you sure?"

The chief steward nodded. "We can't leave it like that. That's where most of the bleeding is from."

Osborne pulled down a large black angle-poise lamp. I could feel the heat from it on my face. Sitting on a wooden chair beside me, he put on a pair of glasses with metal frames.

"This joint smells like a hospital," grimaced the bosun.

I winced with pain as he dabbed a purple substance on my lip with a gauze pad.

"Can't you give him an anaesthetic?"

"Iodine is a local anaesthetic," said Osborne.

"What's that spilling out of his lip?"

"That's fatty tissue. We have to push it back in as much as possible."

"God!"

"This didn't happen slipping on a ladder," Osborne murmured, shaking his head.

"How then, do you think?"

"The only time I've seen anything like this it was the result of a kick with a heavy boot. And look at his eyes – two black eyes. That's not consistent with a fall."

"So he's been filled in?"

"Looks that way."

"I'll kill the swine!" The bosun thumped the bulkhead with the side of his fist.

Osborne fixed me with his eyes. "What's your name, son?"

"Owen," I said with difficulty.

He leaned closer towards me. "Who was it, Owen? Who did this?"

"I fell ... the ladder was slippery."

Osborne shook his head again and began inserting the first stitch. I moaned.

"You're hurting him," protested the bosun. "Have you ever done this before?"

"No. But I've read about it."

"Read about it?" The bosun looked desperate.

Having tightened and cut the silk thread with the scissors, Osborne said to the bosun, "Put your finger here, Jeremy, so that I can tie it off."

After a long silence, the bosun said, "How many is that now?"

"Three. Another one, just here, should do it."

"It doesn't look very tidy."

"It's not like sewing a button on a shirt, you know. Lips are difficult to stitch. They're all floppy."

I didn't know why, but it was at that moment a terrible realisation seeped into my consciousness: I would never see Marit again. That was worse than anything else that had happened to me.

I lifted my head off the pillow as someone switched my cabin light on. I could see the outline of a big man in the doorway, and for a terrifying moment I thought it was Mitch.

"Owen," said the bosun, sitting in the chair next to my bed. "You've got to tell me who did this."

"Why?"

"Because it's not right that someone can get away with a thing like this, with someone so innocent ..."

"I'm not innocent," I said.

The bosun put his hand on my arm. "Something happened in Narvik, didn't it? Whatever it was, you don't deserve this."

"It's not only that." I felt as if my eyes were straining to pop out of my head. "There's something else. It's something I did a long time ago."

The bosun smiled. "It can't have been that long ago."

"It was. About five years ago. I've never told anyone."

"What did you do that was so terrible?"

I closed my eyes. "It was when my sister moved to the secondary school, where I was. Delyth, she's a bit slow – you know, mentally."

"Right. So what did you do?"

"I disowned her." The bosun looked puzzled, so I went on, "I denied she was my sister, said I didn't know her. Instead of helping her, as I should have."

"Listen, you were just a kid. Kids can be so damned proud ..."

"This is my punishment."

He tried to smile. "Just tell me who did this," he said between clenched teeth.

I opened my mouth to tell him, but said, "I can't."

"Why?"

"Because ... I might have killed him. I stabbed him with his own knife!" I covered my face with my hands and sobbed. I shrugged his hand off my shoulder. "Go away! Please, just go away."

Chapter 48

The girl with the brown fringe smiled as she served my second chocolate muffin and cappuccino in Caffè Nero's. I'd seen her somewhere before, but couldn't think where. I must try to make this last until lunchtime, I told myself as I carried the tray to a table well away from the door. My mobile rang. It was Charity.

"I was just wondering how you are," she said. It was good to hear a friendly voice from the university. "Have you got the date for the hearing yet?"

This was something I didn't even want to think about. "No, not yet."

"Well, don't worry. You'll be fine. In the end it probably won't be as bad as you expect."

"Yes, I suppose so."

"When will you be back?"

The question is, *will* I be back? While I hesitated, she went on, "Ewelina misses you. Says she's struggling to cope without her mentor."

"She'll be okay," I mumbled.

"I'd better go. Lecture to prepare. At least you're having a break from all that. Take care."

"You too."

I was about to press the off button when I heard Charity again. "Oh – are you still there?"

"Yes."

"Do you remember Irene, that ward sister?"

A cold shiver ran down my spine. "Yes."

"She visited the ward yesterday. She had a child, a daughter, with her. She got divorced and married an Indian doctor. Imagine!"

I sat looking around the café as if I had just realised where I was. I felt as if I had lost Irene for a second time. Things had worked out better for her without me. The café's doors were propped open because of the heat. So different from that winter when I went back to look for Marit ...

It had been an arduous journey, first flying to Ålesund and then onto snow-covered Narvik. Then there was the problem of finding the girls' house – I no longer had the address. When at last an older, wearier version of Torruld's mother opened the door, it took her some time to recognise me. She looked at my mouth, and there was an unasked question in her eyes.

"Come in, Owen." I was surprised that she remembered my name.

She made me a cup of coffee – black. The Norwegians always drank their coffee black, so I didn't bother asking for milk.

"Why did you come back?" she asked.

"To see Marit," I said. "Will you tell me where to find her?"

"She is here."

My eyes darted around the room.

"She is staying here for the weekend," she clarified. "She will be back soon."

I stirred my coffee. "How is she?"

"She's okay now. The nightmares, they have stopped and she can go out alone again." So she did know. "She is happy. She has a boyfriend now. A Norwegian boy. You can wait for her if you want."

She left me sitting by the window while she carried on with housework, glancing at me from time to time. Her eyes made me uncomfortable, but I couldn't leave without seeing Marit.

At some point I heard laughter. Through the window, I saw her and a young man coming up the drive. They looked so right together. I watched them coming nearer, before getting up and putting my overcoat on.

"I'm going now," I called to Torruld's mother. "Please, don't tell Marit ..." I hesitated.

Torruld's mother dried her hands with a cloth. She glanced through the window behind me. "But she will see you."

I pulled on my dark grey balaclava. "Not even my mother would recognise me in this."

I walked past Marit as quickly as the snow would allow me. Still in the other man's arms, she stopped and stared at me, puzzlement on her face. All she could see were strained eyes and a mouth. And the mouth was different from the one she'd known.

Fiona and Brad were having lunch in the garden when I got home. Both were wearing sunglasses. Fiona's covered half her face.

"You're spending less and less time at the university lately," she commented.

She took a bottle of white wine out of a cooler, poured it into a glass, and handed it to me.

"It's a bit early for me," I said.

"Nonsense." The sunny weather had elevated her spirits. Clinking my glass, then Brad's, she said, "Chin-chin. *Salud, amor* and *pesetas.*"

"Shouldn't that be *euros* now?" Brad laughed.

"*Salud, amor* and *euros?*" she said. "No, it doesn't have the same ring to it."

I found the wine a bit dry, but didn't say anything. Fiona was being unusually friendly to me. It was amazing what a bit of unexpected sun could do.

"A letter came for you," she said, handing it to me.

Fiona sipped her wine, looking at me from the corner of her eye. The university's red franking stamp was on the envelope and it was marked Private and Confidential. She must have thought it odd that the letter was sent to me at home instead of put in my pigeonhole at the university. My hands trembled as I opened it. As I feared, this was it. Looking as innocuous as an invitation to a birthday party, it informed me of the date of my disciplinary hearing.

"What's wrong, Dad?"

"It's nothing. I'm okay."

"Nothing!" said Brad. "You're so bloody secretive."

"Bradley!" his mother intervened.

"Well, it's true, Mum. And it's so annoying."

"Your father can't help the way he is."

Thrusting the letter into my trouser pocket, I jumped to my feet, accidentally knocking my glass of wine over. I felt their eyes following me as I rushed across the lawn and into the house.

In the attic, I went straight for the rope and made a hangman's noose at the end of it. Then I threw it over the beam above the trapdoor. I stared at the noose so intensely that my eyes, and my mind, became unfocussed. The next time I blinked, the bell-rope in the wheelhouse of the *Albatross* swayed before me.

Chapter 49

Captain Frazer entered the wheelhouse while I stood with both hands on the helm. In the half-light, he stood gazing ahead at the raging sea. Stratton, the second mate, who was nervously pacing from one side to the other, was startled to see him.

"Oh, good evening, sir," he said, stubbing his cigarette out.

"Good evening, Stratton. Are you okay?" Frazer was calm, despite the concerned expression on his face.

Stratton nodded.

"Rough weather is normal in the Norwegian Sea at this time of year," said Frazer.

"Have you ever seen it this bad?" Stratton asked.

Frazer glanced at him before answering. "No, never like this," he said. "It's essential that we keep heading straight into the wind so as not to catch one on the beam."

"That's what I've been doing, as much as possible. But we're way off course – west by south west, instead of due south."

"We have no choice. Where's Mr Whitby?"

"He asked me to swap watches with him. It was his anniversary yesterday and he was worried he might get a bit drunk."

"Even though his wife is a thousand miles away," Frazer chuckled. "That man never misses an opportunity to celebrate."

Frazer became aware of me, a pale figure behind the wheel. I must have looked a mess, with two black eyes and four stitches in my lower lip. Marcos had looked at my mouth and said, "I'm not very impressed with Osborne's work. I've seen haggises sewn up better."

"Are you okay?" Frazer asked me.

I was standing with my feet apart to keep steady. "I feel sick, sir."

"Second, relieve this man," Frazer ordered.

As soon as Stratton's hands touched the helm I rushed towards the door of the bridge, covering my mouth with my hand.

"Not that way – lee side!" shouted Frazer.

I turned and staggered against the roll of the ship towards the port side door. As I leaned over the wing of the bridge, the freezing air on my face, I heard Frazer say, "The last thing he needed was to have his own vomit thrown back in his face, poor sod. Did you ever find out who gave him that beating?"

"No. Still says he fell down a ladder."

They showed no sign of having been talking about me when I went in and took the wheel again. "Steady as she goes, Roberts," Stratton grinned.

"Steady as she goes," I muttered.

After the two men had stood next to each other looking ahead for about ten minutes, Stratton said, "I think the wind's changing direction."

Frazer studied the heaving sea for another minute. "Yes, you're right. Starboard easy."

"Starboard easy, sir," I repeated and turned the wheel a quarter to the right.

"My God, look at that!" cried the second mate, his eyes widening.

"Hard a-starboard!" called Frazer.

"Hard a-starboard, sir." I turned the bronze wheel fully as fast as I could.

But it didn't seem to be fast enough for Stratton, who yelled, "Hard over! Hard over!"

The two men were mesmerised by something. And then I saw it. A wave that towered above all the others, running towards our starboard side. At last the *Albatross* began to react, turning slowly.

"We're not going to make it!" squealed Stratton.

The helm trembled in my hands with the strain on the rudder. But it was too late. Even I could see that. The *Albatross* fell steeply into the trough in front of the wave and then attempted to climb the huge wall of water. Stratton almost fell backwards as his eyes followed the crest of the wave. Frazer stood motionless. As for me, I let go of the wheel and crouched behind it.

Thousands of tons of water thundered down onto the ship. I heard a grinding and groaning of steel from the main deck. Water was pouring off the bridge and the decks when we were met with the monstrous sight of the second hatch prised open.

"Oh, my God!" cried Stratton.

Grimly, Frazer said, "While you're at it, you'd better ask Him to help us."

The second mate turned and looked at Frazer.

"There's nothing to stop that hold filling up with water," Frazer answered his unspoken question. "Note the time. Enter it in the log."

Frazer picked up the phone. "Sparks, get a call out to all vessels in the vicinity. Yes, it is critical. Mayday, Mayday, Mayday. We have thirty-five souls on board. Our position is latitude 62 degrees 472 minutes, longitude 0 degrees 659 minutes."

"Mayday?" Stratton said when Frazer put down the phone.

The captain nodded. "Stay calm. You must be a good example to the crew. Starting with him." Frazer nodded towards me.

Stratton shuddered.

"What's our course now?"

I squinted at the erratic gyro compass. "180 … 185 degrees, sir."

"Okay, port to 160 degrees."

"Port to 160 degrees, sir."

I turned the helm a half a turn to the left. With the next large wave, we could see water gurgling into the open hold.

The mate, his ruffled hair and beard testifying that he'd just got out of bed, appeared on the bridge behind me. He stared at the scene on the main deck with wide eyes. "Is there anything we can do, Captain?"

"All we can do is try to sail straight into the seas and pray the storm ends soon."

The mate snorted. "I'm afraid I can't help with that. I'm an atheist."

"Within the next twenty minutes there'll be no atheists on this ship," Frazer said.

I struggled to keep the ship on course, but the giro compass was swinging like mad.

"Can't you keep a steady course?" Stratton shouted. He turned to the captain and asked, "Shouldn't we get an experienced seaman up here?"

"I don't think anyone else could do better," said Frazer, and I silently thanked him. He came and stood behind me. He touched my right shoulder and pointed to the sky in front of us. "See that star – just to the left of the brightest one? Steer towards that. Ignore the compass."

"Yes, sir." I hardly recognised my own voice – I sounded like a child.

The *Albatross* began rolling more steeply. It wasn't just the tumultuous sea, but also the water inside the hold flowing from side to side.

During a particularly steep roll the second mate, leaning at almost 45 degrees, cried out, "We're turning turtle! We're all going to die!"

"Any more of that, Stratton, and I'll confine you to your cabin," Frazer shouted.

"I'm sorry," Stratton whimpered.

It was at that point that the bosun appeared at the port side door of the bridge. He paused to steady himself, holding on to the frame of the door. "What shall I do?"

"There's nothing you can do," said Frazer. "No one is to go on the main deck. It would be suicide."

"But we haven't got a chance if we leave that hatch open," protested the bosun.

Stratton opened his mouth to say something, but then thought better of it.

The ship was rolling so steeply that occasionally the handrails on one side or the other would dip into the sea.

Frazer appeared to be deep in thought for a minute. Then he turned to the second mate and said, "Sound six short blasts on the whistle, followed by one long."

Stratton's eyes widened. "Abandon ship?"

"No," said Frazer. "*Stand by* to abandon ship. The order to abandon ship has to be by word of mouth from me."

Stratton pursed his lips. He crossed to the starboard side of the bridge and pulled on the lanyard that was attached to the ship's whistle. The deep blasts cut through the howling of the wind.

Then Frazer turned to the bosun. "Prepare the starboard lifeboat for launching."

The bosun looked out at the violent sea before replying, "Is there any point, sir?"

Frazer took a deep breath. "At this stage, all we can do is follow the correct procedures."

I looked out at the scene of moving mountains and valleys. The ship was going to sink, and there was nothing anyone could do about it.

Chapter 50

I fumbled to get my ringing mobile out of my inside pocket in Nero's. It was Neville. This was the first time I'd heard his voice since the mock hearing debacle.

"You've had the letter about the date of the disciplinary hearing?" he asked me.

"Yes," I said, immediately feeling sick.

"Well, we'd better meet to talk about it." I heard him turning the pages of his diary. "How about next Tuesday morning ...?"

I groaned. "No sooner?"

More turning of pages. "Nope ... but I've had a cancellation, so I could make it now if you're not busy."

"I'll come now." I took a deep breath, then went on, "I'm really sorry about last time. After all your work ..."

"Just call me when you get here. Okay?"

I finished off my tepid coffee in a couple of gulps.

No wonder he referred to it as his cupboard. There was hardly enough room in Neville's office for the grey filing cabinet, a table and three plastic chairs. There was no window; a bare bulb hung from the ceiling. Water pipes were visible on the wall behind him. Being tall, Neville made the room look even smaller than it was.

"Take a seat," he said, indicating the chair on the opposite side of the table from his. "This used to be a female toilet, you know. By law, they had to provide me with an office. I think they were trying to tell me something by giving me a converted toilet."

The kettle on top of the filing cabinet began to whistle. "Tea or coffee?" he asked, getting up.

"No thanks, I've just had one." The truth was that I couldn't have held anything in my stomach at that moment.

"Just as well," he said, examining one mug after another. "There seems to be only one clean mug."

When he sat down with the coffee, I asked, "Do you know who will be on the panel yet?"

"Yes. Shit, I think this milk's gone off ... There'll be a woman from personnel. And a colleague of yours – Charity."

I already knew about Charity, but I didn't tell him.

"There's a rota for being on these panels. I'm surprised you haven't been on one of them."

"I always missed them for some reason – usually holidays or teaching commitments."

"Hmm. Pity. It would've been good to have experienced it from the panel's perspective."

"Who else? You said there'll be three."

"Oh, yes. Professor Kemp. He'll be chairing the hearing. You know him?"

"Vaguely."

I was silent for a moment.

"What are you thinking?" Neville asked.

"I've always found him very courteous."

"You're lucky you've got him. He's a just man. You're sure to have an impartial hearing."

"What are my chances, then?"

Neville took a while to answer. "If this were a criminal case, I'd say you'd have a fair chance of being acquitted."

"But it's not criminal. So my chances are better than that, right?"

"Wrong." Neville fiddled with his pen. "A higher standard of proof is required in criminal law. You have to be found guilty beyond reasonable doubt. It's lower in civil cases, where it only has to be proved that on the balance of probabilities you did it. But what we're dealing with is employment law."

I could feel the blood draining from my face. "What does that mean?"

"It means they only have to prove that they have reasonable suspicion."

"That's not fair!"

The force of my objection made him lean back, almost imperceptibly. "Perhaps it isn't, but that's how things are. What's your relationship with Charity like?"

I'd bumped into her in Harrow shopping centre a few days earlier. Before we parted after a quick chat, she'd said, "I shouldn't speak to you about this, Owen, as I'll be on the panel at your hearing. But I think this accusation against you is ridiculous."

"We've always got on well," I told Neville. "We go back a long way."

"Well, that helps." He seemed to weigh things up before continuing. "The personnel woman will ask a lot of probing questions, but in the end she'll go along with the other two. And with Kemp chairing ... I reckon you've got a fighting chance."

"If things did go against me ...?" I took a sharp breath.

"You know the answer to that, Owen. You'd be sacked. You'd lose your pension. And at your age, I doubt very much that you'd get another teaching job."

"I'd have to go back to nursing," I murmured. My father-in-law came to my mind. I saw the look of satisfaction on his face as he was proved right, that I would always be just a nurse.

"You might not even be able to do that, not if you're put on the POVA list."
"*POVA?*"
"Protection of vulnerable adults –"
"I know what it is," I interrupted. "I meant, what's it got to do with this?"
"A foreign student in an unequal position with you, trusting you ... who knows what people will make of that? Another thing, Owen: I'd advise you to wear a suit and a tie to the hearing."
"I've always despised such hypocrisy," I said. "If I normally come to work like this, why should I dress differently for the hearing?"
"It's a matter of expectations. Anything could tip the balance."
He opened the file on the table in front of him. "I've received a couple more statements. Here are your copies."
Looking at the first one, I caught my breath. "Karolina Czech."
"Czech?"
"That's what I call her," I said. "But what could she say in my defence?"
Neville stared at me for a moment before saying, "That's part of the evidence against you."
While I struggled to find the words to express my disbelief, Neville went on, "The other one is from Wencheng. In your defence. But it's little more than a character reference."
"But doesn't that count for something?" I was feeling desperate. "No one knows me better than him."
"That's like the guy who testified that OJ Simpson must be innocent because he'd had breakfast with him the week before and he hadn't killed anyone then."
He leaned back in his chair and gazed at me, and for the first time I thought I saw a hint of compassion in his eyes. "Owen," he said, "Have you written your statement yet?"
"Yes." I took it out of my briefcase and handed it to him.
He read the eight pages, then summed it up. "So you confess to having sex with her, but not to helping her cheat."
I tried to get comfortable in the plastic chair. "It wasn't that straightforward."
"It never is. But that's the essence of it?"
"Well, yes, I suppose so. So," I gestured towards the statement he was holding, "How does it look?"
"Not too good."
"At least I'm honest about having ... that experience with her. They've got to see that."
"You've got no choice." His brief laugh disconcerted me. "She described the furniture in your house, for goodness' sake."

Chapter 51

Willy fumbled with the door outside the wheelhouse when he came to relieve me. The sound of the storm increased as the door slid open and lessened again as it closed behind him. As he walked towards me he stopped to steady himself against a steep roll to port. His face was white. He wore a life-jacket.

"So that's what it was," he breathed, looking out of the water-splattered bridge window. "It sounded like we were struck by thunder."

"Number 2 hold is filling up with water," I said. "We're going to sink."

"That's enough of that," snapped Frazer. "Just hand over and go below. Put your life-jacket on and report to the bosun."

Willy put his hands on the helm. I turned to go.

"Aren't you forgetting something?" the second mate asked.

"Oh, it's one-nine-zero," I told Willy, who had been staring at me blankly. Willy looked down at the gyro. "A bit off course, aren't you?"

"See if you can do any better, dimwit!"

The second mate glared at me as I walked away, but I thought, what the hell, we're all going to die, anyway.

"Owen," said Willy.

I stopped and turned around.

"See you later," he said. It sounded like a plea.

"Yes, see you later, Willy. Sorry."

He shifted his weight from one foot to the other. "You mean for what you said or ...?"

"For what I said."

Most of the ship's company was on the starboard boat deck when I got there. Like me, everyone was wearing a life-jacket. I was astonished to see Mitch standing at one end of the lifeboat. My revulsion at seeing him was mixed with relief that I hadn't killed him after all. Besides being deathly white and putting his hand on his abdomen when he moved, there was no indication that he had been stabbed in the gut the day before.

Paddy was at the other end of the lifeboat. They were both standing by to wind the davit, on which the lifeboat was suspended, out over the ship's side. Dai was in the boat, untying the rope that kept its canvas cover on. I spotted the bosun near the lifeboat, leaning over the rails to look down the ship's side, his oilskin cape and sou'wester buffeted by the wind. I shouldered my way towards him.

"I'm here, bosun." I raised my voice above the roar of the wind. "What shall I do?"

He smiled. "Remember your job?"

"Yes," I replied. "Ship the rudder and put the plug in."

"That's it! And it's very important. We won't go far if the plug isn't in."

We had laughed at that at lifeboat drill. Who would have thought a lifeboat had a plug, just like a kitchen sink? But this wasn't just another drill. This was for real. I looked at the frenzied sea behind him and tried to imagine the lifeboat, full of men, floating on it. I couldn't.

"Just stand by here for now. We can't do anything else until we get the order to abandon ship." He took my arm and moved me a few feet further inboard. "Not too close to the ship's side."

As he turned his attention back to the lifeboat, I looked at the anxious faces around me. Some of them I had never seen before. We were all in this together, yet all of us were alone. I heard someone praying quietly at my side. Paddy. His lips and the tip of his nose were blue with cold. I hope God is good at accents, I thought. Paddy asked, "Are you after praying, son?"

"No."

"Why not?"

"Well, we're not a hundred percent sure of what's going to happen yet."

Paddy snorted. "Talk about cutting it fine!"

Stratton elbowed his way past us to speak to the bosun. I couldn't hear what they were saying, but they were pointing at the lifeboat and the ship's side. Turning to face us, Stratton pulled his camera out of his coat pocket and took a couple of photos.

"Don't know why you're bothering, Second," Kirk laughed.

"I know. But I might as well use up the film."

Brian was wearing the purple great coat with gold braid that he'd bought in Carnaby Street. Paddy looked him up and down. "You're going down in style, anyway."

"It's not that," Brian replied. "It's just the warmest thing I've got to wear."

"The day before I joined the *Albatross* I was put on standby for the *New Yorker*, a cargo liner bound for the States, because one of the ABs hadn't come back from leave," John said. "They were due to sail from Swansea that night. I went aboard with my all my gear, ready to sign on. But he had turned up, so I went home with a day's pay and expenses. If he hadn't turned up, I wouldn't be here now."

"The same could be said for all of us, one way or another," sighed Sidney. "You make a different decision, you miss a train – we all could have ended up somewhere else. But the fact is, we are all here. And there's nothing we can do about that."

"What makes it so hard," said John, "is not seeing the baby even once."

Sidney asked, "Do you think it would be any easier if you had?"

I saw John wiping away a tear. "No, probably not. I went up to ask Sparks if I could send a message to my wife. He said there was no chance because he had to leave the channel open every second."

"I suppose he can't make exceptions," reasoned Sidney. "Everyone on board would want to send a message to someone."

"Bet he sent a message to *his* wife, though," said Paddy through clenched teeth.

"I doubt any message would get through from here, anyway," observed Sidney.

"Talking about wives," Osborne said to Riley, "at least you won't have to tell yours that you caught a dose off another woman."

"I want to tell her," Riley wailed. "I'd give anything to be able to go home and tell her!"

"I wonder how long she'll take to sink," mused Pussy. He was wearing a woman's fur coat, with a pink bag hanging at his side.

"The *Titanic* took nearly three hours," said Osborne.

"That was the ship even God couldn't sink," Paddy put in. "This isn't."

"Does it matter how long it takes, anyway?" questioned Sidney.

Pussy looked at him in astonishment. "Don't you want to know how long you've got left?"

"Time is relative. If you wait ten minutes for a bus it feels like forever. But if you're waiting for a bank loan to be approved it's nothing."

"And if you're waiting for a ship to sink, taking you down with it?" asked Pussy.

Sidney smiled. "I'll let you know. One thing's for sure, within just two generations, your family won't know who you were. At most they'll have heard of a grandfather or great uncle who died at sea. That might give them something to talk about in the pub. But they'll have no conception of what you went through, tossed around on the deck of a ship, cold and wet, terrified of not being."

Pussy blinked. "Of not being what?"

"Just that," Sidney replied. "Of not being."

Pussy shuddered. "You give me the shits, talking like that."

"Don't worry," said Kirk. "No matter how rough it is on the surface, it's always calm at the bottom of the sea."

"Oh, fuck off!"

Behind John, I saw the mate steady himself on the ladder as he came down from the bridge.

"What are we waiting for? Why don't we go while we still can?" Pussy shouted at him.

"That's for the captain to decide," Whitby replied. Looking at the sea, he added, "And I wouldn't want to be in his shoes right now."

"I just hope I'm not sitting next to that bastard," I muttered, glowering at Mitch.

"Don't worry," said Paddy. "You wouldn't be sitting together for long."

Mitch glanced my way and our eyes locked. He was expressionless, his eyes lifeless. I tried to stare him out, but in the end broke away and looked down at the deck. When I looked up, he was still staring at me. I was trembling all over, and didn't know if it was through cold, fear or anger.

I turned away and went inboard to the housing where there was some shelter from the icy wind. Here, joining Riley and Larry, I could smell the fresh paint we had applied the day before.

"There'th something I want to tell you," Larry was saying to the second steward. "I uthed to hide from you, Riley. Ethpecially when you were looking for thomeone for toilet cleaning."

"It's okay. I knew."

"You knew? Oh, that makes me feel even worse."

"It's okay." Riley patted him on the shoulder. "I was an ordinary steward myself once."

"But I feel really guilty about it –"

"For goodness' sake, I said it's okay! What more do you want? Now piss off and leave me alone!"

A rocket screeched upwards from the bridge, leaving a white trail. Every pair of eyes on the heaving deck was turned upwards as it exploded into brilliant red stars.

"Oh, grand!" said Dai. "Squibs to cheer us up."

As the *Albatross* lurched forward and to port, the bow of the lifeboat swung inwards. The bosun leapt clear, falling onto the wet wooden deck. But Kirk wasn't quick enough. The lifeboat bore down on him, pushing him forward and trapping him against the ship's rail, which buckled and snapped.

"Heave away left and right together!" the bosun yelled as he struggled to his feet.

Marcos took Kirk's place on the left side of the davit and he and Mitch, on the other side, wound furiously to lift the lifeboat up. Kirk was screaming in agony. I joined the others in trying to pull the boat off him. The smell of grease warmed my nostrils. I thought my boots were slipping on it, but when I looked down I saw it was blood. When at last the boat released its grip, we saw that Kirk's right leg was pinned to the ship's rail. He yelled in pain as Paddy and Sidney lifted him off it.

Kneeling beside Kirk, Osborne tore his jeans along the seams, revealing a gaping wound in which could be seen something yellow and white. I realised it must have been his thigh bone. The bosun turned his face away.

Osborne snapped open a black medical bag and took out a roll of bandage. He looked around briefly. "You, come and help me tie this tourniquet on!" He shouted at Brian. "As tight as possible."

Brian's hands trembled as he helped Osborne wind the bandage around Kirk's leg. The bandage was turning red. Someone pushed me to one side to see what was going on. It was Marcos.

"You're putting it in the wrong place," he told Osborne.

"What?"

"That'll only increase the bleeding," said Marcos.

"How would you know?" Osborne snapped, before continuing to apply the bandage.

"You should put direct pressure on the wound."

Osborne looked up at Marcos angrily. "Get on with your own job, lad, and let me get on with mine!"

Kirk's face was contorted with pain and fear.

"It's okay," Osborne reassured him. "I'll give you a shot of morphine as soon as we've got this on."

If Kirk heard him, he wasn't impressed. "Just do as Marcos says," he groaned. "He may be a weirdo, but he knows what he's talking about."

Osborne hesitated, then began unwinding the bandage. "Oh, what the fuck. It's only academic. We're all about to cash our chips in, anyway!"

Chapter 52

"Owen!"

My eyes turned from the short wake of the *Albatross*, which was quickly obliterated by the storm, to the desolate scene on the windswept boat deck. I didn't know who was calling me until I heard, "Over here," in a Glaswegian accent.

Then I saw Callum's head sticking out from one of the housing's portholes. He was in his cabin. He beckoned for me to come.

"I'd better go and see what he wants," I said to Sidney.

"Don't be long," he replied.

I looked at him questioningly.

"Just kidding," he said.

I found Callum sitting in his easy chair facing the door of his cabin.

"What do you think of that?" he said, his speech slightly slurred. He was holding a three-quarters full bottle up for me to see.

"Whisky," I said.

"Not just any old whisky. It's a Macallan 1946. The captain's best."

"Does he know you've got it?"

"Hell, no. But he won't miss it now, will he? It'd be criminal to let it go down with the ship. Unless it's in me, of course." He hiccoughed.

He poured some into a tumbler for me. "Straight or with water? Straight, I think – we'll be having enough water soon." His shoulders moved up and down as he laughed at his own joke.

"How can you drink and joke at a time like this?" I asked.

"Look, the way I see it is like this. What difference does it make if I stay here nice and warm, drinking the captain's best whisky, or if I join that lot out there, soaked to the skin and freezing their balls off? You *ken* what the Red Indians say, don't you?"

"No, I've never met one." I could hear the panic increasing in my voice.

"It's a good day to die."

"It's not a good day for me to die. I'm only seventeen. I don't want to die!"

"Neither do I, *hen*. Neither do I. But I *dinnae ken* we had a choice."

He handed me the tumbler while he went on, "Death will have to come and look for me – here, in this iron box that's been my home for the last three years. Taste that. Wait, wait." He reached out and stopped me. "Smell it first. Swirl it around and look at the colour. See the light reflecting off it. Savour it. That's how you drink whisky of this quality, *hen*. With all your senses."

I did what he instructed. For a moment, with the fiery liquid in my mouth, I ceased to hear the roaring wind, the waves crashing against the *Albatross*, and the occasional anguished cry. Only for a moment. Unlike Callum, I was unable to sustain it.

"You're only fooling yourself." I put the glass down with a thud.

"About what?"

"About reality."

"Reality? Whose reality is the right one? Those out there, or mine in here? And is there only one reality – or do we all create our own?"

"You sound like Sidney."

"The professor? Well, perhaps I've learned from him, although I'd never admit it. Oh, dear," he hiccoughed, "I just have, haven't I? I wonder how he's taking all this shite."

"I don't know."

"Well, if you see him, ask him to pop in for a drink. I've still got a case of Stella Artois to get through." He drained his glass.

I jumped up. "This is horrible! Did you hear what happened to Kirk?"

"The Estonian? No."

"He was crushed by the lifeboat."

Callum shook his head slowly and sucked his lips. "He was a good man."

"He's not *dead*."

"No?" He sipped his whisky. "So what happened to the wanker?"

Stratton, eyes wide and panicky, appeared in the doorway, steadying himself against the roll of the ship, holding a clipboard and pen. "What the hell are you two doing here? You should be standing by to board the lifeboat."

Callum gave a short laugh as he glanced out of his porthole at the frantic sea.

"And why haven't you got your life-jacket on?" the second mate went on.

"The colour doesn't suit me."

"Don't you know what's going on?" asked Stratton incredulously.

"We did notice something," Callum replied.

"So – what? You just sit there and accept it?"

"We all fight in our own way." Callum was almost serious for a moment.

"You're full of shit!"

"Why don't you come in and have a wee tipple yourself?" he grinned.

"This is crazy." The second mate's eyes were bulging. "You're crazy."

"You got any better ideas? It's got to be better than deluding yourself. You think you're going to bob along happily on this sea in that wee boat?"

Stratton pointed an angry finger at Callum, but instead of saying anything he picked up my tumbler and knocked back the whisky. Then he turned and rushed out, wiping his mouth with his sleeve.

Callum leaned toward me. "Why do you think the old man hasn't given the order to abandon ship?"

I shook my head.

"Because he knows we'll survive less time in the lifeboat than on the ship."

"So shouldn't we be – I don't know – praying or something?" I queried.

"You go ahead, if you like." He raised his glass. "Again, we all pray in our own way … I didn't know you were religious, anyway."

"I'm not, but – well, you know, at a time like this."

"Just in case, eh?" Callum winked. "Tell you what, if I were God I wouldn't listen to you now – not last minute like this."

"Don't talk like that!"

"Okay, okay, keep your hair on." He refilled my tumbler. "Here, stop snivelling and get that down yer neck."

We heard a pair of shoes squelching along the passageway, slowly approaching us. It was Larry who stopped at the door, shoulders drooping and a wayward strand of blond hair hanging over his forehead.

"You'd better come now, Callum," he said in a tired voice. "There'th not much time left."

"You look a mess, Larry," I said.

"Well, it's hard graft, enjoying yourself," said Callum. "Come and have a wee dram of the water of life."

"No, no. We need to get out there," Larry insisted. "The mate thaid we were waiting to thee if the thtorm would thtop, ath that wath our betht chanth. But if we leave it too late to go, the lifeboat could be thucked down with the ship."

Callum tilted his head to one side.

"No, it'th true," said Larry. "That'th what they thaid in *A Night to Remember* about the Titanic."

"Maybe it was true about the Titanic, the biggest ship in the world on a sea as calm as a duck pond. But I wouldn't worry too much about that on the *Albatross* in this weather."

Callum opened a drawer and took out a rolled up pair of socks, which he tossed to Larry.

"Change into them, at least. You'll catch your death with those wet socks."

Larry looked down at the red and green tartan socks in his hands. Then he dropped down onto the edge of the setee and levered his shoes off.

"I wanted to be a doctor, you know," he said, reaching for a towel to dry his feet. "I jutht thought I'd thee the world firtht, then become a pop thtar; have a bit of fun. It theemed like there wath all the time in the world. But now …"

Callum was staring at him with his arms folded. Then he turned to me. "How about you, Owen? What would you have done with your life if this hadn't happened? Would you have stayed at sea?"

I swallowed. "I always wanted to become a teacher."

I was thinking about Marit and what might have been.

"Time is so strange. Look at this," said Callum pulling out a thick book from his bookshelf.

"*Cassell's Spanish/English Dictionary.* I bought this in Glasgow with my big sis years ago. She said I should buy a smaller, cheaper one to start off with, but I said no, I'll buy this one because then I'll feel I have to learn Spanish. But I never got around to looking at it. Never had time, you *ken.* But when I heard we were sinking, I felt guilty about it. Can you believe that?"

"No," I said. "I could never imagine you feeling guilty about anything."

Callum winked at me. "That's because I've got my reputation to think of. Anyway, I leafed through it and you'll never guess which Spanish word I picked out at random … Go on, guess."

"*Mañana,*" I said

"Why *mañana?*"

"That's the only Spanish word I know."

"Mind you, that's pretty good. Because it looks like there'll be no more tomorrows for us. But no, the word was *miedoso.*"

"So? What does that mean?"

"It means a coward, a scaredy cat. It was like a message, you *ken.* And I decided then and there that I wouldn't be a scaredy cat. Problem was, I was scared …"

"Well, that'th your reputation down the drain," said Larry.

"… just like you two are now. Then I remembered having to fly to Northern Italy to join a cargo ship back in '56 or '57. I was terrified of flying. But after a few glasses of red wine on the plane, I didn't give a monkey's. I was in seventh heaven."

"So you decided to pinch the captain's whisky," I said.

"Aye. For Dutch courage. As far as I *ken,* that's the only thing we have to thank the Dutch for."

"What shall I do with theth?" Larry dangled the wet socks from his fingertips.

"Oh, just drop them on the deck," said Callum. "I'll tidy up in the morning."

Again he was the only one who laughed.

"Do you believe in reincarnation?" asked Larry.

"What sort of dumb-arse question is that?" said Callum.

"I've never thought about it, Larry," I said. "Do you?"

"It'th hard to believe that it'th all been for nothing," sighed Larry. "Everything you've learned and done ..."

"Aye, all those chords and Tommy Steele lyrics," said Callum.

"You're bound to wonder," Larry went on, ignoring the interruption, "when the end ith thtaring you in the fathe."

"I don't know about reincarnation," I said, "but I can't imagine not being here. I mean, yes, I know the ship is sinking and we're going to drown, but I can't imagine not talking to someone about it afterwards, telling them what it was like ..."

"Yeth, weird, ithn't it," Larry agreed.

"If you did come back," I said, "who would you like to come back as?"

"Ath me, I thuppose."

"Well, that's not going to happen." Callum lifted his glass to his mouth, grinning. "When you're dead you're dead. Anyway, according to reincarnation you're more likely to come back as an animal, aren't you? And aren't you supposed to progress to a higher form each time you come back? Maybe next time you'll be a cockroach."

"There'th no call for that," Larry complained, rising to his feet. "And I don't know about you two, but I'm not going to be left behind when that boat goeth."

As he strode out of the cabin, Callum called after him, "Hey, Larry. How about a song before you go?"

Callum chuckled and took a swig of whisky, swirling it around in his mouth. Then he looked down and his forehead furrowed. I followed his eyes and saw that the whisky in the glass was at an angle of about 60 degrees.

"Is it my imagination," he asked, "or are we rolling more steeply?"

"We're rolling more steeply," I said. "It's the water in the hold sloshing from one side to the other. The mate said this would happen."

"That's all right, then," grinned Callum. "For a minute there I thought it was me."

Chapter 53

"Dad."

Brad had said that a thousand time before, but this time it was different.

His voice vibrated with anger. I looked up at him from the sofa, the paper-
back still on my chest where it had dropped when I started snoozing.

"What's up, Brad?"

He shuffled his weight from one foot to the other.

"I've got to talk to you. Where's Mum?"

"She's doing a Reiki treatment … can it wait half an hour?"

"No. It's you I've got to talk to. Just you."

Without taking my eyes off him, I sat up.

Trying to sound conversational, but through clenched teeth, he said,
"Have a good day at the uni, did you?"

"It was okay …"

"Liar!"

"What's this about, Brad?"

"You're lying to us! Melissa works in Nero's. She said you spend hours
there every morning."

"Melissa?"

"My friend from middle school."

"Yes, I remember her."

"You obviously didn't recognise her, though. But she recognised you. Why
are you making a fool of us?"

"I'm not!" I knew I sounded defensive, just as Brad used to as a child.

"What's wrong with you? Is it reading that diary we found in the attic? Is
that what's upsetting you, making you act crazy? If it is, I'll burn it."

"You don't understand. It's the opposite. It's that diary that's keeping me
sane."

He peered at me through narrowed eyes. "Sane? You call this sane?"

"Look, Brad," I said. "The diary was written for my future self. I realise that
now. Did I foresee at that age that I would need it much later in life? At the
age I am now? I don't know. All I know is that I feel gratitude for that
teenager."

"Which teenager?"

"Me! Myself, when I was seventeen."

"I don't understand. Let me see it."

I considered that for a moment. "No, Brad. The diary was meant to be read
only by me. I can't let you see it. It's too honest, too brutal … too embarrass-
ing. Showing it to someone – even you – would be like a betrayal of the
person who wrote it."

"The person who wrote it? But … Dad, perhaps you'd better see someone."

"Like who?"

"I don't know. But in your job you must know people, someone who can
help you."

"The diary is helping. I couldn't have coped without it. It's like age
regression therapy – I don't know if you've heard of that?"

"Don't try to bullshit me!"

"It's like going back to that time when I was seventeen, when some horrible things happened, and reliving it."

He looked at me incredulously. "How the hell does that help?"

"I don't know."

"What do you mean, you don't know? You're a mental health tutor, for f – goodness' sake!"

"Yes, but you're not one of my students. You're my son. I'm not going to quote authors to you and give you abstract examples."

"Why not – if it'll help me understand what this is all about?"

"I don't know. It'd be like trying to distance myself from you."

"But what the hell's wrong with you?"

I hesitated a moment. "I've got problems at work."

"At work? It looks like you're hardly ever there!"

"The truth is, I'm *never* there." I tried to avoid his eyes. "I've been suspended, Brad. There's going to be a disciplinary hearing. I might lose my job."

He seemed to be struggling to take in what he was hearing. "But you'll get another one – won't you?"

"I'd have to if I lose my pension. But it would be difficult in teaching."

"But why? What have you done?"

"I don't want to talk about it now."

"Dad!" He sounded desperate. "What the hell is going on?"

"They've accused me of gross misconduct with a student."

"What does that mean, exactly?"

"It means – having relations with her."

"Sexual?"

I looked down and nodded.

"I can't believe it. How can they say that at your age? Even though I'm sure this sort of thing must happen sometimes. There are bound to be a few loose cannons amongst the students …"

"It's more than that. They've accused me of helping her to cheat in her exam. I didn't do that!"

He stared at me. "But you did have sex with her?"

"Yes – but I didn't help her to cheat."

"What's she like …?" He seemed to be struggling for something to say.

"She's just a student. From Nigeria."

"She's black?"

"Yes. What's that got to do with it?"

"Nothing. It's just that I'd have never imagined you and … Why did you choose a black woman?"

"I didn't choose her. She chose me."

"Huh! So you're saying it's her fault."

"I'm not saying that at all. It's just that, your mam and I, we don't …" I closed my eyes.

When I looked at Brad again, his usual arrogance had disappeared. He looked confused, stunned.

Hearing Fiona chatting with her client as she saw her out, neither of us said anything else.

Chapter 54

Below in my cabin, I took off my life-jacket and dropped it on the deck. Curled up on my bunk, my head pounded as I imagined water flooding in through the door, filling the cabin. I'd struggle to stay above it, my head at an unnatural angle against the deckhead as I sucked in the last few inches of air, until all I'd be sucking in would be water: a goldfish in a metal box.

My mind drifted back to Narvik, to Torruld's house with its warmth and love, the wood-burning stove, the icy wind that brushed the snow from the window ledges, to Marit.

I heard the bosun's voice. "What are you doing here? Why haven't you got your life-jacket on? The lifeboat's ready to be launched."

I looked up at him, my eyes stinging. "What chance have the lifeboats got in this storm?"

He stared down at the deck for a moment, wide-eyed. "Better than a sinking ship."

"That's not true. Tell me the truth!"

He looked down at the deck again. "Our chances of surviving in the lifeboat are little more than on the ship. But the *Albatross* can't stay afloat much longer. The hold is filling up. There's no more ballast to pump out."

At that moment the complete hopelessness of the situation rammed itself home and I started to cry. I felt the bunk dip as he sat down next to me, then felt his arm around my shoulders. This only made me sob more.

"Can't you do anything?" I must have sounded pitiful.

This was met with silence. Behind the bosun I saw a hooded figure standing in the doorway. It was Mitch. Shaking his head in disgust, he turned away.

The bosun had become very still, eyes turned upwards, thinking hard.

"Yes, there may be something," he said. "Owen, I won't let you die."

He got up, his eyes glistening. "But it's now or never."

Hurrying to my cabin door, he paused to pick up my life-jacket and tossed it to me. "Put this on."

I caught it as an automatic response, staring back at him.

"Now," he ordered. "And get up to the boat deck."

I was still on my bunk with the life-jacket in my hands when water came gushing in through the door. The end was near. I didn't really want to be on my own when it came. I slipped the life-jacket over my head and tied it with a double bow as I hurried along the waterlogged passageway.

On the boat deck, the mate was saying, "Sorry, bosun. I can't authorise you to go onto the main deck."

"But it's the only chance we've got," the bosun insisted.

"The old man was very specific about this. No one is to go onto the main deck. No human sacrifices."

"If that hatch isn't closed, we're all fish food."

"You wouldn't stand a snowball's chance of doing it, anyway."

The bosun looked angry. "Well, I'll tell you something, *mate* – I can try."

The strain in the mate's red-rimmed eyes showed as he stared back at him. "Okay, I'll see what he says."

He turned and went up to the bridge.

"We can't wait while they have a conference," said the bosun after a minute and started making his way down to the crew's accommodation deck.

"Oi, where are you going?" Dai called.

The bosun swung around and shouted, "First I'm going to lower the hatch wheels. Then I'm going to the fo'c'sle head to get the biggest block and tackle I can find. I'm going to rig it to the starboard side and pull the hatch straight. Then I'm going to attach a wire to the front of the hatch, run it to the windlass, and pull that blasted hatch closed."

"Oh, that's okay, then," said Dai. "I thought you were going to do something difficult."

"So if I don't make it back, you can tell the mate that's what I was trying to do."

Leaning on the rail, I watched the bosun continue down the starboard ladder onto the main deck, where the wind buffeted him. Water swirled around his feet.

"No, don't do it!" I shouted.

The bosun turned around and stared at me for a moment. Then, pointing at me but looking at Sidney, who was at my side, said, "Watch him. Don't let him do anything stupid."

Other men were now coming down to this deck to see what the bosun was doing. The bosun heard someone's footsteps coming down the metal ladder behind him and turned around to see Dai.

"Where do you think you're going?" he demanded.

"To help you."

"No, you're not. Go back. It's too dangerous."

"And it's not dangerous for a superhero like you, I suppose? What makes you think you can do it on your own?"

"I don't know if I can – but I'll die trying."

"Then I will too. Who'd miss a piss artist like me, anyway?"

"Go back, Dai. That's an order."

"I've never listened to you before, Jeremy. I'm sure as fuck not going to start now."

Over Dai's shoulder the bosun saw our anxious faces looking down at them. His eyes met mine and they softened. Then he turned and began to make his way along the exposed main deck, followed by Dai, both men struggling to stay upright with the erratic movement of the ship.

When they had got about halfway to the fo'c'sle, being careful to always be close to something secure to grab each time a wave came up and threatened to wash them overboard, we heard a crackling sound above our heads. Looking up, I saw the captain leaning over the wing of the bridge with a megaphone.

"You two men on the main deck," came his voice, distorted, "return aft immediately."

The mate appeared by the captain's side. They exchanged some words, then the captain pointed the megaphone at the main deck again. "Bosun, return aft and bring that other man with you. There's nothing you can do there." Electronic interference ... "putting your lives at risk."

Paddy gave an ironic laugh. "So the old man is after having a sense of humour after all."

The bosun and Dai turned their faces up at the bridge, cupping their hands behind their ears, as if trying to hear above the storm.

"I know you can hear me. This is gross insubordination. Return to your post on the boat deck at once." The captain was yelling now.

The bosun and Dai looked at each other again, shrugged, and carried on towards the bow of the ship.

A wave broke over the main deck and engulfed the two men. We caught our breath. The spray swept aft, blinding us for a moment. When it cleared, we could see the men below still holding on to the side of the stricken hatch.

Between the relentless wind and the seas crashing onto the deck, I thought they would never reach the fo'c'sle, but they did. They disappeared inside the fo'c'sle head and reappeared a few minutes later, both carrying a hatch wheel spanner. They began lowering the small cast iron wheels on the sides of the hatch, which stuck up into the air at an angle of some forty-five degrees, the bosun working on one side and Dai on the other.

"Oh, come on, Dai," Paddy murmured. "Just leave the ones you can't reach!"

Next Dai shackled the three-sheaved block to a metal post on the starboard side while the bosun tied the other end of it to a couple of the wheels. I became aware of the crowd of men around me, shoulder to shoulder, watching the drama unfolding on the main deck.

The bosun and Dai started heaving on the other end of the rope, which was soon as tight as a piano wire. Straining every muscle in their bodies, they carried on pulling the rope through the block, inch by inch.

The two wheels tore away from the hatch. We gasped as they flew towards the bosun and Dai. With the sudden release of pressure on the rope, the two men fell backwards onto the deck. Lucky they did, I realised, as the iron wheels whizzed past where they had been standing, one clanging against the post, the other continuing out over the turbulent sea.

The bosun got to his feet and went into the fo'c'sle head again, reappearing with another heavy rope hanging from his shoulder. He reeved it through the block and made it fast, then took the other end to the dislodged hatch.

"What's he trying to do now?" Paddy moaned. "Pull some more wheels off?"

"Looks like he's going to try to make the rope fast to the other side of the hatch," said Sidney as we watched the bosun scramble over to the port side. There he wound it around the corner of the hatch that was sticking out and made it fast.

"That's what you call seamanship," Sidney whistled in admiration. "It's as tight as a crepe bandage on a sprained ankle."

"Have we got time for all this?" asked Riley.

John gave him a sideways glance. "Why, you got a date with someone?"

"Keep it tight," the bosun yelled to Dai as he made his way back to the starboard side.

The bosun grabbed the rope behind Dai. "Heave!"

The rope tightened and strained. But there was no sign of the hatch moving. Dai was doubled up, his face red; the bosun was clenching his teeth. The rope splayed open – first one strand, then the next, then the third. They fell backwards onto the deck again as the rope parted.

"It's no use," said Paddy. "It's too heavy. We're fucked."

The two men on the main deck were visibly exhausted, especially the stocky Welshman. They dragged themselves to their feet, and the bosun stood beside Dai, saying something which we couldn't hear. Dai shook his head.

They went into the fo'c'sle head again. When they reappeared, a heavy block and tackle, just like the first one, hung from Dai's shoulders. He unshackled the block with the broken rope, letting it clang to the deck, and replaced it with the new one. The bosun again attached the end of the rope to the back of the hatch that jutted out towards the port side.

The bosun stared at the hatch, his brow furrowed in concentration. Then he was explaining something to Dai, gesticulating with his hands. They both held the rope tightly, one in front of the other, but they were not pulling.

"Why the hell are they just standing there like dummies?" asked Paddy.

"Because it's impossible," said Brian. "They know it as well as we do."

"We should abandon ship," cried Pussy. "If we don't go now, we're done for."

John's eyes narrowed. A wave came over, hiding the two men from our view. It receded to reveal the two men still standing there holding the rope.

After this happened several times, John breathed, "That's clever. That's bloody clever!"

My gaze turned from the windswept deck and rested on John.

"They're heaving only when a wave comes over and puts upward pressure on the hatch," he explained, even though he didn't seem to believe it himself. Then he laughed. "They're using the very thing that was causing us to sink to save us!"

"My God, it's moving!" shrieked Pussy, clutching his pink bag to his chest. "The horrid thing's straightening out!"

We watched in awe as the hatch descended, moved back to its proper position, the steel wheels clonking back onto their tracks. Dai made the line fast while the bosun dashed up to the fo'c'sle head. He switched the windlass on and put it in reverse, unwinding a greasy wire from its drum, which he passed down to Dai on the main deck. Dai attached the eye at the end of the wire to the ring bolt at the front of the hatch.

The wire groaned as the bosun put the windlass into forward gear and gradually increased the power. The hatch was dragged forward.

"Easy does it, Jeremy," Dai shouted. "That's the boy. If this wire breaks we won't have another chance."

We all knew this was true. Our lives depended on these two men. We held our breath. Now the only sounds were the sea, the wind and the occasional grinding of metal on metal as the hatch slowly covered the hold.

As the *Albatross's* bow pitched down, the hatch ran forward the last few feet. It closed with a thud.

"That's it!" yelled the bosun, slamming the brake on the windlass to keep the wire taut. "Let's raise those wheels, Dai, to make sure it doesn't move again."

We stared in disbelief as a wave crashed over the ship's side and ran harmlessly across the hatch. Pussy whooped with joy and threw his arms into the air, and we all started cheering and hugging each other.

Chapter 55

Brenda, the librarian, waddled up to me. Her shape always made me think of a juicy pear. "Holy moly, you look good, Owen," she exclaimed, linking her arm around mine. "Have you been working out?"

"Not really," I said. That was the first time we'd ever touched each other. It was warm and comforting. "So you're back from Canada?"

"Yes. I had a great time there, visiting my daughter. A sort of celebration after my divorce. I thoroughly recommend it."

"Divorce?"

She laughed. "Yes, that too."

She let go of my arm and left when Neville stepped out of the lift. For a second I didn't recognise him. He was wearing a suit and a tie, and although the collar of his shirt stuck out a little, he looked impressive.

As he signed me in at the security desk, the new guard looked at me through the corner of his eye. Under "Purpose of Visit", Neville wrote: "Union business".

We went up to the third floor in the lift and as we walked along the corridor, he said, "How are you feeling?"

"Don't ask."

His mouth moved into a sort of smile. "In that case you won't be pleased to hear the bad news."

"Bad news? Being here is bad news. What could be worse than this?"

"It's Professor Kemp," he said, stopping outside Room 308. "He's rung in sick with the flu."

"Oh, no!"

"Don't worry, he'll be all right if he stays in bed and takes plenty of fluids."

"That's not what I meant."

"I know. Just kidding. Anyway, Crawford is prepared to chair the hearing in his place."

Seeing the look of horror on my face, he went on, "But we can postpone it, if you like. Until Kemp is better."

"No, I couldn't go through this waiting again."

"It's okay with you, then – if Martin chairs?"

"No, that's out of the question."

Neville sighed. "Well, it has to be one way or the other."

"I don't know what to do."

"I know, it's the proverbial rock and hard place."

"How does saying that help?" I snapped.

"It's your choice, Owen. We can either adjourn or go ahead with Martin chairing."

I pressed my head between my hands as if to stop it from exploding. Then, breathing deeply, I said, "Okay, I've decided. We'll go ahead."

Neville turned to go. "I'll let Martin know."

"No, wait," I said. "No, we'll adjourn."

"Are you sure? Maybe Charity wouldn't be able to make it next time."

I sighed. "I suppose you're right. So we'd better go ahead now."

After a moment, he asked, "Final answer?"

I nodded. "Final answer."

He took a key out of his pocket and opened the door. "Remind me to take this back to Reception later."

I had ignored Neville's advice about wearing a suit and tie, turning up in jeans and a T-shirt. I thought that might make me feel more relaxed. But as the others arrived, all dressed up, I began to feel uncomfortable about being the odd one out. Even Charity, rushing in late, was wearing a smart trouser suit.

Karolina was the first to give evidence.

"You're not one of his personal students?" Martin asked her.

"No. I'm on a different branch – Maternity. Audrey is my personal tutor."

"So why was he offering to help you?"

"That's just what he's like."

"Was it for money?"

"No."

"Why, then?" Martin persisted.

"You can't expect her to know what was going on in my client's mind," said Neville.

When Martin ignored him, Karolina said, "He just wanted to be friendly, I suppose."

"Didn't he have enough friends on the Mental Health Branch?" Martin smiled at his own joke. "Could it have been because he wanted to have a relationship with you?"

She shrugged her shoulders. "Maybe. I don't know."

"A sexual relationship?"

"He never said anything like that."

Martin smirked. "But that was the impression you got?"

Karolina hesitated. She looked at Audrey and said, "I didn't expect to be asked questions like this."

Audrey looked down at her hands, clenched on the table in front of her.

"Can you think of any other reason he would offer his services to you?" Martin pressed on.

"No." She looked at Neville, as if appealing for his help, but I could see he couldn't do anything. "... I suppose he liked me."

Martin sat back and put his fingertips together in front of his chest. "But you didn't take up his offer?"

"No."

"Why not?"

Karolina shrugged again. "I don't know. In the end, I just didn't phone him."

"Oh?" Martin raised his eyebrows. "He gave you his phone number?"

"Only his mobile." She looked around at the rest of us and her eyes lingered on me for a moment. "I have to say I've always found him to be a gentleman. He is one of the best teachers here – if not *the* best."

"Be that as it may," said Martin. "We are not here to discuss his merits as a teacher. What we want to know about is his proposal to you."

With the tone he used, he might just as well have said "*indecent* proposal", I thought.

"I was leaving the classroom after a teaching session," said Audrey, "when I overheard this student – Princess – complaining to another student about her personal tutor."

"What did she say?" asked Martin.

"She said, 'He would have looked at my essay if my name was Shola'. So I spoke to her on her own. She told me that Mr Roberts was always willing to look at her friend Shola's work and that … that she'd been to his house to make sure she'd pass her final exam."

Martin nodded. "And how would that work?"

"She said it was just a matter of him telling her the correct answers and her filling in the blanks she'd left in her exam booklet."

"So she was saying that he had conspired to help her cheat in her final exam paper?" Martin clarified.

Audrey glanced around at the others present, but avoided eye contact with me. "Yes."

"That sounds straightforward enough," said Martin, sitting back. "Sunita, do you have any questions?"

"Just a couple," she said. "First of all, Audrey, what evidence is there that this student actually went to Mr Roberts's house?"

"Shola described the layout and the contents of it to Princess."

"And how could you be sure that this was accurate?"

"Because I've been there myself." She added quickly, "For professional reasons."

"I see. And what motive do you believe Mr Roberts might have had for giving the student this illicit help?"

"You already know that," Audrey retorted. "That's what this hearing is all about."

"Just answer the question, please," said Sunita.

"For sex." Audrey placed one hand on top of the other on her lap. "She told Princess it was for sex."

"This is hearsay," Neville objected, but not as strongly as I would have liked. "This is all hearsay."

"Not if it's collaborated by Princess and Shola, who'll be giving evidence later," Martin pointed out.

Sunita gave me a sideways glance. "I have no further questions."

"Charity, do you have any questions?" asked Martin.

Charity looked at me as if trying to figure out what she could ask that might help me. In the end, she shook her head. "No."

"Very well." He turned to Neville. "Would you like to cross-examine, Mr McEmery?"

"Yes, I would. Audrey, you say you've been to Mr Roberts's house?"

"Yes. A couple of years ago."

"Would you say it is possible, then, that others from the university might have also gone there for legitimate reasons?"

"I suppose so."

"So it is possible that Shola might have heard details about his house from someone else?"

"It's possible." She almost laughed as she added, "But not very likely."

"I'm not sure where you're going with this," Martin came in. "Mr Roberts doesn't deny entertaining the student at his home."

I wasn't sure either. Neville was grasping at straws.

"I'm just trying to establish the facts," he mumbled.

"Very well," said Martin. "You may continue."

"Thank you, Mr Chairman," said Neville. "I have no further questions."

"Yes," Shola said. "I did go to his house."

"With the intention of cheating?" said Martin.

"No."

"Why, then?"

"In case I failed again. For him to show me how I could do better next time."

"That's not what you told me!" shouted Princess.

"Shut up your mouth, girl!" Shola shouted back across the table. "You're only jealous!"

"Me? Jealous of you?"

"Yes, you! Don't think I didn't know how you felt."

"Order." Martin rapped the table with his knuckles. "You will not squabble during this hearing!"

What did Shola mean by that? I wondered. There had been something in Princess's eyes when she looked at me when she first came in. I couldn't identify what it was … anger, disappointment …?

"Couldn't he have seen you at the university?" Martin was saying.

"No," Shola replied. "He was too busy here."

"You knew he had the exam booklets at home to be marked?"

Shola appeared to calculate for a moment before saying, "Yes, I knew. But it was only in case I had to take the exam again."

"Again?" Martin feigned confusion. "But I understand this was your fourth attempt?"

She nodded. "Yes."

"So there wouldn't have been a next time, would there?"

"Unless there were mitigating circumstances," said Shola.

"And were there?"

"Not that I'm aware of …" Shola's words petered out as she realised the absurdity of what she was saying.

"But surely," Martin gave a cynical laugh, "mitigating circumstances can't suddenly appear *after* an exam, can they?"

"Sometimes you think of something afterwards," she murmured.

I realised Martin's question must have been rhetorical as he went on, "Therefore there were none, which means there would have been no further attempt. So that cannot have been the reason you went to Mr Roberts's house."

"You were only using him to help you cheat!" yelled Princess. "You're disgusting!"

Shola leapt to her feet. She leaned across the table, eyebrows knitted together, red-varnished fingernails extended, teeth flashing. "You're only saying that because you fancy him, you horny bitch!" she snarled. "But you won't get away with it. I'll put the evil eye on you!"

Princess pulled back in her chair, eyes open wide, mouth gaping open.

"Sit down, Sheila," Martin told Shola, turning another page of the folder in front of him.

Next Martin turned to Princess. "I can see this is difficult for you, but we need to ask you a few questions."

"What I told Audrey was true." She was now sobbing behind the hands that covered her face. "Every word of it, so help me God. It's Shola who lies."

After encouraging Princess to repeat what Audrey had told her, he said, "I don't think we need to distress this witness with any more questions." He turned to Sunita, who shook her head, and Charity, who did the same.

Neville said, "I have a few, if I may."

I felt sure Martin would have refused him if he thought he could have got away with it, but after a moment's consideration, he said, "If you must, Mr McEmery."

"Princess, did Shola ever tell you that Mr Roberts helped her to cheat?"

"Not in so many words."

"So, in how many words?"

"She went to his house to fill in the blanks in her answer book." Princess's fingers were curled into fists, her mouth turned down. "She gave him what he wanted. And then she passed."

"So from that you concluded that he had given her the answers?" asked Neville.

Princess looked at Martin, avoiding Shola's eyes. "It's logical, isn't it?"

Martin nodded agreement.

Neville paused for effect, then said, "Just one more question. You say that Mr Roberts was giving a lot of extra help to Shola?"

"Yes. And it wasn't fair!"

"Is it not surprising, then, that she went on to pass the exam?"

Princess was silent for a moment. Then she blurted out, "She cheated! I know she did!"

Sunita put her hand on Princess's arm. At first this appeared to be a gesture of sympathy, but as she patted it I felt it was more a sign of Sunita's impatience. The student gradually became quiet.

Martin turned his eyes to me. "Now, Mr Roberts, we would like to hear your version of what took place between this student and you."

I could see he was enjoying this. It was as if the witnesses had been appetizers and I was the *piece de resistance*. He touched the knot of his tie as if he were adjusting a serviette in anticipation. "I see from your statement that you do not deny sexually abusing her."

"I object!" said Neville.

"It's here in black and white." Martin pointed to the document on the desk in front of him. "Haven't you read it?"

"Yes, I've read it. He admits that sexual contact did take place, but not that he abused her."

"But given the power imbalance between the two ..." Instead of finishing the sentence, Martin waved his hand dismissively. "Anyway, I don't want to waste time on semantics. The only reason we are here is to establish the truth."

The room was hot. For confidentiality, the door was closed, although the windows had been pulled up as far as they would go, which was about ten inches. The fan on a small table was inadequate. Even so, I seemed to be the only one sweating.

"Now, Mr Roberts, please enlighten us on how this ..." Martin paused as if searching for the right word, "... *situation* between you and this student came about."

Everyone was looking at me. Heart pounding, I covered my mouth with my hand, trying to hide my scar.

"Today would be good," said Martin, drilling me with his eyes.

I cleared my throat. I might have been able to cope with specific questions, I thought. I remembered the dream about having my foot caught in the railway line and not being able to shout for help. This was worse, far worse. I cleared my throat again. Then I coughed. And coughed and coughed. I seemed to be drowning in my own phlegm.

"Oh, my God," Martin drawled. "I hope someone here is up-to-date with CPR."

Through bleary eyes, I saw Charity put her hand up. Crawford glared at her.

Neville handed me some tissues and as I dried my eyes and nose, he said, "Mr Chairman, could we have a brief recess?"

"What for?" queried Martin.

"As you can see, my client is experiencing some difficulty. This is very stressful for him."

"He should have thought of that before," Martin muttered under his breath.

"Pardon?" Neville reacted.

Before Martin could answer, Sunita leaned towards him and said, "Perhaps we should adjourn until tomorrow."

"Why?" asked Martin, irritated.

"It's getting late," she reasoned. "And we must be seen to do everything we can to give him a fair hearing."

"I agree!" enthused Charity.

Martin gave her a cautionary glance. Then he looked at his wristwatch.

"Very well. Ten o'clock tomorrow? Anyone have a problem with that?"

"It's okay with me," confirmed Neville.

"I'm interviewing," said Sunita. "But I can get someone to cover."

"I'm teaching," said Charity.

"Give them self-directed study," Martin snapped. "Okay, until ten sharp tomorrow."

My legs were shaking as I went up the stairs to the toilet on the next floor. There I vomited the little that was in my stomach. When I came out, still drying my mouth with a paper towel, Neville was waiting for me.

"Let's go and sit down somewhere," he said.

"No. I'm going home."

"We need to talk first. We need a strategy for tomorrow. You can't just sit there with your thumb up your arse."

"It's no use. I can't face them. Anyway, the result is obvious."

"No, it's not. Those two students are fighting like cat and dog. God knows which one will be believed in the end."

"Martin will make sure it's Princess."

Neville thought for a moment before saying, "Looks like it was a mistake going ahead with Martin. But we can appeal against the way he's chairing the hearing."

"What would happen then?" I asked.

"There'd be another hearing, with a different chairman. I'd try to get Kemp."

"I couldn't go through this again." My voice was steady and decisive as I added, "I know what I have to do." I touched Neville's arm. "I'm sorry. You did everything you could."

He stood there watching me walk away, my file under his arm.

"Owen," he called just before I turned the corner. "I'll be here at nine tomorrow morning."

Without looking back, I raised my arm to show I'd heard him.

Wencheng was waiting for the lift, briefcase in his right hand and a light jacket over his arm. He saw me before I could turn and go down the stairs, so I carried on until I was standing next to him. He looked surprised to see me.

"Hearing's finished already?" he asked.

I shook my head.

"Adjourned?"

I nodded. "Till tomorrow morning."

He studied my face for a moment before asking, "How's it going?"

"Well, I'd say the *superior man* is well pissed off." I was shocked by my angry tone as I referred to the recent I Ching reading.

But Wencheng didn't react to the attack. He just pursed his lips. I knew my anger was misdirected, aimed at the person who least deserved it – perhaps because I knew he could take it. I touched his arm and said, "Sorry. I just want to get home and be on my own."

"How are you going?"

"Underground."

"No way. I'm not leaving the *superior man* travel in the underground in such a state. I'll give him a lift home."

"No, no. It's miles out of your way."

I hardly spoke at all during the journey in his car. At first he tried to get me to talk, but in the end he gave up and he was silent as well. From time to time I rocked forward and back, resisting the temptation to moan. More than once, I saw him shooting me a sideways glance.

When he pulled up outside my house, he said, "I'll come in with you."

"No. There's no need."

He didn't look convinced. "Will Fiona be in?"

"I suppose so."

As I got out of the car, he said, "I'll see you tomorrow. Before the hearing."

I hesitated, then went around to his side, resting my hands on the open window. "Thank you, Wencheng. For everything you've done for me over the years."

He put his hand on my arm. "Owen, let me come in with you."

I shook my head and tried a smile, but I knew it was twisted and grotesque. "It's okay."

Fiona met me in the hall, coming out of the kitchen. "I've been trying to get in touch with you, Why don't you answer your mobile?"

I took my mobile out of my pocket to give me time to think. "I was in the library. Must have forgotten to take it off silent."

She looked doubtful. "I've got some bad news for you, Owen ... Roger called ..."

I knew what she was going to tell me, and my legs went weak.

"When did it happen?"

"At 2.15 this afternoon. Roger said it was very sudden in the end. I'm so sorry."

"Oh, no." I shut my eyes tight to keep back the tears. "Why couldn't it have been me?"

Panic showed in Fiona's eyes for a moment. "I know you're upset, Owen, but ..."

She carried on speaking, but I wasn't listening. I was already rushing upstairs.

The attic ladder screeched as I yanked it down. The aluminium steps seemed to shake and squeak more than ever as I climbed up. With trembling hands, I untied the rope with the hangman's noose from the beam.

Chapter 56

I left the jubilant men and crossed over to the port side, waiting at the top of the ladder for the bosun. Mitch lit a cigarette as he came and stood beside me, dropping the lighted match on the waterlogged wooden deck. The bosun was lowering the last few wheels on the port side of the hatch before coming up from the main deck. Mitch held onto the rails to steady himself against a steep roll of the *Albatross*. What did he want? Was he going to apologise?

"Looks like we might make it after all," he said, as he watched the water wash safely over the newly closed hatch. "Incredible what a queer and an alcoholic can do between them."

"You bastard!" My anger was even stronger than my fear of him. "They risked their lives for you."

He laughed. "Their lives? What are *their* lives worth?"

"A thousand times more than yours!"

"You reckon?" He exhaled a plume of white smoke. "You know what I was thinking about as we were waiting to abandon ship? About that girl in Narvik. About her being my last fuck – in this life, anyway. And I was so glad that I'd made the most of it. A genuine blonde, too. Matching collar and cuffs. I actually got a semi-hard on thinking about her. Imagine that! Up there on the boat deck. Freezing cold, half-soaked, both hands on that icy steel handle ready to wind the lifeboat out, and I get a semi. I promised there and then that if by some miracle we survived, I'd go back to see her again. But don't worry," he put his gloved hand on my arm, "I'll give her one for you."

I jerked my arm away and pushed his chest. He went back a step, laughing. "What's up, pansy? What do you care now, anyway – now you've found true love with the bosun?"

His eyes shone with amused curiosity as I took my right glove off and dropped it onto the deck. Perhaps he thought I was going to take him by the collar and threaten him. He certainly didn't expect me to grab the gold medallion that was hanging outside his white Fairisle jumper, just visible under his donkey jacket. The chain broke open as I yanked it from his neck.

Now deadly serious, he put out his hand. "Give me that, son."

I took a couple of steps backwards. My hand was puny and blue with cold. But I held in it the thing Mitch treasured most.

"Come on, give it to me. This isn't funny anymore."

My fist tightened on his dead father's medallion, the chain dangling down. I looked at the sea behind me. He knew what I was thinking.

"Don't do anything silly," he warned.

"Why not? There's nothing else you can do to me now."

He lunged forward as I raised my hand behind my ear to throw his precious possession. "No!" he shouted.

I turned and threw it as hard as I could. It didn't quite clear the ship, falling onto the main deck below. Mitch drew back an enormous fist and aimed it at my face. He stopped, calculating. Then he turned and rushed down the ladder to the main deck. The bosun looked at him as if he were crazy as he got onto his knees on the deck.

A wave exploded over the starboard side, sending a wall of water racing towards them. They were both swept to the port side rails. Having nothing to hold on to, they instinctively grabbed each other. The bosun managed to jam himself against the ship's rail, but Mitch went over the top of it. As the *Albatross* rolled back to starboard, I saw Mitch hanging over the side with the bosun holding his arms.

"Help me!" Mitch yelled.

The bosun started pulling him up, his face contorting with the strain, while Mitch struggled to get a foothold on the watery side of the ship. Mitch's jacket splayed open. From under his torn shirt hung a bloodied bandage. Their eyes met.

Then the bosun looked at me. "It was him, wasn't it?"

I stared back in horror.

"Wasn't it?" he roared.

I shouted, "Yes, it was him!"

Mitch made a noise like a pig being slaughtered. The strain on the bosun's face increased by the second. A thick vein was now visible in his neck.

The bosun turned his glistening, tormented face to me again. "What shall I do?"

"Just let him go," I gasped, fighting back the tears.

The bosun continued to stare at me for a moment. Then he looked down at Mitch and said something between clenched teeth. The *Albatross* was rolling back to starboard, revealing a huge expanse of its side beneath Mitch, who tried frantically to propel himself up the sloping hull. But the side of the ship was smooth and slippery. His legs spun like a hamster's on a wheel. He tried to grab the rail, missing it by inches.

The bosun's face set like stone as he said something else to Mitch. I couldn't hear what it was above the roar of the sea. Then he let go of Mitch's other arm. Mitch screamed as he slid down the hull to the water far below, arms still reaching upwards. His face turned to me as it bounced off a jagged metal plate, and I saw the red gash it left. As the *Albatross* rolled back to port, there was no longer any sign of him.

Chapter 57

Stuffing the rope into a plastic bag, I returned to the top of the ladder. Through the opening, I saw Fiona's upturned face peering into the attic, brow furrowed. I tried to go down the ladder less frantically than I had gone up it. As I pushed the ladder back up with the pole, there was a hysterical edge to her voice as she demanded, "What are you doing?"

"Nothing. I have to go out."

"What's that?" she asked, pointing at the bag.

"What, this? This is – nothing." I turned and hurried down the stairs.

Just before I slammed the front door after me she leaned over the banister and cried, "Owen!"

Although I was trying to stay calm, I over accelerated when leaving the drive, sending the wheels into a spin. I needlessly stopped and waited at a red light. Getting out of the car in Old Redding, I paused to press the button on my keyring to lock the door. Why? I wondered, shaking my head.

A middle-aged woman with hair the colour and consistency of straw, who was loading a collie into the back of her estate car, looked at me suspiciously. A man in this woodland without a dog or a partner was always suspect.

As I hurried along the path between the trees, avoiding the exposed roots that crossed it like varicose veins. I left the ridge of clay and pebbles, picking my way through twisted rhododendrons with their colourful flowers. And then I was standing in front of it. The hidden oak. Just as I had three weeks earlier, when I first found it.

I took out the rope and let the bag fall to the ground. "That's litter", I imagined Fiona saying. "You should take it home with you".

"Oh, shut up," I said out loud. "I'm never going home again."

Separating the coil into two, I bowled the part with the noose over a horizontal branch about ten feet from the ground, just as I had practised bowling a heaving line from the fo'c'sle of the *Albatross* on the way to Norway. But this time there was no bosun to smile and give me the thumbs-up. I tied the other end to a lower branch with a simple clove hitch.

It's much quicker if you break your neck in the fall. Strange how everyone knows that morbid fact. So I would let myself drop from that higher branch with the noose around my neck. This was one time when that weight I had lost would have been useful. But how could I prevent the instinctive grabbing at the rope to protect my neck? If only I could have tied my hands behind my back.

As I climbed up, I wondered what would happen to my dead body. How long would it hang here before being discovered? Was it true that the first thing the crows eat are your eyes? Who would eventually find me? Not that it would be me by then. Would it be someone curious about the stench and the flies? Or illicit lovers? Or children playing hide and seek?

I paused and looked up at the waiting noose. Don't pause too much, I told myself. I had to act quickly, before I lost my nerve and failed, just as I'd failed in everything else. Try not to think, I told myself – try not to remember. Memories of Marit, Mitch and everyone else to do with the *Albatross* had lain dormant for so many years. All I had to do was suppress them for the last few minutes of my life. Then they would be gone forever, together with all my present day problems. But now the pale blue sky behind the rope and the stillness reminded me of that morning after the storm in January 1967.

Chapter 58

As the white disk to port gradually separated from the horizon, the storm-damaged main deck became visible. I could now see the buckled hatch with two wheels missing and others out of kilter. The parted wire snaking across the deck. A stay hanging uselessly beside the mast. Puffy white clouds on a pale blue background. There was no need for a lookout now.

"Okay, you can stand down," the mate called from the port wing of the bridge. "Come and take this to the officers' dining room."

Leaning over the rail of the monkey island, I saw his bearded face turned up towards me, a stainless steel bucket in his hand.

When I joined him he was kneeling down pouring a clear liquid into the bucket. "Rainwater," he said proudly. "Some heathens use water from the storage tank to dilute rum, but there's nothing like pure rainwater from above the sea. The old man really appreciates it in his whisky."

The image of Callum drinking the captain's best whisky flashed through my mind.

"Why do you add water, anyway?" I asked.

"This rum is over-proof, which means it would blow your head off. We add two parts water to one-part rum. And it's still strong."

I gazed at the red-brown liquid creeping up and smelled the heady aroma.

With a naughty glint in his eye, the mate asked, "Do you know what they call this container in the Royal Navy?"

I shrugged. "A bucket?"

He laughed. "No, it's called a rum fanny."

While I pondered on this quaint term, the mate put the half-empty bottle down on the deck and replaced the steel lid on the container. "Okay," he said, "take the fanny along to our dining room for tots-up at ten hundred hours."

"The officers' dining room?" I questioned, thinking I must have misunderstood him.

"Yes. This is a very special occasion. The captain will be addressing the ship's company."

The second mate had strolled out of the wheelhouse onto the wing. He snorted. "It's a bit rich that we have to have the crew trampling all over our dining room."

It was almost reassuring that he'd returned to his arrogant self.

"Were it not for certain members of the crew we wouldn't still have a dining room," said the mate.

"Yes," Stratton conceded. "I suppose it is a small price to pay."

It was the first time I'd ever been in the officers' dining room. No wonder they called ours the messroom. Here the deck was carpeted and there were high-backed, padded wooden chairs. Brian and Larry were moving the tables and chairs to the sides to allow standing room for everyone.

"Just leave the fanny there," said Osborne, indicating a table with a lot of glasses on it.

The dining room was full when I returned at 10 o'clock, after having a shower. I guessed about thirty of us were there. Looking around, I asked, "What about Kirk?"

"Still in sick-bay," said Osborne. "His leg is in a bad way."

Standing on a makeshift platform and reading from a few sheets of paper, Frazer recounted the events of the day before, which now, as we cut our way south through a milky calm sea, seemed incredible.

"I commend you all for your courage," he went on, "especially the two men who," he cleared his throat, "who, even though they disobeyed my orders, were responsible for saving the *Albatross*. Bosun Jeremy Doyle and able-bodied seaman David Jones. We owe them our deepest gratitude. Tragically, able-bodied seaman Colin Mitchell died in the storm, despite the bosun's valiant attempt to save him."

The bosun's eyes met mine. I looked away.

"Let us observe a minute's silence to show our respect to the man we sadly lost," said Frazer, looking down.

During that minute, every little sound was amplified. The subdued cough of someone at the other side of the room. Someone's stomach rumbling. The faint creaking of the ship as she rolled gently.

Then Frazer was speaking again. "You might have noticed that we are very low in the water. Our original intention was to pump the water out of number 2 hold, although that would have been difficult as it is mixed with the iron ore."

"A bloody nightmare that would've been," Ivor blurted out. "The pump being stopped and de-gunged every five bloody minutes."

Frazer smiled. "Thank you for that impartial assessment. Also it would have meant dumping hundreds of tons of valuable cargo. So we decided that as long as the weather stays as it is now we can make it to the UK with the extra weight. We are going to Swansea, where the ship will be checked and repaired in dry dock …"

Riley, who was staring straight ahead as if in a trance, said quietly, "I'll have to go home and tell my wife about my VD."

John laughed under his breath, shaking his head. "Some people are never satisfied."

Larry and Brian, in their white uniforms, had begun taking the tots of rum around on trays, starting at different ends of the room.

Paddy raised his glass and said, "Down the hatch!"

"I just hope the skipper doesn't intend celebrating with his best whisky," Callum whispered in my ear. "Osborne would kill me!"

As we were leaving, Paddy, who was already carrying a glass of rum, took another off Larry's tray. "This one's for Kirk," he said, his words slightly slurred.

"If Kirk getth half the rum people claim they're taking for him he really will be legleth," said Larry.

Osborne glared at him. "That's sick."

"Thorry, Chief."

Osborne took a swig of rum without taking his eyes off Larry, then added, "Bloody funny, though."

The bosun was going down the ladder to the starboard boat deck in front of me. He turned and smiled. "You'll be able to spend some time at home while we're in dry dock."

"I'm signing off," I said.

"Oh. Well, don't leave it too long before you sign on another ship, other-wise you never will."

I looked at him quizzically.

"You need to get straight back on the bucking horse," he explained.

I looked at the deep scratches on the lifeboat. The buckled rail around it. The dark stain on the wooden deck where Kirk had almost bled to death. The cracked porthole on the housing.

"What a mess," I breathed. "Just like my life."

"Nothing that can't be put right." The bosun caught my arm. "Come with me, Owen. Let's get on a ship going south and enjoy some good weather – now this is all over."

I pulled my arm away. "It's not over for me. It'll never be over for me."

"I can understand you feeling guilty about Mitch. Even after what he did. So do I. But it will soon pass. It's like when you stamp on a cockroach –"

"I can't believe you killed him," I interrupted.

"But it's what you wanted. You said to let him go."

"I didn't! That's not what I meant. I meant just let him go ... to not do anything to him, to let him go."

The bosun seemed to be struggling to understand. "Derek Bentley," he murmured.

"Who?"

"The bloke who said to his friend, 'Let him have it'. He claimed he meant give the gun to the copper, but his friend thought he meant to shoot him. Bentley was hanged for it. Perhaps it was a misunderstanding after all."

"I heard about that. But ...?"

"Don't you see? I thought you meant for me to physically let go of him."

I could hardly speak with rage and frustration. "You thought I wanted you to murder him?"

"It wasn't murder."

"It was Bentley they hanged," I said, the terrible significance becoming clear to me. "Not the one who pulled the trigger, but the one who told him to do it."

The bosun almost smiled. "No one is going to hang you."

I turned to him with narrowed eyes.

"He was an animal," he went on. "He had no right to live."

"Who are you to say that?" I demanded.

"What's done is done!" he shouted, his eyes wild. "I'll throw flowers on his grave next time I pass this way! Will that make you feel better?"

I recoiled at the force of his voice. He stepped forward and embraced me. "I'm so sorry, Owen."

I knew he meant for intimidating me, not for killing Mitch.

Chapter 59

As I reached up for the noose, my hand moved in slow motion. Like when I used to try to catch the budgie to put it back into its cage. Blue and white it was, with pin-hole nostrils in a calcified beak. It was long gone. Like so many people – parents, friends, teachers, lovers, and now even Gwen. It just went to show that dying was easy; it was living that was horrific.

Now I would go with Gwen. Not that I believed in survival after death or that I would be with her or any of that nonsense, but I would die on the same day as her. I remembered climbing the apple tree in our garden with a bowl to pick apples for her to make an apple pie for us. I couldn't recall how old she was then, but she was wearing high heels. She stood under the tree, looking up and directing me.

"That one," she'd said, pointing. "That big one."

"I can't reach it."

"You can if you try. You can reach anything if you try. Just be careful."

And that was what I was doing, reaching for the noose, when I heard a rustling in the undergrowth behind me. Turning to look, I lost my balance. I was falling backwards, again in slow motion. My hand went out to grab a branch, but there wasn't enough time. There would have been when I was a boy, in that apple tree, but not now. I crashed down to the ground. Bright lights exploded in my skull.

When my eyes gradually opened, they took time to focus. Seeing the towering tree above me, I realised I was lying on my back. The noose, silhouetted by the sun, was black. Although my head was throbbing with pain, my one thought was to get up and try again. This time I wouldn't let anything distract me. I'd be as blinkered as a pit pony. After all, I had finished with this world and everything in it.

As I raised myself onto one elbow, I heard the rustling again. It was only a blackbird foraging amongst the dry leaves. But behind it, partly hidden by a rhododendron, was something else. I screwed my eyes up to see more clearly. It was a human form. As the foliage parted, I saw the bosun of the *Albatross* peering out at me. But it wasn't possible. He was out of place – and time. It couldn't really be him because he looked exactly the same as he did back then, nearly forty years before. He was even wearing the same T-shirt and jeans. His forehead creased with concern, he came and knelt down beside me, cradling my head in his arms. He soothed both my body and my mind. *That* was real.

My eyes hurt as I looked up at him. "You should have let me die then, on the ship," I said.

He smiled and shook his head. "I didn't let you die then. I won't let you die now."

Chapter 60

The deep pink flowers on the cherry tree appeared more beautiful than ever as I pulled into my drive. An attractive middle-aged woman opened the front door. Everything seemed so bright and colourful. *Is this what Wencheng calls enlightenment?* I wondered, and smiled to myself. I sat in the car gazing at Fiona, as if seeing her for the first time. Her face was tense with anxiety. She stepped over to the car and yanked the door open.

"Where have you been?" she demanded.

"Old Redding," I said as I got out, holding the plastic bag.

"All this time? You've been out for hours." Her voice was higher than usual. As I passed her to go into the house, she grabbed the bag from my hand. "What *is* this?"

She pulled out the rope. When she saw the sinister knot, she dropped it with a gasp, as if it were a snake. "Oh, my God! What are you doing?"

"Nothing." I could hear the weariness in my voice. "Not now."

As she followed me into the sitting room, she screamed, "You're bleeding!" I put my hand to the back of my head and felt the matted, dry blood.

"Red and white," I said. "The Welsh colours,"

"If you think that's funny, I don't! I've been worried sick."

"*You* – worried about *me*?"

"No, not about you. Worried that you'd do something else to shame the family."

I let myself drop onto the sofa. The patio door's curtain moved slightly in the breeze. She perched on the edge of the armchair opposite me.

"*Something else*?" I echoed her words.

Her eyes narrowed as she hissed, "I know what you've been doing."

"How did you ...?"

"It was the way you left, in such a state. Then you were out so long, with your mobile ringing upstairs. I was so frightened. I didn't know whether to call the police or Bradley. I called Bradley."

"So Brad told you?"

"He didn't want to at first."

I nodded. "He's always been loyal."

"Loyal!" She laughed bitterly. "He said he didn't want to do your dirty work for you. He told me about that woman. I wasn't surprised. I know what you're like. *Everyone* knows what you're like."

I clenched my jaw and closed my eyes for a moment.

"So what happened to you while you were running around like Albert Pierrepoint today? Why are you in such a mess?"

If it weren't for the intense anger directed at me, I wouldn't have been able to keep my eyes open. I tried to figure out a way of telling her what had happened in the woodland without sounding crazy. But I was also tired of deceiving her. So I just told her the truth. With complete honesty, with no embellishment or omissions – in the same way as I wrote that diary in the sixties. She listened. The first time she had listened to me in years.

When I finished she said, "Haven't you humiliated us enough already? What would people have said about us if you'd succeeded in killing your-self?"

I turned my head and stared at her. "Is that what you're concerned about? What people would say?"

"Well, we're the ones who'd have to live with it." She buried her head in her hands and began to sob. "And you and that woman. Sooner or later everyone will know about it. It looks so bad for me."

"Why should it look bad for you?"

"What's wrong with you? Are you stupid? Don't you know what people will say?"

"What? That I wasn't getting it at home?"

"Oh, you got it at home all right. But not off your wife!"

"I haven't got a wife."

Her head came up and she glared at me through her tears. She picked up the remote control from the coffee table and threw it at me. I brought my hand up to deflect it, but it missed me and clattered on the parquet floor behind me – in several pieces, by the sound of it.

She leapt up and, with a stifled cry, rushed out of the room. I heard the tap running and her spluttering and coughing in the kitchen. All I wanted was to go to bed, but I felt too weak to walk up the stairs. I was lifting myself off the sofa when she appeared in the doorway, her eyes red-rimmed and her hair sticking out as if she'd been pulling it.

"Who was she?" she demanded.

I sat back down and stared at her.

"I have the right to know!" she insisted.

"But what do you want to know?"

She faltered, not knowing what to say. "Was she a student?"

"Yes."

"How old was she?"

"In her thirties."

"Don't you know exactly?"

"She was thirty-six."

"What was she like? Was she pretty?"

"No."

"Don't lie to me, Owen." The threat couldn't have sounded more menacing if she'd brought a knife from the kitchen.

"I don't know. It's a matter of opinion. I suppose she was attractive, in a way."

"Did you have sex with her?"

I hesitated. That was enough of an answer for her. "Where did you do it?"

"Where?"

"Yes, where? What is this? You don't understand English anymore? Where? In your bed? In mine? In the dining room? In this room?"

"In this room."

"Where, exactly?"

"Where?"

"On the floor, on the sofa, against the wall – where?"

"On the sofa," I mumbled.

Her eyes swept the length of the sofa, with an expression of disgust on her face, as if she could see us lying there,

"No, it wasn't like that," I said.

"Like what?"

"Like you imagine it. It was a fiasco."

"I want the truth!"

I massaged my temples. "Can we talk about it later? I need to rest."

She clenched her fists and took a step towards me. "I wish you *had* killed yourself!"

She turned and went to the door. Before slamming it after her, she yelled, "I never want to see your horrible face again!"

I heard her running up the stairs. Then there was silence. I imagined she was lying on her bed, crying. My eyelids were heavy. It was only when I heard her moving about above me – in my bedroom – that I realised I'd been sleeping.

I became aware of Fiona standing in the doorway looking at me. She had combed her hair. I expected more anger, more insults, but her voice was soft as she said, "I should take you to A&E to be checked out. After banging your head and losing consciousness ..."

"No, no. I just need to lie down for a while. I'm so tired."

"That's why you need to be checked out. *You* know that better than I do."

She sat on the armchair and took a tissue from the box on the coffee table.

"I'm sorry about what I said. Thank God you didn't ..." She dabbed her eyes with the tissue.

"It was the sight of the bosun, and what he said, that stopped me." I was struggling to understand it myself. "It was my imagination, of course."

"You think so?"

"Yes. He's probably not alive anymore. If he is, he'll be in his eighties. Anyway, he looked just like he did in 1967, so it was impossible."

"It was your guardian angel."

I shook my head. "You know I don't believe in that sort of thing."

"Guardian angels tend to present themselves in forms we are familiar with."

"No, it was just a hallucination."

"Do you really think that's more plausible than my explanation?"

Without warning, she buried her head in her hands and cried, making a sort of moaning sound. I reached out to touch her arm, but stopped myself just in time.

"Okay," she said, taking another tissue from the box. She dabbed her eyes one last time, then sat up straight. "I'm okay now. I've laid out your clothes for tomorrow – your dark blue suit, white shirt, the tie you like."

"Oh, yes," I said. "The hearing."

"You forgot?"

I nodded.

"Isn't it important to you?"

"It is important. But so are other things. I realise that now."

I eased myself to my feet and made my way to the door.

"Owen," she said, "If things go badly, you can always make a new start."

Turning to look at her, I said, "At my age?"

She tried to smile. "If not teaching, you could go back to the wards."

The clothes were immaculate on the wooden chair beside my bed, shiny black shoes on the floor in front of them. As I undressed, I noticed Fiona's dressing gown hanging behind the door. The room smelled different, too. Of perfume. *Chanel No. 5.* Too tired to do anything else with my dirty clothes, I rolled them into a ball, like the long-stay psychiatric patients in the big asylums used to do. I opened the second wardrobe to throw them in. Instead of the usual pile of obsolete computer accessories, files and books, Fiona's clothes were there.

"I put your rubbish in the spare room," she said, leaning against the doorway.

"The spare room?" I murmured. "You mean your room?"

She folded her arms. "I know what I mean."

Too weary to try to figure it out, I pulled back the quilt to get into bed. The quilt was tucked in, not just thrown over the bed, as I normally left it, and the linen had been changed. *Things are not as I had left them,* I thought, as I closed my eyes ...

It is summer in Narvik. Mount Fagernes is now green instead of white. As the *Albatross* comes alongside, Marit and Torruld are waiting for me on the quay, waving. I run down the gangway to them. I kiss and cuddle them.

"You came back," says Marit. Although she is laughing, her blue eyes are full of tears.

"Of course. I told you I would."

I slip the diamond engagement ring onto her finger. She gazes at me, then presses her beautiful mouth against mine. Drawing apart slightly, I touch my lower lip with my finger.

She looks puzzled. "Something is wrong?"

"That's strange," I say. "There's no scar."

"Scar?" She laughs. "Why there should be scar?"

I laugh too, wondering why such a thing should have occurred to me. There is just the three of us with our arms around one another, melting into one ...

I awoke to the awareness that I was smiling. And then I noticed the warmth and softness of a woman lying next to me. The fragrance of perfume was stronger now. Fiona was lying with her back to me. Through her almost transparent nightdress I could see the faint outline of her spine. Her eyes were open, I imagined. As I put my hand on her shoulder, I wondered if she would draw away. But she was still. Everything was perfectly still.